# WHO SHE WAS: A SYLVIA WILCOX MYSTERY

## BOOK 1

### BRAYLEE PARKINSON

# WHO SHE WAS

Braylee Parkinson

# COPYRIGHT

# PROLOGUE

*etroit, Michigan: "Poor Brightmoor" - July 2011*
A stench rose from the rusty dumpster behind the liquor store. The smell was evidence enough for Ali Mansu to know that there was a dead body nearby. The store owner mumbled prayers to Allah as he felt the hairs on the back of his neck stand up. The hot, putrid smell of rotting flesh filled his nostrils, causing him to drop the bag of garbage and peer into the dumpster. A fearful glance revealed only bags of trash, but behind the dumpster, in a thicket of overgrown weeds, a pale, leathery hand lay outstretched, reaching towards the sky.

The fingers, stiff with rigor mortis, were curved into a claw. Between overgrowth and debris, a pool of blood, blackened by the passage of hours, had formed beneath the perforated skull. Strands of wayward blonde hair drenched in blood were stuck to the cement. Even in the body's diminished condition, it was clear that this woman did not belong to Detroit. The degraded hand showed signs of a recent manicure, and the large diamond dangling from her finger told a story that went beyond robbery. Five bullets had been used. The first one would have done the job, but whoever had murdered this woman had been angry. Money hadn't been the motive. Ali's heart raced as he scampered towards the back door.

Police from the 8th Precinct arrived within the hour. The overworked and underpaid detectives examined the scene and talked to Ali, but he had very little information to share. The store had only been open a couple of weeks, and he didn't know much about the neighborhood yet. The detectives took the storeowner's statement, headed back to the alley, and waited for the medical examiner to show up.

# 1

This is what you get for being in the office on Christmas Eve, I thought, as I watched a car parallel park in front of my office. It was my fourth year of widowhood, but I still hadn't figured out how to have a successful holiday season at home. After spending the past few Christmases out of town, I'd convinced myself to stay home this year. Unfortunately, I'd overestimated the amount of business that would present itself in December, and most of my days had been spent organizing and filing paperwork. Now that it was Christmas Eve, a specific pang of loneliness throbbed in my throat. My husband, Derek, had been a Christmas fanatic: he'd start streaming lights around the edge of our house the day after Halloween. Every time I closed my eyes, memories of the warm, refreshing scent of pine, or the aroma of a huge, hot, bubbly piece of apple pie slipped into my thoughts. The sights, sounds, and smells of the season permeated my senses, even though I hadn't participated in any festivities since Derek's death. I had wonderful memories, but now, being at home during the holidays meant facing a silent, empty homestead. That was why I was at the office organizing receipts for tax season.

To drive away the pangs of loneliness, I'd started the day with a shot of vodka. Normally, I stayed away from alcohol, but there were days when the bitter poison slowed my thoughts and helped me to forget. By 10:00 a.m., I was combing through mounds of receipts. After about an hour, I took a break and paced the office, noticing how loudly Martin, my brother-in-law/assistant, was snoring at the adjacent desk. I poured myself another shot. Even though we had nothing on the books, Martin had decided to come to work. We were both there for unspoken comfort. I walked over to the picture window, drank the vodka down in one swig, and sat on the ledge. Michigan was playing its usual bipolar weather game. The previous week, a foot of snow had fallen, but now temperatures were in the low forties, and a cold, unforgiving rain had been beating against the window for the better part of three days. I was staring at Michigan Avenue, admiring the stillness of the town below, when the car came whipping into view. I watched the sporty, black Mazda 3 squeeze itself into the tiny space between Martin's Camry and an old, rusted Bonneville.

I smacked the bottom of Martin's hiking boot.

"Look alive! Someone's coming up."

"Huh?"

"We have a client."

"Where?"

"On his way up."

"How'd ya know it's for us?" Martin asked, leaning back in the chair and attempting to return to his nap.

"Because no one else in this building is stupid enough to be open. Get up," I said, pushing the back of his chair to an upright position.

"Geez, Syl," he said, scratching his head before sitting up straight.

I tossed the bottle of vodka into the bottom desk drawer, pushed the receipts aside, and opened my laptop. A few seconds later, I buzzed the man into the office.

He was drenched from head to toe.

"Hello," I said, before holding out my hand and waiting as he pulled off his rain-soaked parka. He waved my hand away and gingerly hung the parka on the coat rack. When he looked up, I immediately recognized his face.

"My name is Sylvia Wilcox. How may I help you?"

Carson Stark was his name, and he'd been on the nightly news for months following his wife's untimely demise. He was just as lanky as he'd looked on television. About six foot four and bald, with huge, haunting blue eyes, and he had a long, sharp nose that was slightly off kilter, indicating that he had probably broken it at some point. The crow's feet in the corners of his eyes told me that he was older than he seemed, but his body was sleek and trim, like that of a long-distance runner.

When he failed to respond, or move, I decided to prompt him a second time.

"Hello, I'm Sylvia Wilcox. What can I do for you?" I asked, stretching out my arm once again for a handshake. He gave my hand a gentle shake, headed towards the desk, and dropped into the chair next to Martin without any explanation.

I took a quick mental inventory of the man. Carson Stark reeked of old money. The sporty but economical Mazda 3 reinforced the fact that he had nothing to prove to anyone. He'd always had money, and always would have it, so there was no need to be flashy. His creased brow was a direct result of his wife's murder, because this was a man who had been able to fix just about any problem that had come into his life. Losing his wife and not having answers was killing him.

"You need a private investigator."

He nodded but didn't elaborate. After a long, uncomfortable pause, I said, "Start from the beginning."

I sat down in front of my laptop, opened a new document, and cast a sideways glance at Martin, signaling that he should leave. Martin introduced himself and quickly disappeared into the tiny room next to the office, shutting the door behind him. During my brief stint as a private detective, I'd learned that it was better to do an initial consultation one-on-one. Clients were more apt to be candid if they were spilling their guts to a single person.

"My wife..." began Carson Stark, only to have emotion choke his throat closed. He dropped his head, his eyes shut tight. "My wife was murdered. I want to know what happened to her. The police have no leads, and they've interrogated me to the point of harassment. Now, they aren't even really investigating the case. I have to know what happened." Tears welled in his eyes. I pulled out a box of tissues and pushed it towards him.

"How long has it been?" I asked.

"Seventeen months."

"Who do you think would do this?"

"That's the thing—I don't know. She was a beautiful person and I can't think of anyone who disliked her. She was a great mother, wife, and friend. The world was better when she was here."

He couldn't think of anyone who would hurt his wife, but the reality was that someone had done more than hurt her. Someone had taken her life, and life-taking, although sometimes the random endeavor of a stranger, was more often a passion-riddled deed carried out by an acquaintance.

"I will need more information before I decide if I can help. What angles did the police share with you?" I asked.

"The police think it was me, only they have no proof because it wasn't me. She was murdered on the west side of Detroit, and I have no idea why she would be there. Without GPS, I personally don't even know how to get to the spot where her body was found."

"Any other suspects?"

"None that I know of...although there was speculation that she was having an affair."

I remembered the story well. Carson Stark, a Northville Township doctor, had lost his wife to murder. She'd been shot in Brightmoor, an incredibly poor section of Detroit on the edge of Redford Township. I'd worked in the area patrolled by 8th Precinct—where the murder had taken place—before becoming a private detective. Most of my old colleagues thought that she had been having an affair with a drug dealer.

"I remember the story from the news. She was shot, right?"

"Yes."

"Do you think she was having an affair?"

"No."

"Do you have a photo of her?"

"Of course." He dug into his jacket pocket and pulled out a small stack of pictures. He gazed lovingly at the photograph on top before handing it to me. Liza Stark had been almost perfect. Five foot six, about thirty-five years old, with soft aqua eyes that stared into the camera, and a well-practiced smile featuring her straight, white teeth. Her strawberry blonde hair was pulled into a ponytail that cascaded down her back. She was posing next to a petite woman with beautiful sable colored skin. They stood arm in arm, wide smiles on their faces. Both women were striking, but there was a hardness in Liza's otherwise pretty smile—something I couldn't quite put my finger on.

"Liza is the blonde, correct?"

"Yes."

"Who is the other woman?"

"Madelyn Price. I thought it would be good for you to know what she looks like as well."

"Why is that?"

"She was the last person to talk to Liza before she... They were supposed to meet for a coffee date, but Liza never showed up. Madelyn waited for a while, but eventually left and called to let me know that Liza had stood her up."

"Do you suspect that Madelyn Price had something to do with the murder?"

"Oh, no. It's just...I just thought you might want to talk to her. She and Liza were best friends."

"Yes. I will definitely need to talk with her. I'm very sorry you lost your wife," I said, handing the photo back to Mr. Stark. He didn't reach out to take it.

"Can you help me?"

Good question. Murder is hard to solve even when you have an organized police force on your side. I was a one-woman agency with a law-school-dropout assistant. The case was too big for me, and I'd promised myself that homicide was off the list for my agency.

"Mr. Stark, I want to help, but I have a small operation here and I don't really take homicide cases. I have—"

"You've lost a spouse and it changed your life. You know what it's like."

I pushed the laptop aside and stared at Carson Stark. He

had investigated me. That was common, but people usually wanted to know about my credentials, not my personal life.

"Don't be alarmed. You come highly recommended. An officer in Detroit greatly admires you. He told me your story and why you left the police force. Said you couldn't take not knowing. That you fought and fought until you solved cases. Made you unpopular amongst the other officers. He also told me you have a master's degree in criminology—near the top of your class."

I didn't know whether to be impressed, or if I needed to contemplate filing a Personal Protection Order.

"Well, I guess you've done your homework. I assume that means you also know that all those highfalutin tricks that fictitious PIs use will land me in jail. Once I turned in the badge, I turned back into a citizen. Private investigating isn't as glamorous or as fun as it looks. Intuition, feelings, and what people say guide the way. Sometimes the police are helpful, but other times they're offended by the intrusion of an outside entity."

"That's the thing: whatever happened to Liza won't be discovered through a traditional police investigation. I need someone who can feel and discern the small details. You have to be able to see things that aren't seen by the typical police officer's eye."

I had lost a spouse under mysterious circumstances. The truth had been hard to find, but I hadn't stopped searching until I knew exactly what had happened. I'd worked diligently to uncover the truth. It was an ugly truth, but it's always better to know what happened. Even when it's a dirty secret you never speak of to anyone else, you feel better knowing. But...this case was too much for me. The reminder that spouses are sometimes unjustly taken away, the idea that there was a selfish killer out there that needed to be caught...It would be too much for me. I would get caught up in the case, and lose myself.

But...I had a yearning for justice, and Carson Stark deserved that. The case had fallen away from the active roster at the precinct. Liza Stark had been written off as a cheater who had gotten what she deserved. But she deserved better; her husband deserved better.

"Okay, Mr. Stark. I'll do my best."

"Please find the person who did this to her. They left my children motherless, and me..."

"I'm sorry for your loss," I said again, before giving him a few moments to regain his composure. Once the lines in his brow eased, I began a battery of questions.

"Let's start with that morning. Did anything out of the ordinary happen?"

"She was herself—nothing out of the ordinary. A bit flustered with the kids perhaps, but that had been the case for a while. Isabel was two and Shane was three at the time. We'd just hired a housekeeper and part-time nanny to help."

"Was this something new?"

"It had been going on for a few weeks. The kids are seventeen months apart. I think Liza was just exhausted from the stress of the previous four years. It was hard for me to be there as much as I wanted to be. I had only been at the hospital a few months, and the workload was much heavier than it was at my previous assignment. That's why I suggested that we get her some help."

"When was the nanny scheduled to leave that day?"

"Seven p.m. Neither of our kids have ever napped much, so they go to bed early. The nanny was originally scheduled to work a few hours a day, but by that time, she was working from one to seven p.m., five days a week."

"Tell me about the hours that led up to your departure for work. Any details, regardless of how small, might be helpful."

"We bathed and played with the kids. After that, we headed for lunch and spent time at a park. Liza told me she was going to run errands, get a manicure, and meet a friend for coffee."

"So, the nanny was there to watch the kids while Liza ran errands?"

"Yes. She was originally just going to do housekeeping for us, but she really clicked with the kids. And Liza needed more time to herself."

Having two toddlers is stressful, so it made sense that Liza needed a break, but it also brought up questions about what she did during those breaks.

"Do you think Liza ended up in Brightmoor of her own accord?"

"I don't think so, but she was driving and her car was found unscathed. That makes me think she had to have driven there herself, which leaves me with more questions. I don't know...Maybe she got lost or something, but there really is no excuse for her to have been there."

Interesting way to phrase the explanation. A good reason didn't have to be present. Sometimes people are irrational and sometimes, people have secrets. Brightmoor was a wasteland of firebombed houses, drug houses, and party stores. There wasn't really a good reason for nonresidents to be in the area.

"Liza was meeting a friend...Madelyn, correct?"

"Yes, Madelyn Price—her best friend. The other woman in the photo."

"Did Liza make it for coffee?"

"No, but she called Madelyn and told her she was

running late. That was around three p.m. She sent another text message around twenty past four. That was the last activity on her cell phone."

"Is Madelyn in Northville too?"

"No. She lives in Ann Arbor, not too far from here."

"Do you know where they were meeting?"

"No. At the time it didn't seem important."

"I'll need her information."

Carson nodded and an awkward pause filled the office. I wasn't sure where to start with this case. I hoped it wasn't an infidelity case gone wrong, but from what I was hearing, the possibility was there. Most of my work came from former trophy wives turned soccer moms who wanted proof of infidelity so that they could get a sizable divorce settlement. Men are notoriously bad cheaters, so those cases were always simple and fast. But women who cheated on their husbands...Those cases could be tough, and solving a murder that took place in a city that vies for the murder capital of the country on a yearly basis was an entirely different story.

"Does Liza have family in the area?"

"Yes."

I waited, but nothing came.

"May I have their names?"

"I'd rather leave them out of it."

"That's not possible. If you want me to take the case, I need all the information. Things might get uncomfortable. If you don't want that, we can't move forward."

A pained look came across his face. Murder can drive a serious wedge between family members, but there was no getting around talking with them.

"Mr. Stark, I understand how hard this must be for everyone involved, but I will need to talk with Liza's family.

Did she have any siblings? Are her parents alive and in the area?"

"Liza has a brother, Peter Abernathy, but they weren't close. I doubt he'd know anything. Her parents-Ralph and Janice Abernathy-live in Livonia, but we rarely saw them."

I paused and allowed Carson to rattle on about the insignificance of Liza's family. The curious thing about marriage is that it provides a false sense of familiarity. You live, eat, and sleep with your spouse. The repetition of seeing that person every day creates the fabrication that you know them better than anyone else, and maybe you do, but then again, maybe you don't.

"I would still like to speak to Liza's brother and parents, just to be thorough. May I have contact information for Peter, Madelyn, and Mrs. and Mr. Abernathy?" I asked, forcing a smile that I hoped was reassuring.

Carson continued the unbroken eye contact. A few silent, motionless minutes passed before he pulled out his phone. His pupils were faded and coarse, like blue jeans that had been washed too often. His movements were rigid, but stealthy for a man of his height; calculated and mechanical. He gave me the information and slipped back into that blank stare. I could almost hear the wheels in his head turning.

"Do you need money now?" Mr. Stark asked.

"Just the retainer. You can transfer the money online when you get a chance."

We shook hands and I walked him out, informing him that I'd be in touch when I had information to share. After that, I gently closed the door and took a moment to compose myself. The past bubbled up in my soul. Losing a spouse was one thing, but losing a spouse and having no idea why they were gone was unbearable. The feeling was all too familiar. I shook off the thought and called Marty into the office.

"We've got a case."

"Yes!"

"Don't get too excited. We're in over our heads."

_____

## 2

We closed up at six that evening. I pulled a gift-wrapped box out of my desk drawer and handed it to Marty before turning out the lights.

"Syl...you didn't have to get me anything."

"Don't make a big deal. It's Christmas, for goodness sake. Everybody needs a gift."

I watched him blush.

"Let's get outta here. You got plans? Midnight Mass is on tap if you're free." I said, grabbing my umbrella.

"I do have plans, but thanks."

Probably a lie, but I let it go. As we headed out down the narrow staircase, Martin fired off a series of questions about Carson Stark. Do you think he did it? What do you think the cops will say about you taking the case? What do you want me to do?

At the bottom of the staircase I turned to face him, remaining silent. My first inclination was to snap and tell him to settle down, but then I remembered how much I owed him. He had given me a purpose, and for that, I was eternally grateful. I adjusted my features, softening my hardened frown. Recognizing the look that said, "Slow down; pace yourself," Martin nodded gently. I unfurled my umbrella and opened it before stepping out into the rain.

"Want a ride?" Martin asked.

"No, thanks. I'll walk."

"Sylvia, it's a downpour out here."

"I know. That's why I wanna walk. Merry Christmas." I blew him a kiss and headed for the crosswalk.

Living five blocks from the office made it nearly impossible to drive, even when the weather was miserable. As Martin pulled away, the chilled rain began to turn into sleet, and the slosh of my boots in the cold puddles increased my feelings of loneliness and regret. The meeting with Carson Stark had pushed me deeper into a somber mood. There's something depressing about spending the holiday alone in a place where you should know people. The opposite is true of out-of-town Christmas vacations and I wondered again why I hadn't booked a flight.

I'd spent the previous Christmas in Quebec City, sipping Ice wine and nibbling on poutine in a cozy bed-and-breakfast. I'd spent a week in the old section of the city, making temporary friends of random strangers and meandering along the frigid, snow-covered cobblestone streets. The companionship of the strangers I met was too short to sour, but long enough to satiate the need for human contact. I'd returned after New Year's Day feeling refreshed and ready to get back to my world of all work and no play.

I was born and raised in Detroit and had spent most of my life in southeastern Michigan. My parents, who still lived in Detroit, tolerated yearly visits, but we had not been close for a long time. At ten years old, my twin brother, Simon, had disappeared one day when we were playing at the edge of the dead-end street adjacent to our house. The loss of Simon had destroyed our family, causing me to seek refugee somewhere far away from my parents.

I'd attended a boarding school in Connecticut as a teenager, but something had drawn me back to Michigan for college. Ironically, Michigan is the place where I feel most alone. My haunted past had followed me around the state, with the ghost seemingly incapable of leaving Michigan. During my time in Connecticut, I'd been free of the guilt of being the twin that hadn't been abducted, but returning to Michigan had rekindled painful memories of my brother's absence. Currently, I live in Ypsilanti, Michigan, a little college town about forty minutes from Detroit. Ypsilanti is historic-district-meets-the-ghetto, with a cross-hatch of college life. The town is sandwiched in between Ann Arbor and Superior Township in Washtenaw County, and it serves as a cheaper option for those who want to live close to the culture and beauty of the Ann Arbor area. I moved to Ypsi for graduate school and fell in love with the place. It has a Midwest swagger with a hint of southern hospitality and an edge of danger. If you get a flat tire, someone will stop and help you change it, but if you leave your front door unlocked, someone might come in... and maybe take a thing or two. People speak to each other when walking down the street, and hippies, scholars, students, and drug dealers manage to co-mingle without much friction.

Shuddering underneath the umbrella, I felt the chill of isolation. The street was quiet and calm, but the glow of windows warm with Christmas Eve cheer filled my peripheral vision. I should have invited Martin over for a drink, but there was a part of me that didn't want company. The loss of Derek reminded me that some parts of life were dark: there was no way to eliminate them. Accepting that fact had helped me deal with the sorrow. Instead of thinking it would end, or that I needed to fight against the pain, I accepted that most days would be no better or worse than the previous day. Derek would always be in the corner of my mind, silent, but ever-present.

I have learned that staying busy and productive is a great way to repress loneliness, but there are times when busyness fails to distract from the truth. Even so, I was going to do my best to let this new case consume me. As I stuck my key in the front door, I began to organize a plan of action to find out who killed Liza Stark.

I headed to the kitchen and tossed half a box of linguini into a pot. In a second pot, I mixed Parmesan and cream cheese to make a simple but adequate Alfredo sauce. I poured myself a glass of Riesling, tossed the pasta and sauce together, and sat down at the long wooden table for a silent dinner. After that, I sighed and faced reality. The night was not over yet, so I had better start getting myself in order.

Midnight Mass was the last place I wanted to go, but since it was Christmas Eve, it would be a stop along my lonely Christmas journey. There is nothing quite like Midnight Mass, but you don't remember that until you walk through the door of the church. The inclination to curl up with hot cocoa and watch *It's A Wonderful Life* always tempts me to stay home, but once I arrive at church, I remember why I go every year. I'm drawn by the smell of frankincense and myrrh weaving through the air, the flickering flames of candles lit in oblation, and the collective warmth of the people in the overcrowded church, many of whom have not been to Mass since Easter, or the previous Christmas Eve. I never want to go until I get there, but I never acknowledge that truth, until I arrive.

I took a shower before slipping on a cardigan, a long, pleated black skirt, and boots. As I waited for the clock to move closer to midnight, I started to review the preliminary questions that preface all murder investigations. Who wanted Liza Stark dead? Who had the means to kill her? How did she end up in a vulnerable position that allowed her to be killed?

The issue of who wanted Liza Stark dead was important, but not as important as how she ended up being vulnerable to murder. Some people aren't likable, or they make enemies along the way. There might be a few people who would like to see them dead, but very few enemies are going to act on that impulse. Also, a complete and total stranger can kill you if you end up in the wrong place at the wrong time, so there was a chance that Liza's murder was purely coincidental. She was in one of the worst neighborhoods in the country. Getting murdered in Brightmoor was easy, but being in Brightmoor was not. So, the first question was: how did she end up in a time and place that allowed her to be killed?

Since it was Christmas Eve, there was little research that could be done. I wrote my three essential questions on a piece of paper, took it to my home office, placed it on the desk, and forced myself to close the door. Life is more than work, I told myself.

The snow continued to fall throughout the evening. At a quarter to twelve, I reluctantly headed out into the bitter, wet cold. I arrived at the church moments before the procession started. Just about every seat was taken and the air was full of incense. Warmth emitted from the packed pews. I slithered into a small space on one of the back pews, next to a family of six. The toddler was bouncing on his mother's knee and squealing with delight. I flipped down the kneeler and said a few prayers before the music for the procession started.

CHRISTMAS DAY DAWNED WITH A COLD, empty silence that left me distracted and aloof. A light, wispy snow was falling, and the temperature continued to drop throughout the day. I skipped my run that morning and curled up on the couch with a cup of tea. I spent the day alternating between my bed and the tattered beige recliner in the sitting room. My breakfast and lunch consisted of soup I'd made from my Thanksgiving turkey. In the evening, I felt restless and decided to find a movie to watch. After thirty minutes of a sappy story about international house-swapping and falling in love, I stole one last look at Jude Law and turned off the television. Time to do something constructive.

Being a PI is difficult because you're in law enforcement, but you don't have the perks that regular cops do. I have access to public domain information on the internet, but I can't just tap into a database and pull up interesting tidbits about a victim. Instead, I must find evidence the old fashioned and least reliable way...by talking to people. I didn't think anyone would appreciate me interrupting their Christmas dinner to ask questions about a homicide, so I decided to do the cyber-sleuth thing.

The first question about the case was: what the hell was Liza Stark doing in Detroit? Southeastern Michigan living has two very simple rules: know your place and stay there. Liza Stark was a white female from the suburbs—and not one of the blue-collar, United Auto Workers suburbs. There was really no legitimate reason for her to have been in the Brightmoor district of Detroit. There aren't many businesses in that area except for churches and liquor stores, and even those are sparse. It's a safe assumption that people who live in Brightmoor stay in the area and rarely, if ever, venture out of the neighborhood. Someone living in Brightmoor wouldn't end up in Northville Township, an upper-middle-class suburb that is light years away from most neighborhoods in Detroit. Someone living in Northville Township might end up in Brightmoor if they were searching for something they had trouble getting in their neighborhood. Even so, they would have to know someone in Brightmoor. Who did Liza know in that area? How would she have met them? Initially, I thought that drugs might have beckoned Liza below Eight Mile Road, but an article posted a few months after her killing said that an autopsy showed she didn't have any drugs in her system. Carson Stark had already told me about the second theory: Liza was a desperate housewife looking for a thrill with some young have-not. The third one, of course, was that Carson himself had murdered his wife. None of these theories really pushed the right buttons for me, but I thought that the infidelity angle was worth looking at.

It is possible to be madly in love with someone who likes you enough to stay, but who has no problem lying to you. The tears and anguish Carson Stark had showed had seemed real, but who was to say that the Liza he knew was the only one that had existed? Maybe there was some drug-dealing, stolen-car-wheeling guy who had satisfied Liza's primal urges. Since becoming a private detective, the bulk of my work had been focused on infidelity cases. Humans are capable of a high level of deceit. Liza could have gotten herself into a deadly affair; perhaps her lower-class beau had demanded money, and she had refused.

Before the night was over, I had some basic facts about

Liza. She'd attended Stevenson High in Livonia, but no graduation date was listed. She'd also spent two years at Schoolcraft College, but never completed a degree or certificate. At the time of her murder, she was thirty-four years old and a stay-at-home mom—by all accounts just your average suburban wife. Her life before marrying Carson was a little less certain. Her work record was spotty. She'd been a Certified Nursing Assistant for a while, and a substitute teacher, but neither career had lasted long. She'd taken classes in Early Education in college, but they hadn't amounted to much. Some people take time off between high school and college for jobs or to travel, but Liza did not seem to be a part of the working world until she was twenty-two. That seemed odd, but not completely out of the question. Some people are slackers.

I ran Liza's name through the online white pages and found addresses in Livonia, New Orleans, Louisiana, Northville, and Detroit. The dates indicated that she had lived in Livonia as a child, in Detroit as a teenager, and in Louisiana and Northville during her adult life. It was strange that she'd lived in Detroit at all, and it was even odder that she'd lived there as a teenager, but virtual white pages are notoriously inaccurate. The listing probably had another woman with the same name mixed in with Liza's address results.

I also checked Liza's social media pages, but there wasn't much to see. Perhaps she had made sure to keep the security on her social media pages tight, and strangers were not able to view the bulk of her information. I couldn't be sure, but her list of friends was rather sparse. Her page had a picture of Carson and the kids, minus herself, and she had twenty-nine friends. She hadn't posted anything since 2009, two years before she was murdered. Of course, social media had just been picking up steam around that time, so it wasn't too strange that she didn't have much information, but it did pique my interest. Posting on social media and having "friends" is by no means a sign of normalcy, but for a stay-at-home mom in a posh suburb, it would be a great place to boast and possibly brag about your world. She was beautiful, married to a doctor, had two kids, a phenomenal zip code...all the surface things that people think produce happiness. Of course, I know from experience that the more people you include in your life, the more difficult it is to be happy. Perhaps Liza had come to a similar conclusion and decided to keep her life private. Or maybe she'd turned to an outside source for some type of release.

I scrolled through the few posts on Liza's page and found minimal, very guarded information. There were no thuggish-looking folks on her friends list. Next, I checked a newspaper website for articles on the murder. I read a short summary of the crime, and read a few statements from one of the detectives on the case-Kelvin Cole. After a few hours of scouring the internet, my vision was blurred from too much time in front of the computer. I closed the laptop, grabbed my phone, and called Martin.

"She was hiding something," I said, as soon as he picked up the phone.

"Why do you think that? Oh, and Merry Christmas," Martin said. I could hear the muffled sound of a video game in the background.

"Her social media pages are sparse. There's one single solitary photo of her...the rest are of her family, but none of those photos have her in them. She's never with the family because she's different."

"How's she different?"

"I don't know, but she's different from them."

The noise in the background stopped.

"Tomorrow, I will set up appointments with Carson, her best friend, Madelyn, and the store owner. I want to see where Liza lived. After the holiday break, contact her former coworkers. She taught at St. Bart's for a year. Talk to the principal and any teachers who worked with her. I'll also call the 8th Precinct and get in there to see the case file."

"You think that Liza did something to get herself killed?" Martin asked.

"I think that there's something her husband doesn't know that contributed to her murder. I know how it is to have secrets."

## 3

The day after Christmas, I woke up feeling restless, but one glance outside revealed slick, glistening sidewalks. Damn ice...I'd hoped to get out of the house early and get the adrenaline going, but running on ice was impossible. Instead, I decided to work the phones. The goal was to set up appointments with Madelyn Price-the friend, Peter Abernathy-the brother, and the owner of the liquor store where Liza's body was found.

I tried Madelyn Price first. A soft, calm voice informed me that I'd reached Madelyn before the message provided several options. Press one for information on yoga classes, two for mental health services, and three for personal inquiries. I pressed three and left my name, the reason for my call, and my number on the voice service. Next, I called Peter Abernathy and got his voicemail. His voice sounded angry and rushed, but he'd managed to contain himself and record a relatively professional sounding message.

The only person I managed to get a hold of was the liquor store owner, Ali Mansu.

The phone rang twice before someone picked up and said, "Lo."

"May I speak to Mr. Ali Mansu?"

"This is him."

"Hello. My name is Sylvia Wilcox. I am a private detective investigating the murder of Liza Stark, and I would like to come in to talk with you about the murder."

There was silence on the line.

"Mr. Mansu?"

"Yes."

"I am—"

"I don't want nothing to do with that. Long time ago and I already talk to police about it," the man shouted, his Middle Eastern accent thick and heavy.

"Mr. Mansu, I understand. I just need a little bit of—"

"No!"

"Mr. Mansu—"

"No, no, no!"

"Sir, what would happen if the DPD came in and checked your employee roster?"

Silence.

"What if undercover cops were in your store, waiting for a minor to buy alcohol?"

I hated to be one of those PIs, but sometimes you have to pull the police card.

"Fine. What you want to know?"

"I'd like to come by and talk with you."

"That it?"

"Yes."

"Not a bunch of cops?"

"No. Just me."

"Oh. Okay." His voice was calm now. "That is okay. I thought you want to bring a lot of cops."

"Nope. It's best that it's just you and I."

"When?"

"Today. Around noon."

"Fine," he said before hanging up. I showered, dressed in a blue pinstripe suit and dark blue pumps, and headed out. Pushing the Taurus just a few miles per hour over the speed limit, I was able to hit I-96 at 11:11a.m. During the drive, I gave the scene a mental comb-over. Strangers in a strange part of town had found the body. Even though a multitude of murders had occurred in that area, and gunfire was a daily part of life, Liza's murder was unique. She didn't look like typical Brightmoor fare. That corner of the city had little diversity, but the inhabitants had a "look"—deep bags under their eyes, faded faces, slow shuffling walks, and bovine gazes that told a story of hopelessness. If Liza Stark had been slumming it for a piece on the side, someone would have noticed her shiny red Range Rover cruising around.

Traffic was relatively light at this time of day and I was able to cruise to Brightmoor with ease. Passing through Redford Township, I was reminded of the home Derek and I had shared north of Telegraph Road. There was a time when Detroit cops were required to live within the city's boundaries, but by the time we were in DPD, that restriction had been dropped. Even so, we had decided to move into a section of the city where a bunch of retired cops and old-timers who were still on the force lived. Our little neighborhood on the outskirts of the city had been full of cops and other civil servants who needed a Detroit address, but wanted to be as close to the border as possible. Quiet, well-kept lawns lined streets of modest, two-story brick bungalows and ramblers; children played in carefully laid-out streets. The diversity lacking in most of Detroit lived within the five blocks preceding the working-class suburb of Redford. A few mom-and-pop businesses had survived the explosion of shopping malls and corporate fast food chains, making the neighborhood a hidden jewel of community and safety. We were well armed, and all the thugs on the other side of Telegraph Road knew it.

There was little reason to venture across Telegraph Road except for work, but I had driven past the area where Liza's body was found countless times during my time on the force. Even though the murder had taken place over two years ago, and all physical evidence was long gone, talking to the store owner who had found the body still might be fruitful. I pulled up in front of the store at around ten o'clock that morning. The sign on the storefront read simply: "Beer/Wine/Liquor."

The corner store served as the one-stop grocery store, convenience store, and anything-else-you-might-need store. It was larger than average, but it carried with it the tell-tale signs of most neighborhood joints. Once inside the door, I spotted expired food lining the shelves, miscellaneous rotting fruit hanging off the front counter, and greasy processed pizza, chicken, and hamburgers filling the stands close to the checkout window. A thick plate of bulletproof glass separated the clerk from the patrons, and the butt of a shotgun could be seen just underneath the counter...Just your typical Detroit party store.

Ali Mansu wore a knitted cap on his balding head and a cream-colored traditional robe. His smile—thin and forced—was clear, even though he was behind the thick sheet of plexiglass. We'd made eye contact the moment I pushed open the heavy glass door. He gave a small wave, completed a transaction, and dropped a handful of change into the shallow silver well. He called for a young woman in a hijab who was stocking shelves in the food aisle. She looked up, nodded, smiled at me, and headed behind the counter.

"Mr. Mansu?"

"Mrs. Wilcox?" His eyes brightened with a mixture of fear and curiosity.

"Yes, hello. Sylvia Wilcox," I said, holding out my hand and receiving a firm handshake in return from Ali.

"Mrs. Wilcox—nice to meet you. We can talk in the storage room," Ali said, unlocking the cage that separated the cash register from the store.

Ali was close to six feet tall, but he walked with a stoop, which caused him to look slightly slumped over. His face was encased in a thick black beard that was neatly cropped two or three inches from his chin.

"Thanks for taking the time to meet with me," I said.

"No problem," Ali said in a soft tone.

I followed him down a tiny hallway that emptied into a room full of flattened boxes and random stock. He motioned for me to sit on a rusty, gray, folding chair.

"So, you had only been open a short time before you found the body, correct?" I asked. The rickety folding chair wobbled a bit. I said a silent prayer that it would last the length of the interview.

"Yes. We had been open few weeks only," Ali said with a heavy accent.

"Now you've been open for about two years, right?"

"Correct Close to two years"

"Did you know that this was gang territory and a very bad neighborhood when you opened the store?"

"I grew up in Gaza. I'm not afraid of bad areas."

"Would you say that you have the same customers over and over again?" I knew he did, but I wanted to prime him for the next question.

Ali shook his head—yes. He was starting to look bored.

"I know it will be hard to remember, but did anything out of the ordinary happen the day before you found Liza's body? Was it busy?"

"My fourth son was born," Ali said. A smile spread across his face.

"Congratulations," I said. If Ali's son had been born the day before Liza's body was dumped, he would remember the day better than if nothing important had happened in his life. This interview might net good information.

"I was in the store, behind the counter, when my wife called. I jump up and down, told customers I had to close early, and left around eight that night."

"Were there people in the store when you found out?"

"Yes, but I don't remember them. I was too excited about my son."

Some customers would have known that the store closed early that night. They could have spread the word.

"Is there anything else you remember about that night?"

"I was leaving around eight, but ended up staying an extra few minutes because a customer showed up. She was mad because I was closing early. I asked her if it was an emergency; she said no, and after I explained why I was closing early, she understood."

"Do you know the woman's name?"

"Ah, yes. She is a regular. Very nice. Lives around the corner. Nice house. Nice husband."

"May I have her name?"

"Amber. Amber Dukes, I think is her name. Nice house. You can't miss it."

"Thanks. That's helpful. Do you remember posting a sign, or anything like that, to let people know that the store was closing early?"

"No. I didn't want everyone to know—just those who came into the store. Letting the entire neighborhood know would not be smart. If someone stopped by and saw that the store was closed, it would be better for them to think that it was out of business than for me to tell everybody I was closing early."

He had a good point. Broadcasting that he was closing early would have been an invitation for robbery.

"So, the only people who knew were customers who came into the store that day?"

Ali nodded. That meant that the killer had probably been in the store.

"Do you have surveillance tapes?"

"Of course. The police took them."

I'd have to check with the detective who'd worked the case to see if any evidence had been garnered from the tapes.

"Mr. Mansu, is there anything else you remember?"

"The police didn't seem interested, but you might care."

"I do care. What weren't they interested in?"

"The first few weeks the store was open, gangs bothered us. That's why we have the gun. After that lady was found dead in the alley, no more gangs bothered us."

That was interesting. Perhaps Liza had been slumming it after all.

"What were the gangs doing?"

"Breaking windows, graffiti, harassing my daughter."

"And that stopped after the body was found?"

"Yes."

Strange.

"May I see the alley?" I asked.

"Sure."

I followed Ali to the back of the storeroom, dodging cardboard.

"I will wait in the door. I don't want to leave a woman in the alley by herself."

I nodded and headed out into the alley. A pale brown rusted out dumpster sat in the midst of trash and overgrown grass. The alley was lined with abandoned buildings. It was a great place to dump a body. I tried to imagine a scenario that would end with Liza's body behind the dumpster. Why would she have been in this alley?

"Mrs. Wilcox," Ali called from the doorway. "Will you be much longer?"

I'd come back later if I needed to.

"No. In fact, I'm all done. Thanks for your time."

We headed back inside. I bought a pack of gum from Ali, waved goodbye, and left the store. On my way out, some unpleasant kids in gang colors pushed past me. Three loud, boyish-looking girls with cornrows, bandanas, and saggy jeans muttered a litany of swear words as they rambled up and down the aisles. Two of the girls were tall and thin, but the third one, a short, chunky girl, appeared to be their leader. I tried to avoid eye contact, but Chunky Girl fought to lock eyes with me. She was no more than fourteen, maybe fifteen years old, but her face was already hardened from the wear and tear of life. Her forehead bore several lines of wrinkles, and her eyes were a dirty sea-green color that made me think of a contaminated ocean. I nodded and pushed past the girls.

Outside, a skeleton-like body was lurching around on the passenger side of the Taurus. I ran my hand over the butt of my gun and made sure my shoes clicked loudly on the pavement. Hopefully, the being would scramble away as he heard me approaching. When I got within four feet, the emaciated body began to slowly pivot to face me. The remnants of breasts lay flat on her stomach and a white film encircled the woman's mouth. When she tried to speak, the hole in her face produced a hollow pink-and-black pathway that croaked "Spare change?" in a raspy voice. I took my hand off the butt of the gun, dug into my pocket, and produced a piece of lint and two quarters. I dropped them in her hand, and muttered, "May God have mercy."

On my way back to the freeway, I decided to drive past the house of Amber, the woman who had come into the store the night Ali Mansu had closed early. Nice houses in Brightmoor are noticeable because they are the extreme exception. I drove down Dacosta Street and immediately recognized what had to be Amber's house. A modest, but well-kept brick home sat behind a gated fence. I checked my phone for the time and surveyed the neighborhood. Impromptu interviews aren't ideal, but I wanted to at least get a look at the landscape. I looked up and down the block of burned-out houses. I assumed that some of them had been firebombed in drug turf wars. What I assumed to be Amber Dukes' house sat behind a chain-link fence that had freshly shoveled sidewalks and a spattering of salt on the stairs leading to a tiny, uncovered porch. I got out and walked along the street in front of the house. A worn "Welcome" doormat that was caked with gray snow and salt sat on the porch. There was a "Beware of Dog" sign on the chain-link gate, and to back up this warning, two large Rottweilers ran around the side of the house with gusto, barking and making their presence known. I jotted down the address and headed back to the car.

～

THAT AFTERNOON I headed back to the office and did some research on what had been going on in Brightmoor over the past few years. Since my departure from the police force, the neighborhood had shown some sparks of hope. One man had taken to driving around and scaring off people who came to dump trash, or use the services of prostitutes in the area. Other residents had started community gardens and neighborhood watch groups. Even so, Brightmoor was by far one of the most dangerous areas in the city.

By five that evening my eyes were starting to blur. I closed the laptop and called Carson Stark.

"Did you find something already?" he asked.

"I'm working on gathering information. Actually, I would like to stop by your house and get a feel for the place Liza called home."

"She hasn't...been there for quite some time. What good will that do?"

"It's routine. I just want to get a better feel for who Liza was. I also can update you on what I've learned so far."

Dangling the carrot of information helped change Carson's mind.

"Okay. I'm working midnights this week, so if you can come sometime in the morning that would be great."

How about ten tomorrow morning?"

"Perfect. See you then."

The next morning, I was in front of Carson's house by nine-fifty-five. Carson Stark lived in the new part of Northville Township. Oversized mansions that showcased the excesses of the current millennium, but none of the charm of the previous century, filled subdivision after subdivision. The Starks' home was a sprawling structure close to a state park. Carson met me at the side door that opened into the kitchen. He wore a tight smirk as he nodded hello. I stepped onto dark hardwood floors that sparkled with perfection. A matching, polished wooden table had place settings ready for four occupants to settle into the cloth-backed beige chairs. A little girl with wispy blonde hair muttered a shy "hi" and held her brother's hand up to wave at me.

"Mrs. Wilcox—thank you for coming. Welcome."

We shook hands. A quick look around the house told me two things: Liza had picked the location, but Carson was responsible for the interior decoration. The interior of the house had an old-world charm. The exterior was identical to the rest of the houses in the area.

Carson was dressed in black, creased slacks and a long-sleeved, white, button-down shirt with a blazer. His clothes had a modest quality that once again pointed to the fact that he was old money. He looked like he was on the way to a business meeting. Of course, the purpose of our meeting was business, but I was a little stunned at his formal dress.

"Hi, Mr. Stark. Hi there," I said, flapping my hand at the two children at the table.

"Hi," the little girl said again, smiling.

"Please call me Carson. Amelia?" Carson called, and turned towards the foyer. "Can you take the kids?"

A small brown-skinned woman came into the kitchen, muttering in Spanish. Carson responded in Spanish as she gathered the children and left the room. The nanny/house-keeper Carson had told me about...Was she keeping any of Liza's secrets? Perhaps she had some information on why Liza was in Brightmoor the day she was murdered. I would have to talk to her before I left.

"She's our housekeeper and lifesaver. I don't think I could handle the kids without her...So glad Liza found her before—" He sighed and ran a hand over his bald head.

Accepting the loss of a spouse was a continuous process. It was the afterthoughts that reminded you that yes, they were really gone. I recognized that faraway, distracted look only too well.

"Mr. Stark," I said, trying to bring him back to the present, "I have been trying to reconstruct Liza's life. When someone is shot as many times as she was, the perpetrator is usually someone they know. With that in mind, I need to know what Liza did with her free time, and who her friends and family were. I need to know who Liza was."

Carson was standing a few feet in front of me, his eyes were downcast, and his forehead was wrinkled with worry lines. I imagined his mind was dissecting everything I said. After waiting for a response that never came, I tried to figure out how much information to give him. The investigation was new and incomplete, and no one wants to hear that their spouse had another life, so I kept the details sparse.

"I believe, Mr. Stark, that Liza knew her killer. That's why I want to know more about the life you two shared."

"I know that random killings are rare, but I don't think we knew the killer, Mrs. Wilcox," Carson replied before offering me a beverage. I could see that he wasn't ready to believe that Liza could possibly have known someone he didn't. I was going to need a new angle.

"What do you take? Beer, wine, cognac? Come into the bar. I'll make some martinis," he said before I could answer. I followed him through a huge family room with a cathedral ceiling. We stopped when we reached the living room, and he waved me over to a large, beige leather sectional opposite a winding staircase, before he headed behind the rather sizable bar tucked into the corner of the room. A warm fire crackled on one wall, and adjacent to that, a theater-sized plasma television played a twenty-four-hour news station without sound.

"I just read the ticker. Can't stand what they have to say," Carson said, as he motioned to the television before he began making the drinks. I noticed that he had not waited to hear what I'd like to drink, or even if I wanted a drink. Type A personality? Not open to suggestions? That was common among surgeons, and while being anal was a great quality during surgery, it rarely went over well in a marriage. What would it be like to be married to him? I decided to stop him before he went too far.

"Mr. Stark, it's a little early for me, and I'm working, so I won't be able to have a drink."

"Oh. Yeah, I guess it is early for you. I just got off work a few hours ago. Sorry. My schedule gets mixed up. Move over by the fireplace...It's nice," he said.

Carson handed me a goblet filled with water. I took the glass and watched him take a long sip of his martini.

"You really think Liza knew the killer? It's hard for me to believe that. I mean, we had a good life here. She was a great mom. Taught middle school for a year. Then when we had kids, she wanted to stay home to take care of them. We were happy. The cops were big on the infidelity angle. It simply isn't true. We were so very happy."

I looked at the photos on the mantle. There was photo after photo of the family. The housekeeper was in a few, but Madelyn Price, the woman in the photo Carson had showed me at the office, was also in two of the pictures. Her lips were pursed into a tight line that seemed to serve as her version of a smile. Only family members, the housekeeper, and Madelyn...Liza's brother was nowhere to be seen. Her parents and Carson's parents were also absent. Strange.

"Is that Liza's friend, Madelyn Price?" I asked, interrupting Carson's stream of denial.

"Yeah—Liza's best friend and yoga teacher."

Madelyn was the last person to speak to Liza; I'd left her a message the day before, but she had not called back. I made a mental note to try to reach her as soon as I left Carson's house. Madelyn had made the family mantle. Obviously, she was important to the entire family.

"Which came first? The friendship or the yoga instruction?"

"Oh, definitely the friendship. I mean, Liza loved yoga, but she wasn't into the whole lifestyle like Madelyn is."

I looked around the expensive house of excess and imagined that Liza had been far from a yogi.

"Would you say they were best friends?"

Carson sipped his martini, gave me a bewildered look, and muttered, "Liza was my best friend; we were very close. But outside of our marriage, yes, Madelyn was her closest friend."

"She lives in Ann Arbor, right?"

"Correct. Not too far from your office. You should talk with her, but I know she didn't have anything to do with Liza's murder. I hope you aren't thinking along those lines."

Carson was agitated. I tried to decipher whether this was his usual temperament, or if he was just overwhelmed with rekindled grief.

"For me to know who Liza was, I have to meet the people she spent time with. That's all. I have her parents and brother on my list as well."

Carson rolled his eyes and took a long swig of his martini.

"Peter is a total fuck-up. We rarely saw him because he's a drunk...gets loud and mean when things don't go his way.

Abigail, his wife—rather, ex-wife now—is kind. I hope she'll talk to you. She and Liza were somewhat close."

"I will get in touch with Abigail. Is there anyone else you think I should speak with?"

Carson took a sip of his martini.

"I can't think of anyone else."

"May I speak with Amelia?"

"Sure, but she's the housekeeper. Do you think she'll have something worthwhile to share?"

"I won't know until I speak with her. Sometimes people don't even realize that what they know is important. I just want to be thorough."

"Of course. Thank you. I like thorough. I'll take the kids and you can speak with her."

Carson seemed slightly bothered by the fact that I wanted to speak with the housekeeper, but he spoke to Amelia in Spanish and called the kids to his side. They followed him into another room and I went into the kitchen.

"Hola, señora," I said, holding out my hand. Amelia hesitated at first, but then relented and shook my hand.

"Hello, Mrs. Wilcox," Amelia responded with a shy smile.

"Is it okay if I ask you some questions?"

"Yes, yes. It's okay. Sit, please." Amelia motioned towards the table. We both sat down.

"I am trying to find out who killed Mrs. Stark. I know you had only begun working for her a few weeks before her death, but I would like to hear about your relationship with her. What can you tell me about Mrs. Stark?"

"Are you policia?"

"No. I am a civilian, a regular citizen who looks into crimes on my own."

"Like a...what do they call it? Um...freelancer?"

"Yes. That's exactly it. I am a freelancer."

"Ah, okay. Well, I can tell you that Mrs. Stark very nice all the time, but sometimes, she nervous about things."

"How did you know she was nervous?"

"She having quiet phone calls, and when this lady come to the door, she tell me not to answer. She answer herself."

"So, you usually answer the door, but she answered the door for one visitor?"

"Yes. Small lady. She knock on door and give Mrs. Stark a note. That was the day before she die. I never see the lady before."

"Was Mrs. Stark nervous or angry, happy or friendly, when this lady showed up?"

"Nervous. The lady was using a tough voice. Not sure what she say, but it not look good."

"Would you mind describing her to me? What did she look like?"

"Short, black, a little big."

I wrote down the details. So, a woman had shown up at Liza's door the day before she was murdered. She spoke in a mean voice, and she wasn't someone the housekeeper recognized. Not exactly a lead.

"Had you seen this woman before? Do you think she was a salesperson, or someone trying to talk to Liza about religion?"

"No. I never see her before, but Mrs. Stark see her before."

"Why do you think that?"

"Because she knew her before she go to the door. She tell me 'hold on' when the lady was walking to the door. And she not ask who it was. Mrs. Stark always answer the door when she know the people."

"Okay. So, you usually answer the door, unless Mrs. Stark knows the person, correct?"

"Yes. Unless she tell me no."

"Mrs. Stark told you not to answer the door?"

"Yes. She say, 'No, Amelia, I got it, I got it,' and she do this to me." Amelia demonstrated by flapping her hand in a dismissive manner.

"Anything else you can tell me about the woman?"

"She not have a car. No car in front of house."

Strange. You needed a car to get around Northville Township. If you didn't have a car, you were catching a ride with someone. The public transportation system didn't stretch too far into the suburbs.

"That's all I know."

"Did you tell the police about this?"

Amelia rubbed her hands together and waited before answering.

"They never talk to me."

"Am I the first person to ask you questions about Mrs. Stark?"

"Yes. No one talk to me. If they talk to me, I tell them."

"Is there anything else you can tell me about Mrs. Stark?"

"Uh, no. Just that she was nervous a lot."

"Okay. Thank you. I appreciate you taking the time to speak with me."

Amelia nodded, pushed back from the table, and headed back toward the living room where Carson was with the kids.

A short black woman with a little bit of extra weight, without a car came to the door the day before Liza was murdered. It wasn't much, but it was something. Now it was time to get a look at the murder book.

I MET Charles Kettering when I was five years old. We crossed paths for the first time on a day when my twin brother fell off his bike and scraped his knee. While I was comforting my brother, and helping him up, a burly kid with a thick, low cut afro came our way.

"He all right?" the large boy asked in a soft voice.

"Yeah. He just took the turn wrong," I said, wiping tears from Simon's cheek. I was four minutes older than my brother, but as we aged, the minutes seemed more like years. "Can you walk the bike back to our house?"

"Yeah," Charles said. I turned back to Simon and took his hand. As soon as we started walking, Charles zoomed past me on Simon's bike.

"Hey! You can't ride the bike! I said walk it back!" I yelled, dragging Simon behind me as I ran toward Charles. When I caught up with him, I slugged him as hard as I could. He fell off the bike and started crying. All the commotion brought both sets of parents outside, where they found two sobbing boys and one bossy girl standing with her hands on her hips. Over three decades later, Charles and I were still friends.

Charles was out when I arrived at the 8th precinct but I was still able to get to the murder book. A few years ago, due to a major decline in population, Detroit decided to consolidate precincts. A lot of the guys I'd worked with at the 8th had been consolidated into what was briefly referred to as the Northwest Precinct. Now, after all the consolidating and reconfiguring, the "new" precinct was back to being the good ole 8th. I walked through the double doors and spotted Darrell Anderson behind the call desk.

"Sylvia Wilcox...Now what have us lowly folks done to earn the pleasure of your company?"

Darrell Anderson had transformed his natural snake oil salesman persona into a foundation for a successful career in law enforcement. He was the king of the interrogation room; he could go undercover and weave his way into just about any criminal operation.

"You know me. I only come around when I need something," I said, winking before slamming my hand into Darrell's thick palm, and allowing him to pull me into a "bro-hug".

"How's easy street treating you?" Darrell asked, referring to my private investigator status.

"Easier and easier every day."

We laughed and made small talk for a few minutes. After that, I chatted with a few other guys, high-fived my former boss, and then asked to see Detective Cole. He came strolling out of the back of the precinct with a suspicious smirk on his face. I held out my hand as he approached.

"Detective Cole. I'm Sylvia Wilcox, and I am—"

"I know, I know. Kettering already put a bug in my ear. Let's talk."

Kelvin Cole was short and stocky with fuzzy, but well-kept mutton chops bordering his upper lip. His eyes were sharp and dark, and they stood in stark contrast to his light brown skin.

"I hate to have people in my business," Cole said, gripping my hand tightly.

"Understandable. Thanks for talking with me."

He was around five foot six, attractive, and, based on the fact that he was the only guy with his nose in a file when I arrived, probably a good cop. I could tell by his swagger and laidback sense of humor that he'd probably been born and raised in Detroit. A brief chat with my old chief had informed me that Cole was known for being a solid family man, and was already approaching high solve rates, even though he'd only been a detective for four years.

"How's the case?" he asked, flipping through the murder book.

I tried to catch a glimpse of the information as the pages turned. Murder books are great resources because they contain pictures, notes, and information from interviews, but from what I could see, this one didn't contain much.

"It's not moving as fast as I would like it to, but there are some leads."

"Really? Well, that's good. So, you've chosen the PI thing. How's it working out?"

I thought about the large sums of money I'd collected from spouses eager to know if their significant others were cheating on them. One case could net enough money to sustain me for several months, and if the information helped the victim get a nice divorce settlement, they were gracious and paid me even more. When I'd decided to become a PI, I hadn't considered the financial gains. At the time, I didn't want to be part of the police force. I was bitter, and blamed the DPD for Derek's death. Eventually, it was revealed that Derek's death was not the fault of the department, but I still chose not to return from my leave of absence. After the first few cases as a private detective, I realized that my income was going to increase by leaps and bounds.

"Things are good. Of course, this murder case will be tough, but I think we can solve it. We're just missing something. We need a piece of evidence that isn't there."

"What do you think it is?"

"No idea—but looking at the evidence might help."

The evidence was sparse. The only items collected from the scene had been Liza's gold bracelet, her wedding ring, the carcass of a dead squirrel that had been underneath her body, and a bandana that she had stuffed into her purse. The bandana was the item that had made the police think she was having an affair. Brightmoor was known for its interesting Blood and Crip spin-off gangs. Liza was suspected of seeing one of the gang members, and the bandana was thought to be a gift of some sort, or left behind because the killer was interrupted. The other thing that was curious about Liza's murder was the fact that the killer didn't take her jewelry, money, or vehicle. Instead, they shot her and left...Perhaps in a panic, but maybe because they weren't interested in the money or the other items. This was very strange, and didn't support the cheater narrative. A man in Brightmoor could have supported himself for at least a year with the amount of money and jewelry Liza had on her the day she was murdered. If he'd included the truck in the deal, he would have been set for more than a year. Something else was going on.

"No DNA?"

"Nope. Nothing. The scene was clean. We're pretty sure she was killed there, as opposed to being dumped, but that means she was somewhere else that afternoon and evening. Somehow, she ended up in that alley."

"Lured there?"

"Possibly. She was shot from the entrance of the alley, so she could have been lured there, or chased."

I read over the officers' reports. It appeared that Liza hadn't gone into the party store, so that meant she had probably been meeting someone in the alley, or she had been taken into the alley and executed. The killer was familiar with the alley, and the ability to take a life while one was concealed there, so there was a good possibility that the person was from Brightmoor. I jotted down "local" on my notepad.

"How did you get her there?" I murmured to myself. What would draw Liza to that area? Who was it? What was it?

"There was a footprint in the dirt near the body," Cole said.

"What size feet are we talking about?"

"Smallish. The dude must be little."

"Really? Any photos of the print?"

"Sure."

The footprint was around a size eight or smaller. This was exciting. If they had a shoeprint, it would probably be easy to match it up with a shoe.

"What other evidence is there?"

"There wasn't much, but there are a few insignificant things we gathered from the scene. The way that Liza was found, it was clear that she didn't fight back. She knew and trusted the person who killed her. It was a total surprise."

Who would Liza trust? Her husband, of course, but there had to be others as well.

"The store owner called in the body, right?"

"Yep. He didn't find her until ten o'clock the next morning, but she had been there since the night before. He didn't take out the garbage until that time."

The murder book said that Liza died between midnight and 3:00 a.m. What had she been up to before that timeframe? If she was having an affair and things went wrong, that would explain the time of death. But, since there was no proof of an affair, I had to think about other situations that might have occupied her time before she was murdered.

Could she have been held somewhere before being taken to the alley and executed?

"What leads did you guys have?"

"Virtually nothing. We didn't have much in the way of leads, that was part of the reason why we thought the cheating scenario might be the issue. The husband was difficult to deal with, and we had to consider him a suspect, but no one really thought he did it. It seemed like he loved the woman...he was pretty broken up over things. We hated him, but he wasn't a killer."

"Why did you hate him?"

"He was rude; thought we owed him something, which we did, and we knew that, but he treated us like simple servants. Was always throwing big words in our faces and getting all upset because we couldn't tell him why his wife was in the ghetto, or why she was murdered."

"He was never really a suspect?"

"For a minute—but he was at work during the time that she was murdered, so there's no way that he did it. We thought about murder for hire, but the guy had no major motive. Liza didn't have any money, and they seemed to be happy, so there was no reason to get rid of her. Over time, we figured that we just didn't like him personally, but he wasn't a realistic suspect."

Carson had been relatively easy to deal with, but he wasn't a warm and fuzzy guy. It was easy to imagine him clashing with DPD officers.

"I assume that you guys investigated the infidelity angle."

Cole tilted his head to one side, as if he was formulating what he wanted to say.

"The boss wanted us to close the case fast. When we couldn't, we needed to cast suspicion on the victim. It wasn't right, and it wasn't what we wanted to do. That's part of the reason why I'm the only one here to talk to you."

Corruption runs rampant in some precincts. There's no acceptable excuse, but the job breeds internal breakdowns.

"What happened to your partner?"

"He was disgusted by the politics—one of those die-hard, wanting-to-do-the-right-thing, kind of dudes. From what I hear, he was a lot like you: focused and grounded in morals and ethics that don't always fit in with the way we should do things. You know what I mean?"

I certainly did, and that was the reason why I had left the police force.

"He had been on the force for ten years, but he started young, advanced quickly and avoided politics for the most part. All his success was on merit, but this case...There was more to it... Things that were out of our control."

"Was there someone you thought might be a suspect, but couldn't investigate because you were rushed?"

"No, it wasn't anything like that. I just...well, the family was weird."

"Carson Stark? How so?"

"Not her husband so much, but her parents and brother. The only person in that family that was any help was the sister-in-law. She said that Liza had a secret of some sort. She'd been meeting with some dude, but the sister-in-law didn't think it was an affair."

"Interesting. This is the sister-in-law that recently divorced Liza's brother?"

"I didn't know they got a divorce, but it doesn't surprise me. That guy was wound so tight."

"The sister-in-law thought there was something Liza was hiding?"

"Yeah, and she was friendly, unlike the rest of them. You want a lead to chase, contact the sister-in-law."

"Give me a feel for the family. How are they difficult?"

"The Stark family is old money. The Abernathys are new money. Both families feel put out if you ask them uncomfortable questions, and because they are known for donating money to various charities and organizations in Detroit, including DPD, we had to be 'careful'." Detective Cole used air quotes and rolled his eyes.

"What does 'careful' mean?" I asked.

"This is what got Archie. We wanted to dig into the backgrounds of the two families—thought it might be good to talk to everyone, ya know? In-laws, siblings, everybody. Well, we kept leaving messages for the Starks, and for Liza's parents, but they wouldn't call us back. Eventually, we stopped by their office in Plymouth and the receptionist had a fit. She told us they weren't in the office that day, so we left. The next day, Arch had a sticky note on his desk."

"Cease and desist?"

"That's right. No explanation or reason. It just said that the Starks were irrelevant to the case. Of course, we argued that we couldn't say that until we talked with them, but the boss told us to tone it down and leave them alone. Arch got real mad—went to their house one day when he was off. He shouldn't have done it that way, but he had the right idea. He got written up, but we continued to try to pursue the case. We both decided to move forward with it, and we both became a lot less popular here at the precinct, but it was worth it. We thought we might be on to something."

"Were you?"

"Maybe, but we were stonewalled. We weren't ready to give up. Instead, we switched to the Abernathys. Once again, we tried to schedule meetings, but they refused to meet. The mom sent us an email that said, 'No comment.' No comment on their daughter's murder? Seemed weird, but after contacting them a few times, we received a similar message on a sticky note."

"Did you challenge the idea that you couldn't interview people who were relevant to the case?"

"Yep. That's why Archie is now a hippie organic farmer out west. We challenged and they fought back. Eventually, some rumor conveniently got started about infidelity. The media was beating down our door, and the boss wanted results. When we couldn't get cooperation from either family, and it was clear that they hated one another, we were encouraged to let the rumor fester and take off. No one cares about a woman who cheats. We were pissed, but since we were told to leave it alone, yet again, we had to drop it."

"Where did the rumor come from?"

"Ironically, it was started during an interview with the chief. He threw it out there as a possible scenario. The media loved that angle, and they ran with it."

"It was a plant."

"I can't confirm or deny, but it was strange that he would give them that bone to chew on. You know the media loves drama. After Chief threw it out there, it was a part of every news story."

Why did the chief start the rumor? Why wouldn't the Abernathys or Starks talk with police? I wondered if Carson would be able to get his parents to meet with me. Perhaps I could work through the friendly sister-in-law to get to Liza's parents. They were definitely on my list of people to interview.

"Any theories on why this needed to be a cover-up?"

"Not really. The Stark and Abernathy families have donated a lot of money and time to the city of Detroit.

Usually that means that there's a push to solve the case, unless there is a possible scandal. If Liza Stark was having an affair with a lowlife, it would have shamed the family. Maybe they knew that was going on, figured she was offed by a drug dealer, and didn't want that to tarnish their reputation."

"It does tarnish the reputation a bit...Loose-morals daughter throws it all away for drug dealer boyfriend."

"But it's just a rumor—pure speculation at this point. It's better for the public to think that than for it to be proven. It also takes the pressure off DPD, which is an interesting angle, but I'm sure that figured into the chief's speculation."

"I'm sure. Hey, what about surveillance videos? Did you guys collect anything from the store?"

"Yeah, but there wasn't anything on them. They were low quality and they were focused on the front door, and the back of the building. Unfortunately, you can't see anything on the tapes. It's like nothing happened that night. The angles were intensely focused on the store, which makes sense, especially in that area."

"What about the gang angle? Ali Mansu, the store owner, said that the gangs were harassing him before Liza's body was found, but they haven't bothered him since then. Was there any evidence that pointed towards gang involvement?"

"No. It was strange that the attacks stopped after that, but I think that has more to do with what Mansu did after that."

"What did he do?"

"He took a stand for the neighborhood. Instead of leaving or bad mouthing the place, he really stood up for the community. I think he earned street cred and that's why they left him alone."

"Hmm. Interesting angle."

"I know they're gang members, but they have Bright-moor pride in a way. To see someone stick up for their hood makes them feel good."

I nodded, but in the back of my mind, I thought there had to be more to it than that.

"Interesting. Thanks for your time and insider's view. Dinner is on me one of these nights."

"Don't make promises you can't keep."

"For real. Dinner. Hey, can I get Archie's number from you?"

Cole hesitated.

"Give me a chance to talk to him. I'll give him your number and he can call if he wants."

"Fair enough. Okay, think about dinner. You pick the place and I'll spend the night picking your brain."

"Deal." We shook hands and I headed for the car.

## 4

I spent the rest of the afternoon in the office, brainstorming ideas with Martin. My brother-in-law, Martin Bainbridge, was well over a decade younger than my husband. During a business trip to Wales, Derek's mother, Sharon, had an affair that destroyed her eighteen-year marriage and produced a new family member. Martin was a total surprise to everyone involved except Derek's mother. Even though Sharon moved to Wales and married her new love interest, and Derek was brokenhearted by the end of his parents' marriage, he cherished his younger brother. Once Martin was ten, Derek would fly the boy to Michigan for summers and long school breaks. The rest of the time, he was in boarding schools in England until he turned thirteen, and was shipped off to Vermont. Derek's mother and her new husband all but abandoned the boy to live a lavish life of travel.

Martin had been devastated by Derek's death. He'd stayed in town for a few weeks, ambling along, trying to find his way. I had taken a leave of absence from the department and was spending most of my days at home, examining the details of Derek's supposed suicide. Martin would stop by every day to share developments in a gruesome string of animal murders that eventually escalated to human slayings. Of course, my warnings to Martin and my advice to stop looking into the murders were ignored, and before I knew it, I was super-sleuthing with my brother-in-law. That was the beginning of our partnership. After some time, Martin needed a place to live. Against the advice of all my friends and family, I let my brother-in-law move in, and offered him a job as my assistant. Inspired by his dedication and thirst for truth, I decided to start my own private detective business. Martin and I had been through some great adventures together, and now he was like the son I never had.

"Find out anything?" Martin asked. He was sitting at his desk, hunched over a Styrofoam clamshell container filled with steaming Pad Thai.

"Yeah. DPD didn't want the officers on the case to interview the families. They totally shot 'em in the foot. One guy quit. The other one still works for DPD, but he was forthcoming."

"What about the husband? Any new information?"

"Actually, yes. They never interviewed the maid."

"What? Why not?"

"I'm not sure, but part of me thinks they may not have even known about her. The murder took place in an alley a long way from Liza's home, and it's possible that Carson's interviews took place at the precinct. He was difficult, I guess, but it sounds like it was because they had to investigate him as a suspect. That's uncomfortable, but necessary. Anyway, the maid told me a woman came to the house the day before Liza was murdered."

"A mystery woman! Housekeepers usually know all the dirt on the lady of the house," Martin said.

"You're right. Amelia probably knew more about what was going on in Liza's life than anyone else. Unfortunately, her English is limited, and her job could have been on the line if she'd said the wrong thing."

"It seems like we don't know anything about her."

"Well, we have a little bit to go on. Liza was a stay-at-home mom living in Northville Township. A black woman came to visit her, and she appeared not to have wheels. That tells me Liza had contacts outside of Northville. Not having a car fits with someone from Brightmoor."

"Yeah, but it could also fit a large portion of residents of Detroit. Not to mention, just because she wasn't currently driving, doesn't mean the woman didn't have a car somewhere. How do we narrow the focus?"

"We pray and hope we get lucky. Beyond that, I think we can say, until we learn something to contradict it, that the person was from Brightmoor. She shows up the day before Liza is murdered, she doesn't have a car, and she doesn't enter the house. She stays outside of the house, so we're not talking about a friend, but Liza knew the woman. She told the housekeeper that she would get the door. So, an acquaintance Liza was familiar with, from Brightmoor, came to talk with her."

Even though Amelia hadn't shared anything too private, this mystery woman might hold the key to the case.

"What's the relationship?"

"Not sure, but think about it. Liza had to have been in Brightmoor before she was murdered. She knew the lady. I doubt that someone from Brightmoor just stumbled into Northville and met Liza."

"Right. Liza spent time in Brightmoor."

"Yes. Also, the Starks' place is a little far from that main road, and it's busy, so whoever the lady was, she could have parked at the end of the drive and walked to the house. I just don't see her getting to the house without a ride, even if she wasn't driving. If she did park far from the house, I doubt any neighbors would have seen her," I said, heading over to the whiteboard to draw a sketch of Carson's property.

"Yeah, that's possible, but why park at the end of the drive? I think we must consider that she might not have been driving. Of course, it is odd, because she wouldn't have been able to get there without a car. Someone walking in the area would stand out, and it's not exactly the most diverse part of town," Martin said.

"True, but the properties are built for privacy. Everyone has a little land, and there's quite a bit of greenery because of the state park. It would be easy to slip in and out of that place without anyone seeing you." I drew the long driveway and wrote the name of the main thoroughfare adjacent to Carson's property. Then I grabbed a green marker and scribbled around the house to represent the grass and trees.

"Do you think this person was familiar with the area?"

"She came while Carson was gone, didn't stay long, so it's possible, but it's hard to say one way or another. Maybe Liza was communicating with the woman."

"You think they were friends? Dealer and addict? Or something else?"

I wrote the options on the whiteboard, adding question marks behind each choice.

"There weren't any drugs in her system at the time of death, but we shouldn't completely rule that out. Past drug usage is a possibility. Friends? Well, that's possible, but unlikely. Associate makes more sense. I called and left a message for Liza's friend, Madelyn, the one she was going to meet for coffee the day she was murdered, but she hasn't returned my call. She might be able to give me a more accurate picture of Liza's social life." I stuck the marker back on the edge of the whiteboard and went back to my desk.

"How was the murder book? Anything earth-shattering in there?"

"No, but the D told me something interesting. He said that Liza's family wasn't forthcoming with information. The only person who was willing to help was the sister-in-law. He told me to talk to her if I want a lead."

"That's weird. What about the husband? Was he completely ruled out?"

"He was never really a viable lead, but they did investigate him. He was rude, but no one really suspected him. The other thing that's interesting is that the other D on the case quit because of the politics surrounding the investigation."

"Did he elaborate on that? What type of politics?"

"Carson's parents didn't want to be interviewed. The detectives were encouraged to leave both sets of parents alone. First gently, but after the second attempt to set up interviews they were told to cease and desist. Eventually, a rumor got started about Liza having an affair, and the boss kind of wanted them to let that rumor grow and expand. One of the detectives quit. I'm sure there was more to it, but to have a D quit must mean it was pretty bad. There's like a code of silence about that kind of stuff at the precinct. The fact he told me that much showed he was truly trying to help. I'm sure we'll find out more about whatever cover-up there might be, in time."

"Hmm. What's our next step?"

"Hopefully, the D that quit will call me. He's on the other

side of the country now, so he might not care about DPD politics."

"What would you like me to do?" Martin asked.

"We need more information on Carson. I don't think he murdered his wife, but he's odd. Drinks martinis at ten in the morning, doesn't want to consider the fact that his wife may have known someone he didn't...Total denial. There could be something there. He could be acquainted with the killer and not realize it."

"Okay. Well, I can work on his digital info—maybe see if he has a dark side or something."

"Great. I'll look into the Starks. I'm curious about his family and where their money comes from. Also, Carson's a doctor. People know him. Liza's murder could be some type of vendetta."

"You think Carson is dirty?"

"Not really, but he comes from a wealthy family. Sometimes those folks step on toes."

Martin shoveled a few more bites of Pad Thai into his mouth before grabbing his jacket and heading out.

I OPENED my laptop and started searching for biographical information on the Stark family. A simple internet search for Carson Stark pulled up hundreds of hits. I browsed through the listings and clicked on an announcement about his high school graduation. Back then, Carson had worn a shaggy page-boy cut that made him look much younger than a high school senior. A slight smirk creased the right side of his mouth, but his eyes were stern and serious. The Starks had bypassed public school and sent Carson to a private school in Bloomfield Hills, Michigan. He'd excelled in math, science, and English, and played rugby. Below the first picture were several smaller photos. One contained a tall, leggy blonde with the same page-boy haircut as Carson, identical eyes to her son, and a stiff arm around his shoulders. Another photo showed Carson and his father, a man who was at least five inches shorter than his son, with dark brown hair and cool blue eyes. The family portrait that contained all three of the Starks resembled somber photographs typical of those taken in the early 1900s: no smiles or emotion on their faces. By all accounts, Carson was just your average rich doctor, born and raised in a prominent Northville Township family that had been in the area since the late 1700s. At least, that was how it appeared on the surface. The second hit in the search provided personal information on the family. While Carson's paternal side of the family seemed to follow an established pattern of wealthy family succession, his mother was anything but conventional.

Based on Aileen Stark's birthdate, she was now seventy-seven years old. A woman ahead of her time, Aileen McDonaldson's story was a true rags-to-riches tale. Her parents had emigrated from Ireland in the 1920s and lived in a working-class neighborhood on the west side of Detroit. Aileen won a scholarship to a prestigious private school, went on to the University of Michigan, and became a doctor. That meant she had attended medical school in the 1960s— a truly remarkable feat.

In addition to being a surgeon, Aileen hadn't given birth to Carson until she was forty-three years old. There were several pictures and videos of Aileen Stark. She was at least six foot two, blonde and blue-eyed, slender and regal. Aileen had been a celebrity in her own right. As a female doctor and mother, she would have been a darling of the media. I clicked on a blurred video of an interview with a local news affiliate. Aileen Stark was dressed in a blue suit jacket and a crisp white shirt. One long, shapely leg was crossed over the other, and a flat navy-blue dress shoe dangled in the air. Her tone was smooth and even as she answered the interviewer's questions.

"What was it like to be one of two women in the University of Michigan's medical school the year you entered?" The host was a dark-haired man with slight crow's feet at the corners of his eyes. He leaned in after asking the question, his eyebrows rising as he waited for an answer.

Aileen Stark sat with her back rigid and her face stern. She waited, sighing before answering.

"It was exhausting. Constantly working to prove that I was as good as other students was absolutely exhausting, but it wasn't just at school. It carried over to my family, where all my brothers and sisters were getting married, working in the auto plants, or becoming stay-at-home moms. I was in school, single, and childless. I was viewed as a failure of a woman."

"While all the while you were a trailblazer. Interesting. So, what is it like now that you have married and had your son? Is practicing medicine still as worthwhile as it was before you were a mother and wife?"

Aileen Stark threw her head back and let out a robust but controlled laugh. "It's never separate, but the roles are never meshed together, either. The three entities—mother, doctor, and wife—coexist. I love each role and don't think that one diminishes the others. Women can, and should, pursue their career goals. The husband and children will happen if they are supposed to, but no woman should make that her sole purpose in life."

I stopped the video, feeling admiration and intrigue. I wanted to meet this trailblazer.

Next, I read an article in a business magazine that provided a brief summary of the Starks' love affair. Married in 1968, Brian and Aileen first met in 1960 at the University of Michigan, but their paths did not cross again for eight years. The article described how Brian and his friends had secretly laughed at Aileen's ambitious career choice, but when he fractured his hand and went to the emergency room, he was treated by a resident named Aileen MacDonaldson. The article quoted Brian Stark as saying, "I knew I had to marry her. A girl like that is rare." By that time, Brian was vice president of Stark Construction and one of the most eligible bachelors in Michigan. Their marriage, three months after the emergency room visit, had been the talk of the town.

Due to Aileen's age and dedication to her career, children were not expected, but six years into the marriage, Carson arrived. The article went on to detail Carson's accolades and discuss his immigrant ancestor and the rise of the Oliver Stark empire. Oliver Stark had come to the United States from England in the late 1700s. Initially, the family had lived in New York, but Carson's great-grandfather moved to Michigan in the mid 1800s and invested in steel and steam engines. By the late 1800s, the Stark name was associated with success and wealth.

Carson Stark had continued in his parents' footsteps by being a standout athlete and scholar in high school. He'd earned a scholarship to Yale, had finished medical school six years prior, and was a surgeon at the Detroit Medical Center. By all accounts, Carson seemed to be the perfect upstanding, predictable success story. The guy had money, good looks, and power. Liza was a beautiful woman, but it hardly sounded like they moved in the same circles. How had they found one another? A man like Carson could have had any woman. Why did he pick Liza Abernathy?

I considered that he might just be an altruistic, warm-hearted guy, but from what I'd seen so far, that wasn't the case. It wasn't that Carson was cold or pompous, but he didn't exude warmth either. He seemed utilitarian and sterile—qualities that are excellent for a surgeon, but not necessarily great for a marriage. I opened a Word document and typed Carson + Liza? After that, I went back to researching the Stark family.

By the twentieth century, the Stark family fortune had multiplied thanks to a shift into the construction business. Carson's grandfather had gotten in on Detroit's Gilded Age, a time when housing and skyscrapers were being built at a rapid rate. Back when architecture and style mattered, the Starks helped bring classic, but affordable bungalows, Victorian mansions, and Italian revival estates to life. World-renowned architects came to Detroit and partnered with the Starks to sculpt immaculate churches and sprawling estates. Over time, as the tastes and the pocket-books of Detroiters began to change, the Stark family began building simpler homes. Stark Construction built numerous low-income housing developments around Metro Detroit, including in Brightmoor. By the time Carson came along, the fortune was secure and robust. I'd heard of Stark Construction, but hadn't made the connection until now.

Most of the coverage I'd read of Liza's murder focused on the shock of a Northville socialite being found dead in Detroit, but several reports included snippets about Aileen Stark, and how she was a pioneer for women in the field of medicine. She was one of the few women to successfully complete medical school in the 1960s. The combination of the Starks' wealth and Carson's mother's groundbreaking achievements, made the Starks a power couple—movers and shakers in Metro Detroit. I was dealing with a powerhouse in Carson Stark. A quick internet search told me that Aileen and Brian Stark still ran Stark Construction out of an office in Plymouth. Curiosity moved me to hop in the car and head to their office.

## 5

Rush hour was beginning to snarl the traffic, but a jigsaw route of back roads delivered me to the Starks' office in twenty-five minutes. The office was a small, well-kept Victorian house. I parked in the adjacent lot, squeezing the Taurus between a shiny, vintage black Monte Carlo, and a dated Chevy Lumina, and bundled up before stepping into the chilly air. A series of bells announced my arrival and a buzz beckoned me into the cozy lobby. A petite woman, with a name tag that read "Latoya" and skin the color of caramel corn, greeted me with a smile.

"Hello. Welcome to Stark Real Estate and Construction. How may I help you?"

I answered her with a big smile and an outstretched hand. Her tiny fingers, limp and weak, fell into my palm.

"I need to speak with Mr. and Mrs. Stark."

"Okay. Are you a renter or a homeowner?"

"I'm a homeowner."

I wasn't lying. I was a homeowner. I just hadn't bought my property from the Starks.

"Excellent. Give me the address and I will get you in right away."

I gave the receptionist my address, hoping that Mrs. Stark didn't know all of the addresses of her properties by heart. I sat in an elegant bronze chair featuring a lion's head at the end of each arm, waiting to be thrown out of the office. The receptionist strolled down the short hall, stayed away for about five minutes, and came back to the desk.

"Mr. Stark is busy, but Mrs. Stark has agreed to see you."

Aileen Stark was standing when I entered the room. She clasped my hand in a tight handshake, towering over me like a scion. Her thin, blonde hair had a few streaks of gray here and there, but she looked no older than fifty-five. Her body was taut and toned, and she walked the way she had sat in the old interview I'd watched on video: tall, proud, and strong. Her hair was cropped quite close to her skull, with just enough length left for pleasant curls to weave their way around the sides of her head. She had the slightly masculine air that was so common among women who had worked in male-dominated fields.

"Mrs. Wilcox. I've been expecting you."

Nothing mentioned about the deception I'd used with the receptionist.

"Thank you for meeting with me."

"It is a pleasure to meet another pioneer. I've heard great things about you from Carson."

"It is a pleasure and honor to meet you as well, Dr. Stark."

"You've researched me."

"Just a simple collection of data...but no less impressive, Dr. Stark."

A tight-lipped smile spread across her thin lips.

"You are here about Liza. How can I help?"

"As you know, Carson has asked me to look into her murder. It appears that Liza did not have many friends, so I'm talking with family members to get a feel for who she was."

"Hmm—I see. A type of, shall we say, psychological autopsy?"

"Something along those lines. The DPD has been kind enough to share a little information with me, and I couldn't find any information on interviews with you or your husband."

"That's correct. I couldn't stomach talking with petty cops. The comments they made on the news and the way they handled the investigation was appalling. When they insisted on meeting with us, we refused on principle."

"You thought that the police didn't do a good job investigating the case?"

"Mrs. Wilcox, I have much more faith in a determined young woman who seeks the truth than a bunch of young, untrained, and uneducated men."

I thought about the amount of intelligence and college degrees held by the guys on the force. Assuming that the officers were untrained and uneducated was rather arrogant.

"Did the officers offend you?"

"No...They just asked elementary questions. I suspect your questions will be much more advanced. You've already intrigued me with the psychological autopsy."

Police have a different scope and sequence than private detectives. I wouldn't be asking Mrs. Stark any of the basic questions because the detectives from DPD had already done that. I was thankful to them because their "elementary" line of questioning was going to work in my favor. The key to keeping Aileen Stark talking was to remain interesting to her.

"What was your opinion of Liza?"

"I don't know that I had an opinion of her. I loved her because my son loved her. He was happy and that's all that matters to me."

"Okay. Did you and Liza ever have daughter-in-law/mother-in-law dates?"

Aileen Stark laughed and threw her head back.

"Oh, Mrs. Wilcox, you don't know a thing about our family, do you?"

"No, ma'am, I do not. Would you mind telling me what I need to know?"

"Yes, I think we should start there. There are no dates. Not even Brian and I have dates. We have appointments and business to take care of, and we do our best to see Carson and his family on the holidays. Our love is not based on time spent together. The cliché is true—absence makes the heart grow fonder."

"Okay. Makes sense. When was the last time you saw Liza before she died?"

"It had been at least a month, maybe more. Brian and I want to stay healthy, so we keep busy. If we're not at the office, we're out with friends or attending a charity event. Carson and Liza were also very busy, so we mostly reserved the holidays for family get-togethers."

"What do you think happened to Liza?"

Aileen Stark sighed.

"No theories?"

"I'm not a private detective, Mrs. Wilcox. I don't like to speculate."

"I understand, but for the sake of Carson, would you care to wager a guess?"

"An affair gone bad."

"So, you think that particular gossip around the case is accurate?"

"Sometimes common gossip is common because it's true."

"I agree, but sometimes when something happens to a person we're close to, we have our own theories."

"So true. If I had been closer to Liza, I probably would have an assumption or two about what happened to her."

Not shy about the fact that she didn't care for Liza.

"Is that your Monte out there," I asked, attempting to lighten the mood.

"It is."

"Looks great."

"We're into cars. I only drive it on special occasions."

"Nice. What's the special occasion?"

"We have a fundraising event in Novi tonight. Don't worry, I won't be wearing this. My gown will be dropped off before I leave...and before you ask, the fundraiser is for single mothers in Detroit."

"Sounds like a worthy cause."

"Mrs. Wilcox—I am smart, but I also was lucky. I didn't believe the things I was told about womanhood; it made all the difference. So, I give back to those who have fallen prey to the idea that a woman needs a man, or children to be worthwhile. It's still a prevalent theory in our society, so I don't hold it against anyone. Since you're here, I have to assume that you feel the same way."

It was true. I did pity women who thought that they weren't worthy simply because they weren't married or because they didn't have children. Life was more complex than that.

"With that in mind, Mrs. Stark, I still see the value of

being married and a mother, and that is why I am here. There are two children and a husband who will never have their wife and mother back. The woman just happens to be your daughter-in-law. Is there anything else you can tell me to help find out who took her life?"

Aileen Stark waited for a moment; her forehead creased while she considered the question.

"I wish I had something more, something that could help, but I don't. I'm sorry to have wasted your time, Mrs. Wilcox."

Fair enough. It seemed that I had gotten all the information I was going to get from Aileen Stark.

"Thank you for your time, Mrs. Stark. If Mr. Stark has a break in his schedule, I'd like to speak with him as well."

She nodded her head in a manner that told me it was highly unlikely that Mr. Stark would ever be available to talk with me. We shook hands again and I saw myself out.

I HAD an idea of what might have made Carson's family standoffish, but I had no idea what to expect from the Abernathys. The loss of a child was undoubtedly painful, but during my time as a cop, families of victims were often overzealous and determined to give officers every piece of information, even if it seemed completely irrelevant. The fact that they had been uncooperative was strange. It was time to get to know the victim's people. The preliminary information I'd gathered told me that Liza was from a different world than Carson.

After jotting down a few notes, I called Peter Abernathy a second time to set up a meeting. He was less than enthusiastic, but agreed to meet at 4:00 p.m. the next day. After talking with Peter Abernathy, I was able to get a hold of Madelyn Price, and we set up a meeting for the following morning. By the time I was finished with my cyber-sleuthing and appointment setting, it was 5:30 p.m. I decided to close my laptop, relax for the rest of the evening, and start fresh in the morning.

I woke early the next morning, brewed my coffee, and got a run in before 6:00 a.m. Winter was warring with spring, fighting to keep the chill in the air. The breeze was crisp, cool, and refreshing, but the soft rays of early sunlight brought the temperature up to ideal running weather. After my run, I showered, slipped on a gray pantsuit and boots, and pulled my hair into a bun. Madelyn Price had agreed to meet with me at ten o'clock that morning, and Peter Abernathy was scheduled for 4:00 p.m. I reviewed the preliminary information on Madelyn while eating a bowl of oatmeal with fresh apple slices and cinnamon.

Madelyn Price was the last person to hear from Liza, which made her an obvious person of interest, but the fact that she was still a supportive friend for Carson made her a somewhat unlikely suspect. Madelyn and Liza had been scheduled to meet for coffee on the day of the murder, and even though Liza had never made it, they had exchanged texts. It's possible that could have been orchestrated if Madelyn was the killer, but that was a leap in logic at this point.

The phone conversation with Madelyn Price had been strange. She'd spoken in a slow, subtle tone, devoid of the emotion I'd expected to hear from one of Liza's good friends. Her address put her on the outskirts of Ann Arbor, close to the border of Dexter. I took Ann Arbor Trail to a secluded dirt road that I would've missed if not for the pale blue mailbox that read "Price." The bare branches of winter-stripped trees enveloped the narrow, bumpy road. A quaint red-brick converted farmhouse was tucked away behind a thicket of trees at the end of the dirt road. I pulled up beside a row of cars that sat adjacent to the house around 10:00 a.m.

A chilly wind smacked me in the face as I stepped out of the car. I grabbed my briefcase and moved swiftly onto the wide country porch, past the hanging swing bench, and to the front door. A sign that said, "Come in! We're Open!" dangled above the window. A small bell rang as I entered.

Madelyn Price owned a yoga studio that she ran out of the lower floor of her house. Soft lighting surrounded an empty reception desk, and the quiet, calm murmurs of a yoga session crept into the hallway. I proceeded down a dim, narrow staircase into the foyer, took a seat in a wide hallway that served as a lobby, and watched the end of a class through the squeaky-clean glass doors. Madelyn and her students folded into the Downward-Facing Dog before getting into a seated position for cool-down. A collective murmur of "Namaste" came from the room as the class ended. I studied Madelyn's pleasant face as she spoke in a soft tone that bounced gently off the glass doors. After a few relaxation breaths, Madelyn dismissed the class and a crowd of women of various backgrounds and ages gathered around their teacher. She smiled and conversed briefly with the students, flashing a warm, but well-practiced smile. Ann Arbor is full of male yogis—I wondered if Madelyn Price conducted classes for men as well. Within minutes, the room was clear and Madelyn was standing in front of me with a tight smirk on her face.

"Hello. Mrs. Wilcox, I presume?"

Madelyn, who was barely five feet tall, held out a small, incredibly soft and manicured hand. She was a tiny woman with flawless sable skin that conveyed no indication of her age. Her eyes were large, slightly almond-shaped, and such a deep brown that from certain angles, they looked midnight black. Her sharp, strong nails caught the edge of my palm on the release of the handshake. She wore a thin smile and avoided all attempts at eye contact, and her small frame gave off a hint of vulnerability as well as a strange air of caution and comfort.

"Thank you for meeting with me, Ms. Price."

"Of course. We can talk in my office," Madelyn said.

I followed her through the pastel pink studio into a moderately sized, neat and clean space that had probably served as a washroom at one time. A large desk, free of office trinkets, was in the left-hand corner of the room. Madelyn Price didn't have any personal items in her office: it was clean and professional, and two red-cloth-covered seats sat adjacent to the desk. Without turning her head, Madelyn caught my curious glance and creased eyebrows.

I could see her eyes flicking around. Intense peripheral vision...A relic of criminal behavior lying just beneath the calmness, or had I been doing this job too long?

"My office is different, I know. I want my students to feel like we are all on the same level, so we sit side by side when they come to talk with me."

"Interesting. I like that approach," I said.

"Thank you. I hope it creates a sense of welcome."

She smiled and sat down, folding her hands on her blue leotard-clad lap.

"Thanks again for meeting with me. I'm interested in what you can tell me about Liza."

"Yes. I know," Madelyn answered with the tone and composure of Buddha. I attempted to make eye contact, but she continued to avoid my gaze.

"What do you think happened to Liza?"

"It's hard to say. She was my student and associate, but I don't think I have any information about Liza's murder. I can tell you a little about our connection."

"Okay. Anything you can tell me would be helpful."

"We met years ago, when we were both living another type of life."

"Was she also your best friend?"

Madelyn looked taken aback by the question.

"We were acquainted, and she was my student. I first met her in high school when we were, as I said, living a different type of life."

Student and acquaintance? That was a little different than being best friends.

"What other type of life were you two living?"

"Drinking, partying...we were reckless, uninhibited. Our boyfriends were friends. There was a time when we bickered over a loser, but you know how teenage "love" is. We only came into contact with one another a few times. After that, we, fell out of contact, and then came across one another years later. We exchanged information and...well, you know how it is. Old acquaintances promise to reconnect and keep in touch. Most of the time that doesn't happen, but this time it did. We emailed, met for dinner a few times, and became friends. When I opened the studio, I invited her to take classes for free, as I did all my friends. Liza was one of the few that took me up on the offer," Madelyn said

"Carson told me that you would come over for dinner often, and watched the kids now and then. You and Liza must have been close."

"I guess we were friends. I still do those things with Carson and the kids, even though Liza is gone." An absent-minded hand smoothed hair that was perfectly sculpted into a bun.

"It sounds like you and Liza were very good, or best friends. She trusted you."

"Yes, and I trusted her."

"I'm trying to get a feel for Liza as a person. Anything you know could be helpful."

Madelyn nodded her head, but remained silent. She wasn't going to give anything I didn't pull out of her.

I said, "Carson says that an affair is out of the question."

"He's right. There was no affair. Liza loved her family more than anyone I know."

Edgy voice, troubled face. She had turned in her chair to face me.

"You sound sure," I said.

"Absolutely."

"Really? No doubt that there might have been something she didn't tell you?"

"No—not about that. She was not having an affair."

There was too much certainty in her voice, and her hands were gripping the sides of the chair. How could she be so sure that Liza wasn't having an affair? Her small fingers applied enough pressure to lose color. I decided to change the subject.

"Can you walk me through what happened that day you and Liza were supposed to meet for coffee?"

"Sure. Liza called me the night before and asked if we could meet for coffee. Said she had something to talk with me about. No, she didn't give me any hints, and it was late, so I just agreed to meet. We decided on three the next day, Sunrise Café in Farmington."

"What was her tone? Did she sound nervous or agitated?"

Madelyn thought for a moment. "I would say she sounded cautious."

"Any idea why she would need to be cautious?"

"No. Liza was a private person. So am I."

"What happened the day you two were scheduled to meet?"

"I got to the café around two fortyish. Sent Liza a text telling her I had arrived and was going to grab a table."

"Did she respond to that text?"

"Not directly. I sat there until three thirty before I ordered a coffee and a croissant. I ate slowly and enjoyed the weather on the patio. At ten past four, I received a text message from Liza that said, 'Running late, but still coming...' I continued to wait until five thirty. At that time, I was a little annoyed and decided to leave. After I hopped in the car, I thought, 'What if something happened?' I sent Carson a text asking if he'd heard from Liza. I didn't hear from him for several hours. He's a surgeon, so I expected as much, but during that time I called Liza twice, and sent a few text messages. When Carson responded telling me that he couldn't get in touch with her, I called him and explained how she'd stood me up. We were both at a loss."

"Were you able to leave voice messages when you called Liza?"

"Yeah, but I didn't. I was confused and angry. Wasn't sure

what to say, but I didn't want be rude in a message, so I just called and hung up when she didn't answer."

"Did you speak to Carson again that night?"

"Yes. He called around two that morning."

Two o'clock in the morning was within the kill zone. Could the two have collaborated and murdered Liza?

"What did Carson have to say at two in the morning?"

"It sounds strange that he would call me at that hour, right? But who else could he call? Liza's family is estranged. They would not have been any comfort. I told him that he needed to file a police report the moment he got off work, which he did. He called me from the police station to tell me that the officers were arguing about filing a missing person report before the obligatory twenty-four-hour waiting period. I told him that wasn't true. He just had to force the issue and the report would be filed."

Smart lady. There is no law saying that twenty-four hours must pass before a missing person report can be filed. Somehow, that stipulation had slipped into the vernacular of police forces around the country, but it was largely a myth seemingly created in the 1970s, when people were apt to hitchhike, and take off without letting loved ones know where they were going.

"When did you hear about Liza's murder?"

"That afternoon. Her body was found that morning, not too long after the police finally let Carson file the report. Carson called me around three that afternoon. Identification was easy, and the cops were at Carson's door soon after the body was discovered."

"What happened next?"

"I rushed over to be with Carson and the kids. It was chaotic. His parents were there; so were Liza's parents. I know all of them, so it was good to be there to lend a hand. I helped with the kids, made tuna casserole, and tried to comfort his parents and in-laws. Later that day, Peter—Liza's brother—and his family came to the house. The rest is hazy."

Liza had been killed between midnight and 3:00 a.m. Where had she been between 4:20 p.m. and the time of her death? Liza never cancelled her coffee date with Madelyn, which was interesting. She was either planning on making it and got sidetracked by the killer, or she had plans that overlapped. The last text Liza had sent said that she was running late but still coming, which supported the theory that she had run into her killer that afternoon. If the killer was a lover, perhaps they argued, made up, argued again, and the second time the argument ended in murder. Carson had told me that Madelyn called him at 5:45 p.m. asking if he had heard from Liza. They were originally scheduled to meet at 3:00 p.m. It seemed like a long time to wait for someone to show up.

"Why did you wait so long at the coffee shop?"

"Liza was always late. Whenever we were meeting, I knew to bring something to keep me busy while I waited for her to arrive. That time, I took my books from the studio. I was reviewing payments for my online subscriptions and payouts to my assistant teachers. The time flew by."

"Any idea why Liza wanted to meet at Sunrise Café?"

"We meet there often...Good coffee and friendly faces, and it's just a nice, quaint area. We started meeting there when she lived with her parents in Livonia. Back then, we would walk around downtown Farmington—solve all the world's problems."

"So, this particular coffee shop holds a special place in your hearts: would that be fair to say?"

Madelyn thought for a moment.

"You could say that, but we were just meeting for coffee. It isn't inherently a special place. It is nice that they know us there. Kind of makes meeting for coffee even more inviting."

"When was the last time you received communication from Liza?"

"The text message at twenty past four. After that, nothing."

The murder file hadn't explained the gap between the time they were supposed to be meeting and the inquiry from Madelyn. Liza had sent Madelyn a text message just before 4:30. That was the last time anyone had heard from Liza. Carson and Madelyn both called and sent text messages to her phone throughout the evening. When Liza was not home by the time Amelia's shift was over at 6:00 p.m., Carson begged the housekeeper to stay with the children until Liza got home. At 6:00 the next morning, after Carson's shift was over, he headed straight for the police department to file a missing person report.

"So, how'd you get into yoga?" I asked.

"Remember the other type of lifestyle I mentioned? Well, yoga helped me relax when I was changing my life."

"I understand. Got into it myself after my husband died. It was very helpful."

"Yoga is great for many things. I began about fifteen years ago. Got tired of cardio—wanted something that I would get more out of." Madelyn paused and then said, "I am sorry about your husband. Carson told me that was why he chose you."

I was surprised by the comment but managed to maintain a poker face. Carson Stark had done research on me, that I knew. It was strange that he'd conducted research about my dead husband, but it was even stranger that he'd told Madelyn about me. The fact that she was bringing it up felt odd as well—like she was trying to throw me off the scent. But what scent did she think I'd picked up? I pondered the point while she chatted away.

"He said you had all the right credentials; you also know what it's like to lose a spouse. You're a woman, so you would respect his need to know what happened, even though the leads are nonexistent. And you are a chameleon."

"A chameleon?" I'd been called a lot of things in my day, but never a chameleon.

"You're from Detroit. You're black, but you are your own person. You don't fit into the stereotypes put forth for what some would call 'us'."

Madelyn had taken my decision to change the subject and turned it against me. Her eyes were minuscule, haunting slits of darkness. I wasn't entirely comfortable with her, but she had something to tell me and I needed to find out what it was.

"What about you, Madelyn? You aren't a stereotype either. Tell me a little bit about yourself. I want to get a feel for the person that Liza Stark called her best friend."

"Born in Detroit, Michigan; left the city when I was eighteen, and rarely return. I moved to New Orleans for a brief period, but missed living in Michigan. I attended U of M and have a master's in counseling. I teach yoga and do therapy on the weekends. I don't drink, smoke, or eat red meat. I say my prayers to Buddha, Jesus, Allah, and anyone else up there that should happen to listen. Don't own a television..."

"That's it, eh? Where did you live in Detroit?"

"Westside."

"Oh yeah? What neighborhood?"

There was a long pause before she said, "I don't see how that matters."

Standoffish. Irritated by the question.

"Just curious. I grew up around Schoolcraft and Livernois."

"I grew up on the west side of the city."

Extremely vague. It was clear that this was not something Madelyn wanted to discuss.

"Well, what can you tell me about Liza? What was she like?"

"Kind, caring and giving: all the things women want to be, but rarely are. She had found a way to be those things."

"Interesting. And how did she manage to do that?"

Madelyn smiled and shook her head. "Detective, if that answer was easy to come by, I'd be a millionaire."

My interview was starting to go places I didn't want it to go. Madelyn Price was an enigma, one of those people who had a riddle or philosophical conjecture for every question.

"Where did you meet Liza?"

"We met through a chance encounter in the city, close to my high school."

"Where did you go to high school?"

"Why?"

"Just curious...I grew up in Detroit too."

Madelyn hesitated. I saw a crease in her jaw. The past wasn't something she was comfortable with.

"Redford," she said after some hesitation.

Redford High School was closed now, but it had been located a few miles away from where Liza's body was found. Madelyn knew I would pick up on that and start to wonder if she was familiar with the area. Even so, the hesitation had been obvious.

"Where did you live?"

"Around Telegraph."

Another vague response, but not so vague that it would

be strange. But because Liza Stark's body was found a few blocks from Telegraph, it was strange.

"I know that area well," I said. "'Poor Brightmoor', we used to call it. Had some friends who lived there when I was a kid. It was also the beat I worked as a cop. What street did you live on?"

Madelyn took a quick glance at her hands before answering, "Dolphin Street."

I hadn't been to Brightmoor in quite some time, but I remembered the area well. I'd been placed in the 8th Precinct fresh out of the police academy, and quickly learned that Brightmoor was a great place to disappear or die. Children were expected to fall prey to drugs, pregnancy, or death, so no one was watching for wayward youth. Sex and drugs flowed freely through those blood-drenched streets, and women like Madelyn rarely emerged from that part of town. Graduating high school was virtually unheard of, and finishing college was a miracle. Seemed like an odd place for someone like Madelyn to grow up.

"When did you move from Dolphin Street?"

"Mid-nineties."

"Where did you move after that?"

"Louisiana."

"Nice. I love it there. How long did you live in Louisiana?"

"A few years. Then I transferred to the U and moved to Ann Arbor."

"Ann Arbor is a great place to live. Do you ever go back to New Orleans to visit?"

"Sometimes...Not as often as I would like, but a few times every year."

"I spent some time in New Orleans after I graduated from college—great place to visit," I said.

Madelyn nodded. The interview was starting to wane. I decided to ask a few more questions and wrap things up.

"Liza was into yoga, but she pretty much seemed like a soccer mom in practice. Homemaker, red meat eater, Northville Township address...seems like her life was much different from yours. What was the connection?"

Madelyn pondered the question for a moment and smiled. It was the first time her lips had curled into condescendence.

"It just so happens that different people who live different lifestyles can be friends, Mrs. Wilcox. How long were you married?

It was an odd question to tack onto the end of her statement. I hesitated before responding.

"Not long enough." The struggle to keep the pain out of my voice failed.

"Ah. For that I am very sorry, Mrs. Wilcox." This time she was sincere and concerned—the counselor in her coming out.

"I met Derek when I was five. We married in our mid-twenties and Derek died a few months after his thirty-fourth birthday."

"Your one true love..."

"Correct."

An awkward pause hung in the air. My thoughts drifted away from the interview.

"I have a class in ten minutes; I must prepare," she said, pulling a business card off the desk.

"Thanks for your time," I said.

"I know I haven't been terribly helpful, but if you need to speak to me again, feel free to call or email."

Madelyn stood up and handed me the card. She was so

small, but there was a certain sense of power emitting from her. I couldn't put my finger on what it was.

"Thank you again, Madelyn." I shook her tiny hand and smiled, catching a nervous smirk on her lips before I turned to leave.

"I hope you find out what happened to Liza. She was a good person and Carson deserves to know," Madelyn said as I headed for the front door. I noticed that her warm, calm tone had returned.

---

## 6

Madelyn Price was difficult to read, but the fact that she had lived in Brightmoor meant that she had ties to the area where Liza had been murdered. Even though almost two decades separated her residency in the neighborhood and Liza's demise, it was quite a coincidence. There had also been some hesitation in telling me where she'd grown up. Madelyn said she had met Liza when they were living "a different kind of life." She had never mentioned where they'd met, but she had known her since high school. But if they met around Redford High, they were probably somewhere in Brightmoor.

Various scenarios ran through my head as I crept along the narrow dirt road. Liza Stark was killed in an alley in Brightmoor. The alley she was dumped in was one street over from where Madelyn Price had lived. If Madelyn had lived on Dolphin Street between Fenkell and Six Mile Road, it would simply be too much of a coincidence that Liza's body had been found on Dacosta Street between those two thoroughfares. Of course, Madelyn had moved away from Brightmoor sometime during the nineties and Liza's body was found in 2011. Well over a decade had elapsed between when Madelyn lived in Brightmoor and when Liza's body was found. What was the connection?

Madelyn Price knew more than she was saying. She'd also been a little cagey about her life. I made a mental note to find out more about her when I got home. I glanced at the time on the car's dashboard: 10:50 a.m. I wasn't meeting Peter Abernathy until 4:00 p.m. that afternoon, which meant I could swing by Brightmoor.

There aren't many restaurants in Brightmoor, but if Liza had spent time with a side piece, or anyone else, they'd probably stopped by Mickelson's Fish N Chips. It had been in the neighborhood for decades, and their fish was well-known beyond Detroit's borders. I stopped in for the "Famous Fish and Chips." Simple wooden chairs and cafeteria-style tables lined the restaurant. The walls were covered in fishing and shipping paraphernalia, and an old jukebox sat in a corner. I took in the sights and waited patiently to talk with the cashier.

The woman at the counter wore an unremarkable ponytail that brushed the top of her waist. Her face was plain, but pretty, and free of make-up.

"How are things in Brightmoor these days?"

"Same," the middle-aged woman said without looking up from the register. She pointed me in the direction of a rickety two-top.

I sat down and surveyed the room, taking note of the six other patrons. None of them looked like residents of the abandoned and fire-bombed neighborhood that lined Dolphin Street. This was a place that had survived in Brightmoor, but it was not of the neighborhood. The chairs were filled with professionals and elderly couples crowded around rickety, wooden tables. This was a place out of time.

The white flight of the 1970s had taken the regulars to homes in the suburbs, but they returned to rekindle nostalgic memories of their childhoods. After cashing out several patrons, the woman from the cash register came to my table, pen and pad in hand.

"Have you ever seen this lady?" I pulled out Liza's picture and put it on the table top.

"Ya, she's been in here with another lady."

"More than once?"

"Ya, couple of times. Who's asking?"

"Sylvia Wilcox. I'm investigating her murder."

The cashier looked up; her eyes wide with alarm.

"Oh, that's the lady, isn't it? The one that was having the affair and got killed? Probably a gangbanger. She should have known better..."

"What can you tell me about the two women?"

"Nothing special...Just seemed like two friends. They laughed, ate lunch, and talked."

"What did the other woman look like?"

"Short, tiny actually, with black hair in a bun. Pretty."

Madelyn Price? Why would they be in Brightmoor? Neither of them lived anywhere near the neighborhood.

"Were they regulars?"

"No, but they came in a few times. Nothing major. Probably three or four times. We don't get a lot of new people in here, so when newbies come in, we notice. Try to keep them coming back."

The fish and chip shop sat across the street from the alley where Liza's body was found. Why were the women hanging out in Brightmoor? Two successful, attractive women of means traveled to one of the most dangerous neighborhoods in the state to hang out? Why? The fish and chips were delicious, but Brightmoor was so far out of their realm.

Liza and Madelyn weren't of the neighborhood, but they had an affinity for Brightmoor. There wasn't really a better explanation that I could think of. Maybe they came back to stroll down memory lane. But how good could the memories be? Not better than being a successful yoga teacher and stay at home mom married to a doctor. Why live in the past?

"Thank you. Hey, great food!" I tossed a forty percent tip onto the table and left. On my way to the car, I brushed past a group of girls dressed in red, with red bandanas in their pockets and on their heads. It was the same pack I'd seen in the party store the previous week. I turned around and headed back into the restaurant.

"Hey, do the locals come in much?"

The cashier looked up. "No. We don't allow gang colors, so most of the locals stay away. We have a good reputation. People are willing to cross Telegraph for our fish. Gotta keep it safe in here."

I slipped back out the door, looking for the girls, but they were nowhere to be found. So far, I had confirmation that Liza and Madelyn had been in the neighborhood; now I needed more information about why they were there. I had no idea how to find that out. I decided to switch gears and head around the corner to the house of the woman the party store owner had told me stopped in after the store closed on the night Liza was shot. I drove around the corner and sat adjacent to Amber Dukes' house. I watched for signs of life. After about twenty minutes, a small woman with thick-framed glasses came out and walked down the street. She came back about ten minutes later with a cup of coffee in her hand. Amber Dukes wore thick, Coke-bottle glasses that were pushed high on her sharp, pointy nose. Her skin was pale with a hint of orange, common in people who spend time in tanning beds. Her hair was a thick blanket of wild, curly gray hair that fanned out around her head. She opened the gate in front of her house, pulled two dog leashes out of her pocket, and hooked them to the pair of Rottweilers in the yard. I stepped out of the car and headed toward the house.

"I don't want anything, so don't even try to sell it."

"I'm not selling anything. I'm a private investigator looking into a murder of a woman. She was from Northville Township," I said, knowing that mentioning the posh town would trigger her memory. "She was murdered and left behind the party store down the street. I want justice for her family." I spoke loudly to overcome the barking of the dogs.

"Justice? Well, ain't that nice. Kids have been dying in these streets for decades, and now because some rich white lady died, we need to find justice? I ain't got nothing to say."

It wasn't the friendliest response, but it indicated that the woman had been living in the neighborhood for quite some time. I let her anger die down a bit before continuing.

"Ma'am, I worked these streets as a DPD officer for several years. I care about justice for the people of this neighborhood, but I don't think that just because someone doesn't live here, or they are a certain race, they don't deserve justice. I want justice for everyone—especially the little children Liza Stark left behind."

The woman opened the gate and looked back.

"You worked this hood? Prove it."

"In 2008, we ran a sting operation that ended the drug ring that ran from Dolphin to Trinity. This led to an increase in vacant houses, but most of them had been crack houses, so it made the neighborhood safer. Your former neighbor, Jon Jennings, lived two houses down. He was robbed at gunpoint one weekend and shot the next. We caught his killer within a week. Shall I go on?"

The woman freed one hand and turned to face me.

"Amber Dukes," she said, giving me a warm handshake. "Sorry for being so salty. I'm just tired of people looking for justice for only some people. I guess you work all sides, and that's all right with me. What do you wanna know?"

"How long have you lived here?"

"Twenty-five years...Bought my house for twenty thousand dollars. It's not perfect, but it's our little slice of happiness. I didn't know that the drugs and gangs would spring up around here the way they did, but my husband grew up in this area. He wanted to come back for some reason— probably because he's a long-haul trucker and he don't have to be here often." Amber Dukes let out a cackle. The laugh lines showed her joy and happiness.

"Did you know that the woman who was murdered in 2011 lived in that house across the street in 1996?"

"Naw! No way! You gotta walk with me: these dogs aren't going to wait."

I walked beside Amber as the two dogs pulled her down the street.

"Liza Abernathy lived across the street. She would have been young, in her late teens. Any of that sound familiar?"

The woman's forehead creased as she struggled to keep up with the dogs and see if she remembered Liza.

"She looked much different then, but here's a more recent picture." I pulled out the picture Carson had given me.

"Yeah, I remember her. She was living with a no-good loser. He was dangerous. His whole family was into things. There was one time when his sister, who also lived there with them for a while, was dragged down the street by the father of her children. Rumor has it that the baby's dad came back and killed her daddy. Crazy shit!"

"Do you remember his name?"

"Hmm...let me think. Dejuan? No. It was De-something. Maybe Demario...Ya—that's it! I remember it because he ended up getting arrested later on for something. He was on the news and I recognized him."

"Okay, and Demario's father was allegedly murdered by his pseudo brother-in-law?"

"That's what we heard. The father was found in an overgrown field...Was a John Doe for a few weeks. Don't know how true that was, but there was a time when the supposed killer's mother came over to the house and there was a huge argument. They were out in the street screaming and hollering. We called the police. It was ugly."

"How many people would you say lived in the house?"

"Don't know—but the family of the man was always coming and going. One night, a cousin broke the front window. It was one of those things where the family was just crazy: always arguing, always fighting, and every now and then they would shoot at one another or break windows... Not the best neighbors to have. In fact, they are the reason why we have a fence. We were worried because their kids would come into our yard and do whatever they wanted. They got no home training."

"What can you tell me about the girl, Liza Abernathy?"

"Not much. She was just your average follower who didn't really make much of an impression. Her eyes were dull and dim—not the brightest lady, obviously. We never saw any other white people, so her family was not involved in her life. We figured they'd disowned her, ya know? Not because he was black, but because he was no good. The only real memory of her I have is the catfight she had with this girl that came by. She was a little girl, but she was scrappy. They fought over the no-good man, which was just a shame. The black girl had a little one with her. She sat her kid on the lawn and went to the door with a great deal of fury. It was bananas! I watched the whole thing from my window. I called the cops, but they didn't come that time."

"You wouldn't have recognized Liza after she got married, but she drove a red Range Rover. Do you ever recall seeing that truck on the block?"

Amber thought about it for a moment while she waited for one of the dogs to take care of his business. She pulled out a bag and cleaned up when the dog was done.

"Well, now that you mention it, I saw a red truck that was too new for this neighborhood. If you're smart, you don't buy new cars around here. They will be stolen, or they will get you killed. Yeah, there was a red Range Rover around these parts, but I haven't seen it in some time."

Of course—because Liza was now dead. I found myself going back to the fight that must have been between Liza and Madelyn.

"The fight you told me about—do you know what it was about?"

"Yeah, everyone on the block knew. A love triangle. He was living off both of them. Let's just say it was our soap opera for a while. Every day, something new happened."

"Is there anything else you remember about Liza, Demario, or Madelyn?"

"There were rumors that the black girl was smart... Washed her hands of him and moved out of the neighborhood after she graduated high school."

Madelyn Price had come a long way. Impressive.

I thanked Amber Dukes and headed back to the car.

"Hey, keep me updated. I want justice too!" Amber called after me.

"Will do!" I called back to Amber. I had enough evidence to safely say that Liza was in Brightmoor prior to her death, and that information might change the entire investigation.

I WAS MEETING Peter Abernathy at Liv's Diner, a classy little dive on the edge of downtown Plymouth. I spotted a tall, thin man with white-blond hair spiked in every direction. He was leaning against the diner door, engulfed in a cloud of smoke. Peter Abernathy had a hardened look, just like his sister. According to Carson, he was five years older than Liza, ill-tempered, and had rarely gotten in touch with them. I parked in the far-right corner of the parking lot and headed toward the diner.

"Mr. Abernathy," I said, reaching out for Peter's hand.

Peter nodded and held my hand for a moment, applying no pressure before yanking his hand back after a few seconds. I watched him pull the cigarette out of his mouth, stomp out the butt, and apologize for smoking.

"Don't worry about it," I said, holding my breath to avoid inhaling second-hand smoke.

It looked as though life had been hard for Peter Abernathy. His face was worn and leathery, and he looked about ten years older than he was. I watched his gnarled hands reach for the door and wondered what had prematurely aged him.

"Thank you for meeting with me, Mr. Abernathy."

He nodded, said it wasn't a problem, and told me to call him Peter. I followed him into the restaurant where a sign directed us to seat ourselves.

"Any preference?"

"How about that booth over there by the window?" I said, pointing across the dining room. We headed to the booth and sat opposite one another.

A tall waitress with a bored look on her face came over to the table and took our order: burger and fries with a Coke for Peter, a salad with Italian dressing and water for me. Once the waitress was gone, I tried to make eye contact, but Peter avoided it. I heard the creak of the leather booth beneath his shaking leg and wondered if he was having nicotine withdrawal already, or if he was nervous about something else.

"So, you wanna know about Liza," he began with a jerk of the head and an evil sneer, before leaning in close over the table.

"Yes, but first, I want to say that I'm sorry for your loss. I also appreciate you taking the time to meet with me."

Peter snorted and shrugged. I persevered.

"Your brother-in-law has hired me to investigate your sister's murder, and while I understand you two weren't close, I'm interested in what you can tell me about Liza. The detectives on the case are completely swamped and have no leads. Carson wants answers, and I believe that some of those answers will come from me finding out more about your sister."

Peter ran a hand through his hair, leaving it a complete mess, before puffing out his cheeks and blowing cigarette-smoke-laced air my way. I held my breath and controlled my eye-roll as best I could.

"What do you wanna know?"

"What type of relationship did you have with Liza?" I asked, now wanting to get the interview done as soon as possible.

"We weren't close. She had her life and I had mine. We were five years apart, so we never went to the same school at the same time or had the same friends. By the time she got to high school, I was out of the house."

The shaking of his leg had quickened.

"I can understand that. When you have age gaps like that between one another, it can be tough to be close, but anything you can tell me about the years you did spend together would be helpful."

Peter's head jerked again. What was all the nervousness about? Perhaps he just had a tic. Or did he have something to do with his sister's death?

"She was my parents' little angel. She raised holy hell in high school, but they took her back when she came knocking. I was in college then, but I know she ran away and got involved with some bad people." Peter Abernathy wrangled a pack of Camel Reds out of his green army coat. He tapped the pack of cigarettes on the table before putting it back in his pocket. His nervousness was increasing.

"Been three months...Sobriety's a bitch, but it's the only way I can see my kids. Might even get my wife back if I keep it up."

I felt my eyebrows arch in an "ah-ha!" moment. He was an alcoholic—still going through detox. The nervousness was explained...Or was it?

"Congratulations," I said, offering up a warm smile that produced a glimmer of hope in Peter Abernathy's eyes. He had his own demons; probably hadn't spent much time thinking about his sister's. Addicts aren't selfish. Their worlds are built on a self-centeredness that is necessary for any addiction: they don't have the capacity to think about others because they're controlled by a substance. Peter might not have much to tell me, but I pushed on with the interview.

"I'm sure you've heard the speculation about Liza possibly being involved in an extramarital affair. What do you think of those rumors?"

"She liked 'em. I mean, no offense, but she was into black guys before Carson. Growing up in Livonia, we weren't well stocked with 'em, but Liza found 'em anyway. Not the nice ones either. I mean, no offense, but she went for the ones with the baggy pants and braids in their hair. Not the ones...like you."

No offense was taken, but it was interesting to see how antsy the subject made him. He was not necessarily a racist, but someone who was uncomfortable with race. I considered what he was telling me. So, there had been a time when Liza had had an interest in the type of man Detroit typically produced. Had a deadly craving led to her demise? Were the gang attacks at Ali Mansu's store somehow tied to Liza?

"Do you know anything about Carson and Liza's relationship? Did you sense that they were happy when you saw them?"

Peter's top lip twitched before he spoke. "I'm not a fan of Carson. He's a stuck-up punk who wants to control everything."

"Is there anything else you can think of about Liza, her marriage...anything that might help me find out who killed her?"

"I ain't got much to say. We weren't close. It was her choice as much as mine."

"Did Liza have any enemies?"

"Probably. She was strange. Not real warm and fuzzy. Kind of a loner."

"When was the last time you saw Liza?"

"I think it was Memorial Day. It was right around the time Abigail and I started trying to work things out."

"Was Liza herself? Did anything seem off?"

"She was a little quiet and she looked distracted, but she was in the kitchen with the girls, my mom, and Abby most of the day. I was out with my brothers-in-law—Abby's brothers—on the boat. Carson breezed in and out, claiming he had to work."

"You mentioned that Liza was rebellious during high school. Was she ever estranged from the family?"

"Yeah...she ran away in high school and was gone for years. Eventually, she showed up on my parents' doorstep."

"Did she ever talk about where she was during that time?"

"Nope, she just left and stayed away for years. I was pretty pissed at her for putting Mom and Dad through that shit; didn't really talk much to her when she returned. Eventually, Abby encouraged me to make amends."

"Do you think your sister had any ties to Brightmoor?"

"The place where she was killed? Well, I figured she had to know someone there. I've never been there, but I hear it's pretty slummy. She could have been having an affair, but there's really no telling what Liza was up to over there. She wasn't always the best judge of character...Could even have done something stupid, like offered a ride to someone."

"Do you know her friend Madelyn?"

Peter's face softened.

"Yeah...I know Madelyn. She's a good person."

"That's what I've heard. What is your relationship with her?"

"We don't have a relationship, but I've met her a few times. She used to come to my parents' house every now and then. She and Liza would take trips together, hang out at the house...She was a good influence on Liza—helped her get her shit together."

Peter's face was calm and pleasant when he talked about Madelyn. Could there have been a twisted sibling love triangle? Peter loved Madelyn...Liza loved Madelyn...so someone had to be taken out of the picture?

"When was the last time you saw Madelyn?"

"Well, let me...Hey, what is this? Why you asking about Madelyn? I thought you wanted to know stuff about my sister."

The waitress returned with our food. She set the plates down cautiously, noticing that Peter was becoming increasingly agitated.

"I just want to make sure I have a clear picture of who Liza was. For that to happen, I have to know about her friends and family."

"Well, all you need to know is that Madelyn was good to her. She was an amazing friend, so no need to go barking up that tree."

"Okay. Did you know that Ms. Price lived in Brightmoor for a time? She lived about two blocks from where Liza's body was found."

"No, I didn't know that, but I don't see how that could be relevant. I know that Madelyn lives in A2 and has for several years."

Yes, I was reaching, but I'd investigated too many murders to believe in coincidence. What did it mean that Madelyn had once lived so close to the murder scene? It meant something; I just wasn't sure what.

"Did Liza have any skeletons in the boyfriend closet? Men who might be angry that she left them behind?"

"Sure—like I said, she dated bad boys."

"Do you remember any names of men she dated?"

"Not really. Like I said, we weren't close. In fact, the less I knew about Liza's shenanigans, the better. I gotta get back to work soon."

I ate as fast as I could and thanked Peter for meeting with me.

"Mr. Abernathy, if you remember anything else, please let me know."

"Yeah," he said, pushing away from the table, cigarette pack already in hand.

"Thank you," I said, but Peter was almost at the door.

## 7

The meetings had produced mixed results. I wasn't sure if we were further ahead, behind, or exactly where we'd started before the interviews. I turned on my Bluetooth and called Martin.

"Progress is slow on this end. How are things going for you?"

"This isn't going to be an easy one. I haven't come up with much, but I'm headed to St. Bart's to talk with Liza's old coworkers. She was a substitute teacher who landed a long-term sub position. The school couldn't find a permanent teacher for the spot, so she made it through the entire year. Doesn't sound like it was a good experience for the principal."

"Okay. Well, get whatever you can from them, and we'll meet tomorrow morning. I'm heading to the office to do some super-sleuthing."

"Internet?"

"You got it!"

"10-4."

Since I didn't have a suspect, I decided to search for

information on Madelyn and Peter. He was a bitter sibling with his own problems, but his anger about her teenage angst may have been more about his temperament and less about how he truly felt about Liza. Madelyn, on the other hand, had worked hard to present a picture of complete stability and calm; however, she was very guarded when I asked about her life, and she had once lived in the neighborhood where Liza's body was found. At this point, everyone was a suspect, but Madelyn and Peter didn't really fit the profile for suspects. Peter didn't have a motive unless it was bitterness, and the anger could simply be part of his disposition. Recovering from alcoholism was no small feat. If Madelyn had a motive, it involved Carson, but a romance between Carson and Madelyn was unlikely. It would have been an obvious avenue for the police to investigate. Even so, if it was a theory, it didn't hold much weight. Basically, none of the information I had gathered so far really amounted to leads or suspects. I needed something plausible.

Madelyn Price had been less emotional than I'd expected her to be, but in time, any grieving person learns to cope by pushing the pain into a tiny space in his or her heart. It wasn't that they weren't upset and missing their loved one, it was more the fact that one can't be actively mourning and still function successfully. Even so, it was strange that Madelyn had lived in Brightmoor. The odds of her knowing more than she was willing to share were good.

Tracking down address information online isn't difficult, so I decided to embark on the mindless, easy task of tracing addresses. I started with Peter. He had lived in Livonia, East Lansing, Farmington Hills, and Plymouth. The most recent address was in Plymouth, a nice quiet neighborhood on the edge of Canton. A quick search of Peter's social media revealed short, basic posts such as, "So cold out here" and "Missing my girls. All four of them." He seemed to post every couple of months, but, like Liza, he didn't really seem to be into social media.

Next, I decided to search Madelyn's address history. She'd lived on Dolphin Street between 1992 and 1994, which meant she had moved there when she was about fifteen or so. Liza would have been sixteen in 1993, when she lived in Brightmoor—not exactly an age when most young people move out on their own, or have a house in their name. It was odd that both women had left home so early. Was it possible that the two had been emancipated youths? The Detroit address was in Brightmoor, but it wasn't the same as Madelyn's. Liza had lived on Dacosta Street, which was very close to Dolphin. I pulled up the address and verified that Dacosta was just one street over, and the address where Liza had lived was adjacent to the alley where her body had been found. Interesting, but not proof of anything other than the fact that both Liza and Madelyn had lived in Brightmoor.

I went back to the list of Madelyn's addresses. She had lived on Oakman Boulevard, which had been a fashionable street back in the 1980s and early 1990s. Mid-sized homes, middle-class families, and a relatively low crime rate for Detroit had made the area desirable for the city's successful residents. The fact that Madelyn had moved to Brightmoor was strange. Perhaps she'd had trouble with her parents and went to live with an aunt and uncle, or a cousin.

Why would two sixteen-year-old girls who weren't originally from the area be living in Brightmoor? It didn't make sense. Next, I pulled up Madelyn's address and saw that it was within a one-block radius of Liza's former residence.

The two women had both lived in Brightmoor, but that was close to fifteen years ago. What did this mean? Was it possible that I needed to adjust the timeframe of the investigation to include the late 1990s? I'd planned on waiting to check in with the senior Abernathys, but now it seemed imperative. I placed a call to Liza's parents. After four rings, the voicemail came on. I heard a soft male voice, tempered with a hint of confusion, whispering into my ear.

"You've reached the Abernathys. Uh...leave a message, and we will do our best to get back to you." I left a message explaining who I was and asking if we could arrange a meeting. I repeated my phone number twice and disconnected the call.

After the call, I considered strategic searches of the web that would help me decipher information about Madelyn. As a private detective, the internet is your friend. I was registered with all the pertinent social media and networking websites, and I considered which ones might have information on Madelyn Price. I settled on a website that allowed old high school classmates to find one another. Madelyn's name was listed in her class, showing that she'd once registered and logged into the system. Overzealous reunion planners had scanned the yearbook and uploaded it to the website.

Madelyn Price, it turned out, had been president of the French Club, a member of the Honor Society, and a teenage mom. She'd paid for a full page in the yearbook, but most of the page was taken up with photos of her daughter, Kara. She appeared to have been a toddler by the time Madelyn was in twelfth grade. I remembered how cautious Madelyn had been when I had asked about her past. Her daughter would be a teenager now. I clicked on another tab and googled Kara Price. Results from a gymnastic tournament popped up first. A lean, small-boned girl with a bright smile, Kara looked like a younger version of her mother. She had shiny eyes and thick, bushy hair pulled back into a cute bun like her mom's, but, unlike her mother, Kara's hair refused to be tamed. According to the results, she had finished second in the tournament and had gone on to compete at the state level. Another page showed Kara at the statewide spelling bee and stated that she was a student at an all-girls college preparatory school. I was familiar with St. Mary's—the tuition fees were steep. In fact, some colleges were cheaper. Was a paycheck for a stealthy "hit woman" helping to fund little Kara's education? It was far-fetched, but Carson had plenty of money to spare, and if he had wanted Liza dead, it would have been easy to lure her into a trap with her "best friend." Of course, it wouldn't make any sense to hire a PI to investigate a murder you'd orchestrated. I wondered just how much Madelyn was bringing in at the yoga studio.

Madelyn didn't have any social media accounts, but Kara had one that she seemed to use sporadically. Her posts were vibrant and intelligent. The teenager seemed to try, and succeed at times, to be introspective, insightful—and impersonal. The one exception was on April 22:

Happy birthday to my beautiful mother who sacrifices so much for me! She is my inspiration and I will always strive to live up to her impeccable example! Love you, Mom

Kara was respectful, enrolled at one of the best schools in the state, a standout athlete and a scholar. Madelyn had to be a proud mom. The only reason Madelyn wouldn't mention Kara was if she thought her daughter might be hurt, or put in danger by something she told me. Or perhaps Madelyn didn't want to share much because the less she shared, the less I would suspect that she was guilty. I went back to the yearbook website and printed out a picture of Madelyn Price. A teenage mom turned yogi, college professor, and counselor was a somewhat irregular path. I didn't have statistics, but I was sure that Madelyn's life represented the road less traveled.

I jotted down Madelyn's daughter's name and birthday. After that, I ran Liza's name through the system, but couldn't find a trace of her. There was a chance that Liza had simply never signed up to the website, but I wondered if perhaps she hadn't graduated high school. As a troubled youth, she might not have finished twelfth grade.

I spent the rest of the day looking for gaps and holes in the narrative. I needed to reconstruct Liza's life from the age of sixteen onwards. I spent some time searching online for more information; I dug further and found out that Liza had a GED, not a high school diploma, meaning that not only had she lived in Brightmoor, but was a dropout while she was there. I considered all the trouble she could have gotten into as a teenager with so much free time, and wondered what she'd done to keep herself occupied.

Several other names came up in a search of possible relatives. Names that I expected popped up—Peter Abernathy, Liza's parents, and Carson Stark—but there was also another name: Demario Masters. I typed "Demario Masters" into the computer and received several mugshots in the results. I opened another tab and looked for address information for Demario Masters. A few addresses popped up for him. One included Madelyn Price and Liza Abernathy was listed along with Masters, for another address. Liza and Madelyn had lived with the same guy?

"Bingo!" I muttered.

Next, I entered Demario's name into the Offender Tracking Information System and found out that he had committed a few minor offenses in Michigan and Louisiana, but those were all dated crimes. He was currently serving four 15- to 60-year concurrent sentences for sexual misconduct. He also had acquired a felony as a juvenile and been locked up from the age of fifteen to nineteen. It looked like he'd been released in January 1996; Kara had been born in December 1996. That meant he had met Madelyn, who would have been fifteen when he was released, and gotten her pregnant almost immediately.

Attempted murder at the age of fifteen was usually a sign of things to come. It wasn't a stretch to think that Demario had committed the crime close to, if not within the boundaries of Brightmoor. My guess was that he had grown up in that area, and that was why Madelyn ended up living there. My former precinct was just outside the jurisdiction that held the now-defunct Redford High School—the school from which Madelyn had graduated, and I assumed Demario Masters had attended. I searched through a newspaper database using "Redford High School" and "stabbing" as the keywords. Several hits popped up, but only one took place in 1993, the year Demario was incarcerated. Since he'd been a juvenile, no names were used, but the article described a gang fight that ended with one student being stabbed in the head. That definitely fell into the attempted murder category, but that area of the city had been teeming with violence at the time, due to the crack cocaine epidemic. Demario could have been the perpetrator, but so could any other violent youth in the area. I tried to think of old-timers on the police force that might be pining for a stroll down memory lane. The felony had occurred in the 6th Precinct, across the street from Redford High. I wondered if there were still guys around the 8th Precinct who remembered the stabbing, or the kid who had committed the crime. I sent Detective Cole a text asking if he'd heard of Demario Masters. My phone rang a few minutes after the text was sent.

"Hey, Cole. What can you tell me about him?"

Cole was quiet on the other end. After hesitating and sighing, he said, "I'm busy for the next couple of days, but don't move on this thing until we talk, okay?"

"I'll do my best. What can you tell me now?"

"Slow down, Sylvia. Just wait for a few days and we'll meet up." A sharp edge of warning was in his voice. I heeded it.

"Okay. Call me when you're free and we'll set something up."

After I hung up, my head started to spin with questions that were not going to be answered that evening. I closed my laptop, curled up on the couch, and slept until the next morning.

THE COLD MORNING air brought light, fluffy snowflakes. I was snuggled under a beige-and-brown afghan, my head bent at a slightly awkward angle. Shaking off the crick in my neck, I went to the kitchen, started a pot of coffee, and headed for the shower. At 6:30 a.m., I slipped on a pair of black dress slacks and a red, button-down blouse. Next, I sent Martin a text telling him to meet me at the Blue Gill at 7:30 for breakfast. Just as I was heading out the door, Mr. Abernathy called and agreed to meet at 10:00 that morning.

Even though it was only seventeen degrees, I decided to walk to the Blue Gill. I bundled myself up in a knitted scarf and heavy cardigan and slipped on an overcoat and flat black boots. The snow was easy to traverse. My boots crushed the white powder, still fresh and un-shoveled, creating a slippery trail behind me. The crunch of the accumulated flakes echoed with each step as I trekked the three blocks to the restaurant.

Martin's long, lanky frame was folded into a booth at the back of the dimly lit diner. He wore a beige sweater, faded jeans, and brown moccasins.

"Hey," I said, sliding into the opposite side of the booth.

"Morning. You find anything interesting?"

I smiled and shook my head. "You're never going to believe this."

"Try me."

"Liza and Madelyn lived in Brightmoor at the same time. They were sixteen-year-olds, living less than a block from one another, and there's a man who is listed as living at both of their addresses."

"The same guy?"

"Yes! Can you believe that?"

"Oh, man! What do you think is going on?" Marty asked.

A tiny waitress with a smattering of freckles and thick, curly red hair pulled into a bun came to our table. She smiled and asked for our orders.

I ordered an eggbeater omelet with home fries and wheat toast, and Martin ordered a stack of blueberry pancakes.

"I don't know. It doesn't make much sense. These two young girls from totally different worlds—inner city Detroit and Livonia—end up in the same place for one year. They have a man in common. Over the years, they seem to be friends, but twelve years later, one of them is murdered a few steps from where both of them lived."

"But even if they had this man in common, and there was a love triangle, it obviously played out long before Liza's murder. Liza was living the life in Northville and was married with kids. Madelyn is a counselor and yoga instructor, living in A2, and obviously successful. Maybe there had been some trouble in the past, but they seem like smart enough ladies to get over that, right?"

"Sure, but there's one problem with that."

"What?"

"Liza Stark is dead."

"Well, tell me what you're thinking."

"I think Madelyn should have been a little more emotional than she was when I went to talk with her about Liza. I know it's been a while, but if my best friend had been murdered it would take me forever to get over it. Discussing it two years afterwards would still produce some emotion. That's another reason I think Madelyn knows something or is connected somehow...I just don't know how."

"Yeah, death is so permanent. It's not something you get over. Especially since it seems they had known each other since they were pretty young."

"Right. So, we need to find out more about what happened way back in Brightmoor."

"You think that's really connected?"

"I don't know. It was a long time ago, but we should check things out anyway."

The waitress set down our plates. Martin's stack of blueberry pancakes was as wide as the plate. My eggbeater omelet was stuffed full of veggies and cheese.

"Anything else?" the waitress asked.

"No, we're fine. Thanks," I said.

Martin sawed off a hunk of pancake and soaked it in syrup. I stirred my omelet and home fries together before squirting ketchup on the mess.

"The brother was also weird. He was standoffish and a bit rude. I sensed some bad blood between the siblings, and no one dishes like a sibling scorned. He still seems bitter about the parents babying her."

"It's silly to still hold a grudge against a dead sibling. Petty and coldhearted," Marty said.

Peter hadn't shown any remorse or love when I had spoken to him about Liza. My brother had been missing since I was ten years old and there wasn't a day that he didn't cross my mind. I had been in a state of mourning for more than two decades, but Peter Abernathy didn't show any signs of sadness over losing his sister.

"You have a point, but I don't think he has a clear motive. There's not much online about Peter—a couple of social media posts about his family and the weather, but nothing major. Run a background check on him; maybe talk with people from his job. I'm going to set up another interview with him next week and pay Carson a visit at home."

"What's the plan for Madelyn?" Marty asked.

Great question. There wasn't any information on Madelyn Price on social media sites, and googling her name turned up very little. She owned a yoga studio and was a therapist. Normally, that would mean an online presence of some sort. It was strange that her name didn't turn up anything.

"I think Madelyn is hiding something. The Brightmoor connection may be involved in the murder."

"Do you really think that Liza's death is the result of something that happened over a decade ago?"

No, I didn't. But I didn't really know where to start with this case. So far there wasn't any proof that Liza was anything besides an upstanding woman at the time of her death. The fact that her good friend had once lived in the neighborhood her body was found in gave me pause. I didn't know what the connection was, but something was off.

"What do you think this is all about?" I asked Marty.

"I think Liza Stark slept with some guy, he asked her for money or something, she refused, he killed her and dumped her in Brightmoor. Case closed. Sorry, Mr. Suburban Doctor Guy, your wife was sleeping around with some loser."

"Is that some plot from one of those Wednesday night cop shows? Not the kind of answer I expect from my brilliant little sidekick," I said, before throwing money on the table and getting up to leave.

"Sometimes the simplest answer is the right one."

"True, but we don't have much to support that theory. You find some evidence, and we'll go down that rabbit hole."

"Fair enough."

Infidelity felt too easy. There had to be more to the story. I thought about my conversation with Madelyn. She had been a bit vague, but did she seem like Liza's killer? Not really, but that didn't mean she wasn't guilty—or maybe she just knew more than she'd told me. Either way, I needed to investigate.

"I need to know more about Carson and Madelyn. That would be the only way I could see Madelyn being the killer. She and Carson are close, but Peter also really likes her. Personally, she doesn't seem that warm and fuzzy to me, but then again, I'm investigating her."

"And you're a woman. She probably charmed those guys."

"True. Okay, how did it go at St. Bart's?"

Martin handed me a file with Liza's name. "Check out her personnel file."

"How'd you get the file?"

"That's classified," Martin said, winking and letting out a giggle.

"Cheeky, cheeky," I said, wagging my finger like a concerned mother.

I opened the folder and flipped through the pages. Liza had been written up twice in the year she'd taught at St. Bart's for having too many visitors at school. Both write-ups stated that a visitor had interrupted her class. Her personnel file also stated that she had not been invited back to teach the following year.

"So basically, she had too much company and didn't stand out in other ways, so she was fired?"

"That's the gist of it. Also, her coworkers weren't that fond of her. No one seemed to have a grudge or anything, but they were a bit indifferent when I told them that she had been murdered."

"What did they say about her?"

"Generally, she was late for work, not that reliable, and she couldn't get along with students' parents. It sounded like the year she spent there was rough. The principal didn't want to talk to me, but there was this one lady, Mrs. Dawson, who gave me the dirt."

"And the file." I winked and smiled, watching Martin's face fall.

"You always have to ruin my fun."

"That's what I'm here for," I said, suppressing a giggle.

"What did she say?"

"Mrs. Dawson seems to be the only person who had any contact with Liza outside of work. She told me that Liza was only there to impress Carson. They had started dating the summer before. He's a devout Catholic, ambitious, successful, etc., and she wanted to make him think she was a sweet deal. Mrs. Dawson told me that Liza never planned to stay there, so she didn't mind her mother coming up to the school and interrupting her class on a regular basis."

"What? Her mother?"

"Yeah. Apparently, Mom was a little overbearing. Mrs. Dawson told me that she worried about Liza because she wasn't...How did she put it? 'All there'."

"You think this Mrs. Dawson was being straight with you?"

"Yeah. She's probably beyond retirement age—loves teaching; a motherly sort. I could see her taking a new teacher under her wing. Sounds like Liza needed that."

"I wonder what made Liza such a needy case?"

Carson Stark was a great catch. He could have had any woman he wanted. Why did he choose Liza?

"We need to find out more about Mom's connection with Liza. Her showing up at her grown daughter's job is weird. I'm heading over to talk with Mom and Dad today. Will you get some info on the parents?"

"Sure thing."

"I can't understand how Liza and Carson ended up together."

"Yes, seems weird, but that doesn't really matter, does it?"

"Well, I think it does matter. What if some other woman thought herself to be more deserving? Maybe it just took her a few years to work up the nerve to get revenge. Carson may seem nice enough, but he is part of the elite. Sometimes, things us commoners don't flinch at cause irrevocable harm to the elite."

"Hmm. I hadn't thought of that."

"That's why I keep wondering how and why they were together. There might be something more to their marriage."

"I'll see if I can find any connections."

"Okay. I'm going to continue looking up information. Maybe Liza left some hints if she was having some type of affair. Hey, I almost forgot to mention the gang activity that took place at Ali Mansu's store. So, before Liza was murdered, Ali Mansu says that he experienced attacks from gangs. After Liza was murdered, there weren't any other attacks."

"So, you think this is a slumming case? Liza got mixed up with a gangster? But what does that have to do with the store owner?"

It didn't make sense. What connection did Liza have to Ali Mansu and the store?

"We're missing something. I wonder why the other detective quit?"

"Corruption? Does Liza have any connection to the police force?"

"Not that I know of, but we need to leave that possibility open."

I remembered how much pressure was applied when a murder took place in Detroit and the victim was from one of the posh suburbs. The prostitutes, drug dealers, and Detroiters caught in gang crossfire were viewed as low priority, but a young, beautiful blonde was high. Or was she? Why hadn't the police pursued the murder to a greater extent?

"The fact that the chief told them to let the infidelity rumor stick tells me that it wasn't important to solve the crime. It was important to make the crime go away."

"Why?"

"She's different from the rest of the socialites from Northville Township, but still, she isn't the type of person the media usually forgets about. She an attractive, upper middle-class white female. Why was she shoved out of the spotlight so soon?

"For some reason, she doesn't fit into that society."

We looked at each other and simultaneously asked, "Why?"

"Okay. You do some background searches on Liza and her family. I'll keep my date with Liza's parents."

I TOOK Prospect Road down to the freeway and headed for Livonia. During the drive, I thought about the information I'd found online about Liza's parents. Ralph and Janice Abernathy were a middle-aged couple living out a typical, southeastern Michigan suburban existence. Both were retired school teachers, active in the Lutheran church that sat two blocks from their home, as well as world travelers, and well-known philanthropists. I had found several write-ups on them in their hometown newspaper. Peter had been featured a few times when he played high school football, and his parents seemed to make regular appearances in the paper. Liza had five entries. Her birth announcement, notices about the birth of her two children, an announcement about her marriage to Carson Stark, and her obituary.

It took me twenty-five minutes to get to Livonia. The Abernathys' split-level colonial sat on Six Mile Road, just north of Newburgh. As I pulled into the driveway, I noticed that the garage door was up and a snazzy red Corvette sparkled and shone in between an organized system of shelves and tools. A blue, late model Camry sat at the edge of the driveway. I pulled in beside the Camry and headed to the door.

Janice Abernathy opened the door before I could knock.

Liza's mother looked to be five foot seven, about 125 pounds, and resembled an aging Barbie doll. She had the stereotypical blonde hair and blue eyes, and her body was sleek and toned. However, her face was worn, with wrinkled folds of skin, and she bore the same faint hardness that I'd noticed in Liza's photographs. She forced a smile, revealing deep crow's feet around her eyes.

"Hello, Mrs. Abernathy. I'm—"

"Sylvia Wilcox. Yes, I know. Please come in."

Mrs. Abernathy led me to a white leather couch in the living room through a long hallway lined with family portraits and individual headshots of Peter. Brown plush carpet crushed underneath my boots, making me feel like I was walking on clouds. Pictures of the family were also clustered on the mantle. There was Peter in a football jersey during younger, happier times. Liza was pictured with the kids—minus Carson—smiling that blank smirk. Her eyes appeared just as empty as they did in the picture I had of her.

"So, Carson has hired someone to try to find out who killed his wife. Well, it's about time."

Strange choice of words: his wife, not their daughter.

"Yes, he is dedicated to finding Liza's killer, and I am determined to help him get justice for her."

Mrs. Abernathy let out a hard, angry chuckle.

"Mrs. Wilcox, I admire your determination, but you and Carson can't have the same goal."

"Why is that?"

"Because he killed my Liza!"

"What makes you say that?"

"He's a doctor, with money, power, and looks. There's no way he would have chosen Liza over all the other girls that wanted him—unless he had a plan. He profited from her death. He's happy she's gone."

Not the most refined interpretation of the crime, but she was a mother grieving her child. Contrary to Mrs. Abernathy's interpretation, Carson hadn't profited from Liza's death. The couple had forgone life insurance because they had a trust, and a great deal of wealth generated from the Starks' empire.

"I would like to learn more about Liza. What makes you think that Liza and Carson weren't a good match?"

"Liza was...different. She wasn't like your average girl. Early on, we knew she had some trouble processing information, and she struggled in school. It was odd because she loved school, but she was never successful. Teachers enjoyed having her in class, but Liza was lucky to get Cs. Peter has always been the smart one."

I considered inquiring about Ralph Abernathy, Liza's father, but decided to wait for Mrs. Abernathy to reveal whether or not he would be present for the meeting.

"We always thought she would end up with some nice boy: Protestant, factory worker, liked beer and football...You know, a blue-collar dreamboat—know what I mean?"

My stomach churned. Categories bothered me.

"So, you thought Carson was out of Liza's league?"

Mrs. Abernathy let out an uncomfortable laugh, threw her head back in sarcastic amusement, and placed a strong, steady hand on my knee.

"Mrs. Wilcox, you think this is some story of a nice lady shot in a bad neighborhood; a random thing. But I'll tell you, this was some type of revenge plot. Carson caught Liza cheating on him and made her pay the ultimate price. See, Liza had a craving for...well, there's no other way to put it...

black men." Mrs. Abernathy's voice had decreased to a whisper, as if she were revealing a dirty secret.

"Do you have any evidence that Liza was having an affair?"

"No, but I know she was. Liza was very sneaky."

Not exactly the portrait most mothers would paint of their daughters. I felt a tinge of sadness for Liza. Her family did not seem to think that her murder was a great injustice. Her brother and mother seemed to blame her. I was also getting tired of people being so sure of Liza's infidelity. There was nothing that pointed to her being unfaithful, and yet even her own mother was ready to accuse her of infidelity.

"My assistant visited St. Bart's and it turns out that Liza's file contained write-ups for her having too many visitors. Do you know anything about that?"

"It was her first real job. I knew that she would need help, so I took her lunch a few times. Those people made a big deal of it, but it was nothing out of the ordinary. Then again, that's what you get with Catholics: rules, rules, and more senseless rules."

I tried to imagine my mother bringing me lunch at my first "real" job. I worked hard to suppress a chuckle.

"Did Liza like teaching?"

"Well, like I told you, she wasn't smart, but she loved school. She liked being in the school, but she wasn't a good teacher. Carson married her before it mattered, but she wasn't going to be asked back the next year. Teaching wasn't for her."

"Is that why she became a CNA?"

"No. That was all for Carson, and she'd dabbled in that before taking the sub job at the school. She was determined to get him, and by golly she got him all right—and look what happened. He made her pay."

I wondered why Mrs. Abernathy disliked Carson so much. He was a great catch by most standards, and he honestly seemed to be grieving the loss of his wife. Sure, he was a little arrogant, but by all accounts, he appeared to have loved Liza. I decided to change the subject.

"Do you know Madelyn Price?"

"Of course, we know Maddie. She's a wonderful woman; she really helped Liza become a better person. She was the one bright light in Liza's group of friends, but she kept her distance. She's a smarty-pants—always doing something brilliant."

"Liza was on her way to meet Madelyn the day she was murdered, but she never made it for coffee. Do you think it is possible that Madelyn could be involved?"

"Involved in what? Liza's murder? Mrs. Wilcox, Maddie is a great gal. She would never do anything stupid like that."

A man who looked like the Ken doll for an aging Barbie, a.k.a. Mrs. Abernathy, stepped into the foyer. He wore a pale green polo with the sleeves rolled up to his elbows, and a pair of khaki Dockers. A neat crease ran down each leg of his pants. Liza had inherited his ability to look almost perfect. Something was missing, but just like his daughter, he was still very attractive. I took note of his sad aqua eyes, leathery, artificially sun-kissed skin, and two thin slits where lips should have been. He smiled and greeted me with a friendly, but meek wave before taking a seat next to his wife.

"Mrs. Wilcox, I apologize for not joining you sooner. It's hard, but I want to thank you for investigating Liza's murder. We do miss her terribly, but I don't know how much we can help you," Ralph Abernathy said.

"Well, whatever you can tell me will be helpful."

"Liza kept secrets from us. I'm sure the same was true for her marriage."

"I don't like you saying that, Ralph," Mrs. Abernathy said in a sharp tone.

"Honey, it's the truth. You know—"

"I won't have you throwing our daughter under the bus. Yes, she had issues, but Carson killed her, and you know it!"

Mrs. Abernathy bounced off the couch in a fit of anger and stared down at her husband. She had gone from zero to one hundred in no time.

"I just want to tell Mrs. Wilcox the truth. We didn't know Liza that well."

"She was murdered! It wouldn't have mattered if we knew her inside and out—we couldn't have stopped that. Why can't you accept that?"

Mr. Abernathy sighed and glanced in my direction, pleading with his eyes.

"Mrs. Abernathy, would you mind telling me what Liza was like? It would help me to get a feel for who she was," I said, attempting to get her to calm down.

Liza's mother cast a dark stare my way before composing herself and taking a seat. Ralph Abernathy laid his hand on her knee and began to speak.

"Liza was always a bit of trouble. Peter was angry at times, but he was usually an okay kid. Easy to deal with most of the time. Initially, I thought it was because she was a girl, and I never had any sisters, but over time, it became clear that gender was the least of the issues."

"Were you in touch with Liza when she lived in Detroit?"

The Abernathys looked at one another, eyes wide with shock.

"Um, Liza lived in Detroit for a while...We lost contact with her for a few years. It was her choice. She wanted to be with her boyfriend more than she wanted to be with us, so we just let her be," Mr. Abernathy said.

Liza had been sixteen years old when she lived in Brightmoor. The most likely way for her to get to Brightmoor was by being a runaway. It was sad to hear how nonchalant the Abernathys were about their daughter.

"Was she reported missing?"

Mr. Abernathy sighed. "Well, we reported her missing the first couple of times she ran away. After that, Mother and I decided that we shouldn't do that."

Strange. Runaways aren't found if they aren't reported missing.

"May I ask why you didn't continue to report her missing?"

"You have no right to judge us. We didn't want her in the system! Doesn't that make sense?" Janice Abernathy yelled.

I wasn't comfortable with the way this interview was going, but I had to forge ahead, even if Mrs. Abernathy kept behaving like a madwoman.

"I understand that this must be difficult, but it is important for me to find out if there was something in Liza's past that led to her murder. Since she was murdered in Brightmoor and she once lived there, something that occurred in the past might be relevant."

"Well, I seriously doubt it. I mean, wouldn't she have been killed back then?"

"Not necessarily. Sometimes people hold grudges for a long time. They wait for the right moment to strike."

"No. We didn't report her missing. We had our reasons," Mr. Abernathy said in the same soft, quiet voice he'd used on the answering service.

Most teenagers wanted to do things that their parents disagreed with, but the children weren't allowed to just have their way. Why wouldn't two seemingly upstanding citizens file a report when their daughter ran away to a dangerous, drug-infested neighborhood?

"Mrs. Wilcox, Liza was murdered long after her teenage years. I don't think the past matters as much as you think." Janice Abernathy continued to fume in the background as her husband spoke in a calm, quiet voice.

"Mr. Abernathy," I said, making a point of focusing on Liza's father and ignoring her mother's pouty face. "I believe that Liza's murder had something to do with her past. By all accounts, she was living a good life, and there aren't any clues that point to infidelity or wrongdoing on her part, so I want to know if someone from the past came back for some type of revenge."

"Really? Very interesting, Mrs. Wilcox. Now I understand the line of questioning."

"That doesn't make any sense. The cops would have investigated her past if there were clues pointing that way. She was a cheater who got caught, and Carson lost it. You know he has a lot of guns, don't you?" Mrs. Abernathy asked.

There were more questions to ask, but I thought that Mrs. Abernathy might blow. Detective Cole had warned me about how uncooperative the family could be, but he'd also suggested talking to the sister-in-law. That might be delicate, since Peter and his wife had just gotten divorced, but the ex-wife couldn't be as angry as Liza's mother. I decided to test the waters.

"Mr. and Mrs. Abernathy, I'd like to know more about the rest of the family. What can you tell me about Abigail, Peter's ex-wife?"

"Nice girl. It's sad that they didn't hang in there," Mr. Abernathy said, a sorrowful look coming over his face.

"She's okay, but she is a quitter," Mrs. Abernathy added.

"Was she close with Liza?"

"They got along well...better than Liza and Peter. We'll miss having Abigail in the family," Mr. Abernathy said. He gave his wife a stern look before continuing. "Liza had some problems, but in all honesty, she had the perfect people in her life. Carson was good for her; so was Abigail."

"Peter and Liza weren't close?"

"Not at all. They were always competing. Peter more so than Liza. She wasn't really up for a battle, but Peter was always striving to prove himself, don't you think so?" Mr. Abernathy turned to his wife, casting her an interrogative look. She turned away from him and let the question go unanswered.

"Did Liza have cousins or close friends who may have more information to share?"

"Not really. We kept our family unit close. It was really just us and the kids. The extended family is spread out around the country, so there weren't any cousins to spend time with."

"Friends?"

"Madelyn Price," Mrs. Abernathy said.

"Can you think of any reason why Liza would have been in Brightmoor?"

Mr. Abernathy shook his head slowly before closing his eyes. His wife remained silent. A distant sadness had slipped onto her face.

"Is there anything else you can think of that might help us find out who killed Liza?"

"No," they both responded.

"Okay. I just have a few more questions. I'm wondering if you kept in touch with your daughter while she lived in New Orleans."

"What?" Mrs. Abernathy said, her voice increasing in volume. Oh no, here we go, I thought.

"Excuse me?" Mr. Abernathy looked angry.

"In 1999, Liza was living in New Orleans. She moved there for a short time. Did you have contact with her?"

"What are you talking about? She lived her whole life here in Michigan."

"It appears that she lived in New Orleans for a short time."

"Mrs. Wilcox, I don't think we have much to say about this. Liza is gone, and while I respect Carson's desire to know who murdered our daughter—I mean, we want that too—but it has been almost two years since her murder. We're just starting to heal. We don't have anything to add that we didn't tell the officers when it happened," Mr. Abernathy said. His voice was shaking.

After his speech, both of the Abernathys sat in silence, staring at the floor. Their blank faces looked genuine. I felt terrible for taking them down this painful stretch of memory lane. The thick, heavy stillness in the room seemed to go on forever. When the Abernathys simultaneously raised their heads, and looked at one another for an extended amount of time, I knew I'd done enough damage for one day.

"Mr. and Mrs. Abernathy, thank you for your time. You have been a great help. I will be in touch." I eased off the couch, shook both of their limp hands, and saw myself out.

MARTIN WAS at the office when I arrived, tapping away on his computer.

"How'd the meeting with Liza's parents go?"

"Not that great. It was very sad to see how little the Abernathys knew about their daughter. They had no idea she lived in New Orleans."

"Really? Man, this lady had secrets."

"You've got that right. I—"

Before I could tell Martin about the rest of the meeting with Liza's parents, the phone rang, interrupting our conversation. He answered the phone, but couldn't get a word out. Apparently, the person on the other end was in a hurry.

"Um...sure," he said, holding the phone out to me.

"Hello, this is—"

"Mrs. Wilcox. Can you meet me in about twenty minutes?"

It was Peter Abernathy. He sounded nervous and rushed.

"Yes. I'm in Ypsi. Name the place and time."

"You know that little coffee place right across the street from Liv's Diner? Christ, I can't remember the name."

"No worries. I know it well. See you in twenty."

I hung up and grabbed my laptop and notepad.

"Peter Abernathy wants to meet."

"Wow. He sounded like it was urgent."

"I'll be back later. Keep me posted on any info you come across."

Amour is a coffee shop located in the back of a tiny storefront. It's a dark, drafty place lined with old board games and jigsaw puzzles. I hadn't been there for some time, but during graduate school, I had spent many late nights studying in the back corner. I arrived twenty-five minutes after the phone call from Peter.

None of the tables or chairs in Amour matched, and there were several dingy couches in the corners. Peter was standing at the counter. We shook hands and ordered our drinks. Peter went with a white chocolate mocha with extra whipped cream; I ordered a large black coffee. We headed to a dirty yellow couch.

Peter said, "Sorry 'bout the other day. It's been hard. I feel bad about Liza, but I got my own shit going on, ya know?"

I nodded sympathetically and waited for more. Peter took a sip of his drink, sighed, and started up again.

"I don't think this has anything to do with anything, and my parents like to pretend it didn't happen, but Liza used to live in that neighborhood. It's old stuff, but it's weird that she was found dead in that area."

"Really?" I said, pretending like it was the first time I'd heard this information. "It is strange that she lived there and was found murdered in that neighborhood. Please tell me more."

Peter's face was turning red. I could tell that he was about to reveal costly secrets.

"I appreciate you reaching out to me. I'm not here to judge you or your family. My only goal is to find out who killed your sister. Her children and husband deserve the truth, but Liza also deserves justice. We shouldn't just let someone take her life and get away with it."

Peter nodded and folded his hands on the table. He sighed, paused for a minute, and then began with a slow, barely audible cadence.

"It might be hard to find the official address for her. She had an arrangement that kept it kind of secret that she lived there. There is something else. Mom and Dad said it wouldn't be relevant—they don't want to ruin her name, you know? People already think she was having an affair with some black dude, and this would just intensify that theory. I mean, this was a long time ago, and there's no way this would play any part, but I think it might be good for you to know it. Liza lived in Detroit for a while and she didn't live alone. There was this guy who lived with her. He was one of those dudes with the long braids, saggy pants, fucked-up family, and all that to boot. I'm sure he was a drug dealer, probably a gangbanger, and just one of those overall bad people. I can't remember his name, but I know that he originally lived somewhere else on the street."

"They lived on Dolphin Street? What else can you tell me about this guy? You saw him, I assume?"

"A few times. He was very nervous about coming to Livonia. Liza was dumb enough to bring him home for Christmas dinner one year. Idiot."

"So, how tall was this guy?" I asked, trying to steer Peter Abernathy out of the realm of sibling hatred.

"He must have been about six feet...maybe a little more. I don't know about weight, but he was smaller than I was, so I would say slim build. He had a full beard, and a great deal of hair—had it puffed out in a huge afro the time Liza brought him for dinner. She really thought he was the cat's pajamas. To me he was a-"

"Okay," I interrupted. "Tell me anything else you remember from that time about Liza, or her boyfriend."

Peter ran a shaky hand through his hair. He was still withdrawing from the alcohol, I presumed, but to his credit, there hadn't been any cigarette-smoking during this meeting.

"The guy always had a red bandana in his back pocket or tied around his head. I'm thinking he was a gang member, or wanted to be one."

A Blood? I felt my adrenaline rising. If Liza had gotten mixed up in gangs at one time, she probably had other skeletons just waiting to fall out of the closet. The good news was that Detroit had a strange gang structure that discouraged thugs from other states from connecting with them. This unique gang structure was inspired by Detroit's strong tendency to have neighborhoods separated by ethnic group, religion, and race. Gang colors are less important because you are your flag: skin color, religious garb, or last name defined a person. If there was some type of gang connection to this case, it would be easy to rule out people from out of town. Detroit has a special way of killing its own.

"So, he had a red bandana. Okay. That's good. Anything else you remember?"

"They had a messy break-up. Mom and Dad were worried. I guess he got a little physical with her. The summer they broke up—I think Liza was nineteen—my parents sent her to the UP."

The Upper Peninsula is pretty far away from Livonia. If Liza agreed to go that far away, I would suspect that things had gotten very physical at some point.

"I think she filed charges against him. There might be a police record of that."

A police record would bear a name, but I was willing to bet the perp was Demario Masters.

"This is very helpful. Anything else you can remember?"

Peter sighed and dug into his pocket.

"I had to smuggle these out of the house. Don't know if Mom and Dad know these exist, but I remember Liza storing them in the garage. Please don't tell them that I gave them to you. Just make up something, okay?"

I nodded, picked up the envelope, and thanked Peter for his time. I gave him my business card and left. On the way back to the car, I peeked inside the envelope. My jaw dropped as I stared at Liza, wearing a red bandana, her fingers curved into a gang sign. A tall, thin, light-brown man stood next to her holding a baby. "Folks down," I said, recalling the gang lingo I'd heard screamed through the streets of Brightmoor when I was a cop. Liza was in a gang? It seemed unlikely, but there she was in a red bandana, and with a man who clearly, based on his abundance of red, was in a Bloods based gang, or pretending to be a gangbanger. Either way, it was shocking to see Liza mean mugging the camera.

"Omigosh, what did this girl get herself into?" I muttered before sticking the photograph back into the envelope.

Gang involvement, even if it was just for show, opened a whole new can of worms. What if Liza had done something years ago and a gang member had found her and exacted retribution? What if Liza had remained affiliated with the gang all these years? That might explain why she was in Brightmoor, but that theory seemed so outlandish. Mother of two, wife of a doctor, gangbanger on the side? Not a likely scenario, but then again, I hadn't expected Liza to have any type of association with gangs.

"Who the hell were you?" I wondered aloud.

I climbed into the car and pondered this new information about Liza. Secret lives—a lot of us have them, and every now and then a demon we thought was dead and gone comes back to haunt us. If Liza had an abusive ex-boyfriend, there was a chance that he had come back to kill her, especially if she had pressed charges against him. Of course, a great deal of time had elapsed since that relationship, but abusive men rarely change. Now, I just needed to confirm his identity.

While cruising to the freeway, I considered the fact that the case might get dangerous. Martin was a great assistant, but now that gangs might be involved, I didn't feel comfortable using him to gather information. I had dealt with the gangs in the Brightmoor area: they're not to be played with. The ruthless nature of the young men and women in those gangs is incomparable to that of gangs in other areas. I would have to deal with this case without Martin, but I couldn't handle it on my own. I needed help, but it couldn't be from a civilian.

"CHARLES, I NEED A FAVOR." I'd stopped by the 8th Precinct on my way back to the office. This time, Charles was in and available. I would have to get an update on the gang situation in Brightmoor.

Charles was five foot seven and 180 pounds. He had smooth, coffee-black skin and was built like a mini tank, but he was gentle enough when he was out of uniform. He took my hand in his and shook it with vigor.

"What? Now, remember, Sylvia, you chose to go back to being a civilian. You could still have access to all these remarkable law enforcement tools."

"Yeah, but I have a lifelong friend who is a cop, and he knows that we are both fighting for truth and justice, so he's going to hook me up." We shared a laugh.

"Okay, what do you need?"

"You aren't going to believe this." I slid the picture of Liza throwing up a gang sign, and wearing her red bandana with pride across to him. The baby, who was wrapped in a red blanket, was being held by a lanky man with a matching bandana.

"What? I can't believe this! Hey, listen Sylvia, you can't pursue this. The gangs in Brightmoor aren't like they were when you were at the 8th. They've morphed into something much uglier and more dangerous than what we dealt with back then. The Feds are handling most of the gang stuff around here because it's gotten so bad. You gotta back down."

"I just need a little update on the gang situation. I've been paid a hefty price, so I will be continuing the case. With caution, of course."

Charles sighed, but recognized that I wasn't going to stop conducting the investigation, with or without vital information.

"Okay. I'll tell you what you need to know, but you must be very careful. These kids are ruthless. Some of the gangs have turned into hybrids; you can't pinpoint the Folks or the People. Sometimes, there are gangs that have mixed Crip and Blood aspects. The gang thing, the way it was in the 1980s, has gotten old for a lot of the kids coming up now. They want something new, so they've upped their recruiting strategies and tactics. Honestly, they run the gang like a business. Recruitment videos on social media, open-air drug deals, intimidation and murder of witnesses, and a cache of guns and money. I don't know what the victim had to do with those boys, but if it was anything, she was an idiot. How did you make the connection?"

"A little help from my friends." I winked at Charles.

"There you go making friends again; you always were good at that. Well, you've uncovered quite a turn. This lady had a secret life. Are you going to tell the husband?"

"Yes, but I want to wait to see if it's relevant. I mean, at this point, I don't know what the connection is, but because she was murdered in Brightmoor, I'm sure there is one. I just want to wait until I have more information. The poor guy is already suffering. Finding out that the woman he married had a secret life isn't going to make things better."

"True. Okay, what's your next move?"

"I know it's a long shot, but I've got to try to find anyone on Dolphin Street who remembers her and knows more about what went on when she lived there. Do you have any informants in the area?"

"Yeah, there's one guy."

"You think he'll talk to me?"

"Probably. His name's Don. He's still a small-time dealer. Great informant. Has three kids and a house on Dolphin Street. He's one of the few second-generation Brightmoor residents. Too poor to leave; not motivated to do more than collect social security and casually sell drugs. He just got out of jail on small-time drug charges. I don't know if he'll remember anything from that long ago, but I'll set something up."

I LEFT THE PRECINCT, headed to the office, and searched online for more information. Why had Peter decided to provide me with information about Liza's past? What was his angle? Sure, I appreciated the tip, but what was his motive? I began searching for clues.

Peter Abernathy was an upstanding citizen except for the three DUIs he had acquired over the past ten years. That explained his new-found sobriety and his recent divorce from Abigail Abernathy. One area where Peter had been consistent and reliable was at the Michigan State Forensics lab. He'd been employed there since graduating from Michigan State University with a degree in forensics. The excessive DUIs had not affected his employment at the lab, which seemed very odd, but some people pay a higher price than others. Perhaps he had connections of some sort. The rest of the public info was standard.

Peter and Abigail had three children, and they had been married fifteen years before the divorce, which had been finalized two months ago. They'd originally filed for divorce two months after Liza had been murdered. It would be interesting to hear what Abigail thought of her former sister-in-law and her ex-husband. I found Abigail's current address in Plymouth Township, not far from where I'd met Peter for lunch. I wasn't sure if the phone number listed was current, but I decided to give it a try anyway. A phone call should suffice—no need to drive back to Plymouth.

"Hello?" Abigail answered on the second ring. Her voice sounded thin and stressed.

"Hello. May I speak with Abigail Abernathy?"

"You've got her. How can I help you?"

"My name is Sylvia Wilcox, and I'm investigating the murder of Liza Abernathy."

"Oh! The detective! I believe my husband recently spoke with you. I hope he was helpful. I told him to be nice and do his best. How can I help you?"

I hadn't asked any questions, but I was sure that I'd hit the jackpot. Rarely, if ever, were people excited to help a private detective. Generally, people saw a PI as a false detective who was meddling in police business. Abigail's attitude was refreshing. This could be a great opportunity.

"I'm trying to get a feel for Liza as a person and learn more about her family and background. Would you mind sharing your opinion and perception of Liza?"

"Well, I knew Liza for about twelve years. Peter didn't mention her when we were dating, and she wasn't invited to our wedding. Sounds strange, but I didn't know that she existed until after we were married. Of course, I was pissed

—oh—excuse my language, but really, I was far beyond mad when I found out that I had a sister-in-law I didn't know existed. Can you imagine not telling your spouse about your sibling? Weird, right?"

"Yes, that is odd. Did Peter explain why he didn't tell you anything about her?"

"He said that she was dead to the Abernathys. She had run away and after an extensive search, it was concluded that she must be dead—but that's weird, right? I mean, families search for decades for their missing loved ones. I've got three pigheaded brothers, but geez, if one of those yahoos goes missing, we're searching for them "til the day we die, right? No abandoning your family, right?"

"I agree." I thought of Simon, my twin brother who was abducted over twenty years ago. The first thing I did after becoming a police officer was to get his case file and try to find him. Every two years, I revisit the case. There will never be a time when I stop looking for him. I shook off the memories and focused on the conversation with Abigail.

"Why do you think they stopped looking for her?"

"The Abernathys think that everything has to be perfect, but that isn't possible, so they pretend, lie, and create stories until they have the perfect world. Liza was a wild one. She broke their story, so to speak, when she ran away. There was no hiding the fact that they had a teenage daughter one day, but not the next, you see? She wasn't doing what they wanted, so they ex'd her outta the whole deal."

"I see. So, what was it like when Liza returned?"

"Omigosh, it was like she had never left. The parents loved her again, but Peter was upset. He felt like it was so fake to act like nothing had happened. He was hurt that he was no longer the only child. He's not a monster, but up to that point, he'd bought into everything his parents had tried to sell him, you understand?"

"I believe so. What was your relationship with Liza like?"

"Oh, I just loved her. She was the sister I'd always wanted but never had. I'm the oldest of four, like I told you, with three brothers, so I never had that sisterly thing. When Liza came around, I finally had a chance to experience that. She was a great sister-in-law. I loved her dearly."

The quiver in Abigail Abernathy's voice was the first genuine expression of intense feeling for Liza that I'd heard, apart from Carson. The way her voice caught in her throat; the unexpected emotional response involuntarily elicited even though years had passed. The unwavering pain of losing a loved one. This unlikely source of information warranted a meeting. The bitterness of divorce wasn't there, and even though she was technically no longer part of the family, Abigail spoke kindly about Liza. I needed to hear more of what she had to say.

"Mrs. Abernathy, would it be okay if I stopped by to speak with you in person?"

"Oh, yeah—anything to help. Liza deserves justice. I'm free today."

Abigail Abernathy lived in a sprawling new condo complex on the edge of Plymouth Township—spacious units with pale-colored brick veneer, cobblestoned sidewalks, and a wrought-iron fence surrounding the property, which was bordered by large swaths of greenery on all sides. Abigail lived at the end of a cul-de-sac on a street called Devonshire.

A push of the doorbell set off an array of barks that rang out in a calculated manner, telling me that the canine presence was manufactured. Almost immediately, the door opened. Abigail Abernathy was a short, portly woman with an attractive and warm face. She wore a blue flannel shirt, inexpensive stretch jeans, and brown steel-toed work boots. Her hair, bright red and curly, seemed to be fighting its way out of a loosely tied ponytail. Her big blue eyes were nearly translucent, and they sparkled with feverish energy. The freckles on the bridge of her nose wrinkled when she smiled, and her cheeks were fat and rosy. I took her meaty, gnarled hand in mine and gave it a firm shake before stepping into the condo.

"Hey there. Can I get you some tea or coffee?"

"No, thank you. I appreciate your willingness to talk with me."

The condo was cozy. It was decorated with an antique slant, but hints of nature rounded out the decor. The oiled brass fixtures in the kitchen sink and the hardwood floors gave the place a rustic, but Victorian look. The large, simulated wood stumps that lined the staircase complemented the cast-iron grate. A substantial collage of photos, showing three rosy-cheeked teens and Peter, was displayed on the wall. It was interesting that Peter still played a prominent role in all the photos, which reminded me that Abigail had called him her husband on the phone. I glanced at a photo of Peter in front of Mackinac Island's Grand Hotel. His face was beaming with pride as he hugged his three daughters close. He looked so happy—nothing like the man I'd recently met.

"Yes, we were a very happy family except when Peter was drunk. Unfortunately, I had to finalize the divorce for him to stop drinking. Now he is sober. I just wish he could've done that before any of this mess, you know?"

"I'm sorry to hear that."

"Well, he's always been stubborn. Who knows what will

happen now," she said, but her face struggled to hold back a burst of optimism.

"I wish you the best," I said, and even though I had only just met her, I meant it.

"Okay, so here's my concern about your investigation. Liza and Peter were not on good terms most of the time, and there are some red flags you'll probably come across."

"Like what?"

"Like the fact that there was a fight at Thanksgiving three years ago about my father-in-law's last will and testament."

"What can you tell me about the argument?"

"He wanted to add Liza back into his will. I have no idea why my mother-in-law decided to announce it at Thanksgiving dinner, but she did. Peter was very angry, because up to that point, he stood to inherit everything his parents had."

"Do the Abernathys have a fair amount of money?"

"Oh, yes. They live modestly, but they have several real estate investments. My mother-in-law loves to travel, so they've stayed in the Livonia house because it's allowed them to purchase a few vacation homes, and to travel to Europe on a regular basis. Real estate is their thing."

"They're actively maintaining properties at this time? Or are they just buying personal properties?"

"Both. Back in the early 1980s, when the prices of homes in Detroit plummeted, they started buying low-cost homes and renting them. They have since sold most of them, but they still have a few that bring in a monthly income. My father-in-law is a great businessman and money manager. That, on top of the freelance work he does, has made them wealthy."

Real estate in Detroit. I wondered where those properties were located. Pretty sure I already knew the answer.

"Do the Abernathys own houses near Old Redford?"

"Uh, I'm not too familiar with the area where they own houses, but I can tell you it's just below Telegraph Road, on the other side of Redford Township."

Abigail's words were laced with a long, deep inflection on certain words that reminded me of a Canadian dialect, but it was rounded out with the Michigan tendency to drop consonants at the ends of words, indicating that she was probably from the Upper Peninsula. The odds of her knowing what and where Brightmoor was were slim.

"Peter wasn't happy with the idea that Liza would be added back into the will? Any reason in particular?"

"Oh, it's nothing like you think. I just told you that because you're gonna hear about it and I don't want you to think it has any weight, you know? He was just mad, but that's natural, you know? When you talk to my in-laws, I know they're going to throw my husband under the bus. I just want you to know going in..."

Strange. Why would Peter's parents try to implicate him in a murder, especially the murder of his sister? Not to mention, they hadn't actually done that. In fact, in a round-about way, they'd painted Peter as the good child.

"Is there anything else you would like to tell me about Liza, Peter, or the murder?"

Abigail looked around the quiet, still condo, as if someone else were there.

"Well, there is one more thing. I think Liza may have been having an affair."

Shocked, but interested to learn why she thought that, I leaned in close and waited for more. "She told me there was someone she wanted me to meet. Begged me not to tell anyone. This someone was special, she said. I asked questions, but she wouldn't answer them. Just told me to wait until she introduced us."

It was good to know that Liza had felt close enough to Abigail to confide in her. Finally, there was a lead that might explain why someone felt strongly enough about Liza to take her life. This was a breakthrough!

"Okay, I need you to tell me everything you know about this man. Anything she told you might be helpful."

This was the first indication that Liza may have been having an affair, and it was coming from someone who genuinely cared about her. This might be a credible source for the infidelity angle, so I wanted to get as much detail as possible.

"She didn't give many specifics—just that he was from her past, and that he was upset about how they'd broken up. Well, let me try to remember how she said it. I think she said: 'He's mad because I never said goodbye. I just left.' She said she just wanted to make things right. I told her not to play with fire. Peter had told me that she once liked the wrong type of guys. I thought she might be talking about one of them, and that it could get dangerous. Besides, she was happily married; I was confused about why she felt she owed this guy anything."

"Did she mention how long ago this relationship took place?"

"No, but it had to have been before she returned to her parents' house, so that would have been in. Let's see. I'm going to guesstimate that it was around 2000, because Peter and I had been married for a few years, and we already had Reagan. We got married in 1997 and had Reagan later that year. She was an 'uh-oh' baby, but she's our happy little mistake. We were already engaged, so no harm or foul."

"Why don't you think it was someone she met after returning to her parents' home?"

Abigail sighed and waited a moment before speaking. "You haven't been to the Abernathy house yet, have you?"

"I was there yesterday."

"How did that go?"

I thought about the strange visit. "Okay. I see what you mean. Mrs. Abernathy would have interfered."

"Right. Liza couldn't have met anyone nefarious after her return. My mother-in-law is very controlling: she knew Liza's every move. Carson was a happy accident, and the only reason Mrs. Abernathy didn't control that relationship was because he worked in a hospital, and she couldn't gain access to spy on him."

I thought about the conversation I'd had with Martin about Liza's teaching position. She had been written up because her mother had shown up too often at the school. How many times had Mrs. Abernathy shown up for it to be insubordination for Liza? Liza would have been well into her twenties by that time. Why would her mother be showing up at all?

"That is interesting. Do you think it's because Liza ran away? Possibly guilt for not keeping close enough tabs on her?"

"That could be the case, but Liza was an adult when she returned. Yes, she had her problems, and it was a good idea to look out for her just a little bit more than you would other people, but she was capable. It's not like she needed a chaperon."

"What would you say constituted her 'problems'?"

"She didn't have much common sense. Sweet woman, but she needed to be taken care of in that area. It was more of a thing where you would want to counsel her if she had a big decision to make. Odds were that she was going to make the wrong decision, or she was going to base her decision on some skewed logic that wasn't logical at all."

"What did you make of Carson and Liza's relationship?"

"They seemed very happy. Carson was patient and kind, and he liked being her protector. That's why he suggested that she may want to stay home with the kids. Liza was relieved because she wasn't that great in the workplace."

"They were happy, but Liza was having an affair?"

"Well, to be clear, I don't know if it was a full-blown affair. She just told me that there was someone from the past that she wanted me to meet. I think she felt guilty for leaving the guy the way she did, but there was no mention of sex, or anything like that. And I kind of assumed it was a guy, but in her defense, she never said whether it was a woman or a man. Could have been an old friend. She also never complained about Carson. She loved him and the kids."

"I haven't heard anything about an affair," I said. Hoping that my lie sounded convincing.

"Well, there might be something you need to know..."

"Did you mention this to the police? If not, why have you changed your mind?"

Abigail thought for a moment before saying, "Because what else is someone going to shoot you five times for? Right? It's either love or money, and she wasn't robbed, so I guess I just realized that I was hoping that she wasn't having an affair. Besides, the police drew the same conclusion, and I didn't want to sully her name even more than it already was."

"Do you think it's possible that she was being black-mailed by someone? Maybe a guy from her past had some dirt on her?"

"Oh, that's definitely possible. Like I said, Liza wasn't the brightest, so she could have gotten wrapped up in some type of porn thing or taking nude pictures. I could see her being blackmailed."

"What else did she tell you about the guy she was seeing? Anything stand out?"

"She let him come to the house once."

"Really?"

"Yes. Amelia could probably tell you more."

I thought about the conversation I'd had with the housekeeper. She'd said that a woman came over to the house, but not a man. Was Abigail overreaching with the assumption that Liza was having an affair? Was the affair with a woman? Since Abigail was freely giving out information, I decided to take a shot in the dark.

"Do you know Madelyn Price?"

Abigail's brow creased. "Yes, I know her. She's a weird one."

"She was Liza's best friend, right?"

"Hmm. I don't know that they were best friends, but they were associates. Well, I guess you could say they were friends, but I wouldn't say that they hung out all the time, or anything like that."

Carson had pegged the women as best friends. I wondered if that was due to lack of perception, or had Liza and Madelyn convinced Carson they were closer than they were? What purpose would they have had to fake the strength of the friendship? The idea that Liza and Madelyn were best friends hadn't been how Abigail saw it. Nor had Madelyn's mask of calm and happiness fooled her.

"Why do you think Madelyn is weird?"

"It's the way she avoids ever really talking about

anything personal. She's like a mystery, and that's the way she wants it to be."

"In her defense, being a mystery is not a crime, and it could just mean that Madelyn likes her privacy."

"What did Peter tell you?"

I hesitated long enough for Abigail to let the question die.

"Did he tell you anything about the past?"

"A bit. Is there anything substantial I should know about the past?"

"Peter knows more than I do. I don't know for sure, but I think it might be important."

I waited. Abigail's eyes told me she had something to share. Interviewees often want to give investigators information, but they fear the aftermath. It was best not to push, and I didn't want to betray Peter's trust. He'd given me the pictures of Liza in confidence.

"Madelyn and Liza seemed to be associates, like people who work together, but wouldn't hang out for the heck of it —you know what I mean?"

"Yes. People you might see together from time to time, but they wouldn't have a girls' night. Did they ever work together?"

"No. Madelyn is one of those smarties. She is very determined and successful. Liza was never really into the career thing. They would do things together, but they seemed distant. Kind of the way you are with people you work with but aren't friends with."

"So, they were associates," I interjected.

"Yeah. Not besties by any means."

---

## 8

I spent well over an hour at Abigail Abernathy's place, and was rather sad to leave. She made spiced chai tea and continued providing the best information I'd received on Liza so far. By the time I left, it was clear that Madelyn Price would have to be paid another visit. She was hiding something.

If Madelyn and Liza were not close friends, if there was distance, it seemed strange that Madelyn was the last person to speak with Liza before she died. I needed to find out why they were meeting the day she was murdered. I was sure Madelyn had more information than she was sharing. Perhaps Liza and Madelyn had worked together in some type of business, but why would that need to be a secret? Also, why would they meet in Brightmoor? Abigail Abernathy had been very helpful, but I still had more questions than answers.

The next morning, I was out of bed by 5:00 a.m., and behind the wheel headed to Madelyn's by 7:15. I managed to avoid snarls on US-23 by starting out before rush hour was in full swing. It was cold and brisk outside, leaving a frosty layer on the back roads around Ann Arbor. I cautiously maneuvered over what may or may not have been black ice and slowed to a crawl as I approached Madelyn's driveway. I was back at her converted barn by 8:00 in the morning. The Taurus rolled over the frozen dirt roads with ease, but as soon as I stepped out of the car, a frigid wind hit me in the face.

The door was unlocked and the "We're Open" sign was dangling in the door. A little bell alerted Madelyn to my entrance.

"I'll be with you in a moment," she called from the studio. Within a few minutes, she walked out into the foyer and stopped short.

"What brings you by, Mrs. Wilcox?"

"This." I pulled out the picture of Liza, the unidentified man, and the baby. Madelyn flinched.

"What is that?"

"A photo, Ms. Price. Is this the type of different lifestyle you were living when you met Liza?"

"I don't think that is any of your business."

"Do you know who the man is? Speaking of business, did you and Liza have some type of business? I've heard that your meetings weren't exactly the typical girls' night out."

"Mrs. Wilcox, I am sorry that you are having trouble finding information, but that is why this is a cold case. There are just some things we don't know about Liza's past."

"Ms. Price, I'm trying to get closure for a man who lost his wife, the mother of his children. If you have information that will help me do that, I need it. I just want the truth."

"I've told you everything I know."

"Do you know this man in the picture?" I shoved the photo into her line of sight.

"No, Mrs. Wilcox. This is my business. If you have more

questions, feel free to call, but don't stop by unannounced. If it happens again, I'll be forced to call the police."

The Achilles heel of being a private detective. You don't have the right to continuously show up and question a witness or suspect. They have to be willing to talk with you.

I put the picture back in my pocket. "Thanks for your time," I said, turning to leave.

It was clear that Madelyn was lying, but I needed more data to push her over the edge. Back at the office, Martin and I discussed the possibilities.

"Madelyn is doing well, but maybe her business is a front for running drugs," Martin said.

"I don't see Madelyn and Liza as needing to run drugs. Why do it, if not for the money?"

"There's the gang connection. They're both tied to this Demario character. He's in prison, but he might have someone on the outside giving orders. He could have them doing his bidding while he's locked up."

"Are you going to take this to the husband?'

"Not yet."

"Yeah, hearing that the yoga teacher or trophy wife lived a torrid life in the worst slum in Detroit would probably be pretty shocking to the doctor."

"Not exactly the profile you'd expect for either one of them."

"What's the deal with the guy they have in common?"

"It looks like Demario Masters was just a high school fling kind of thing for both of them. I'm pretty sure he's the father of Madelyn's daughter, but he probably has children all over the city. It's not uncommon for Brightmoor babies to have deadbeat dads. Liza probably just got caught up in the mess. I bet that was Madelyn and Demario's baby in the picture with him and Liza."

"It could be a different guy. Regardless, it seems so weird that Liza and Madelyn were friends," Martin said.

"It definitely seems like an unlikely friendship. Then again, I feel the same way about Liza and Carson. I don't see the connection."

I took out the picture of Liza, the man in the bandana, and the baby. Next, I pulled up the image of Kara Price at the spelling bee and held the picture next to the image on the computer. Similar wide-set eyes. The Kara's eyes were darker than they'd been when she was an infant—if the images were of the same child. Of course, that was not uncommon. Infants change so much as they grow.

"What's our next move?"

"I don't know, Martin. Think. Search what we have and find out what we've missed."

"This job doesn't work the way it does on TV."

"I know. The sidekick usually drops a brilliant clue right about now."

Martin gave me a smirk before grabbing his laptop and heading to his desk. We searched for random online tidbits on Liza and her connections for the next half-an-hour. I was getting ready to give Martin the rest of the afternoon off when the office phone rang.

"Sylvia Wilcox."

"This is Archie Paladoski.

Paladoski's voice was deep, his tone careful and calculating. A hint of hesitation was evident in his voice.

"Mr. Paladoski. Thank you for calling."

"No problem."

"I am working on Liza Stark's murder. The murder book is slim, and I'm wondering if there is anything you might know that isn't in the file."

Paladoski was silent for a few seconds before saying, "You talked to the store owner."

"Yes. I spoke with Ali Mansu and he told me that there were problems with gangs before the body was found, but the issues stopped after Liza was murdered. He also said there were surveillance cameras, but I didn't find any tapes."

"Mrs. Wilcox, you worked for DPD, correct?"

"Yes." He'd looked me up before calling.

"Then you know that there are some leads the boss won't let you pursue. For whatever reason, the chief didn't want us to work the gang angle. It was strange. They were gang members, so if we were able to get those guys on anything even if it wasn't related to the murder, it should have been good, right? But we were cockblocked. No idea why."

"Were there other leads you were told not to follow?"

"Well, we never had an interview with the victim's in-laws."

Strange. The first thing you had to do in a homicide like this one, was rule out family members.

"I heard something about that. Were you told not to interview the Starks?"

"No. They refused to meet with us and we didn't really have any evidence that pointed to them, so the boss told us to leave it alone. We did, but there could have been something there. The families, Starks and Abernathys, don't like one another."

"Mr. Paladoski, I hope you don't mind my asking, but I am wondering why this case caused you to leave the force."

Paladoski sighed a few times, as if he was fighting with whether or not he was going to answer the question.

"We took a lot of flack for not closing the case. First, we were being pushed to close the case fast, but after we started getting somewhere, or at least trying to formulate theories, we were stopped from investigating the crime."

"Did you think this was a gang hit of some sort?"

"There was an inclination to draw that conclusion because in the months following the murder, there weren't any attacks on the store. Seemed like that was a viable avenue, but as you know, gangbangers are not just gonna stop. And, rich people don't do anything for themselves, so I thought Carson might have paid the gang members to kill his wife because she was unfaithful."

"That's why you wanted more access to the Stark family."

"Correct. I just thought, them gangbangers would only stop if they had some type of incentive. That was my original theory, but we had to handle the family with kid gloves. It was sickening. The families despise one another, and the husband is an only child. His family has had money a long time. The Abernathys-not so much. Carson was this golden boy hero type that had everything. His parents had him after they'd given up on having kids, so he's kind of a miracle. He's used to getting his way. What happens if his wife steps out on him?"

Due to Carson's status, his union with Liza was even more strange. Golden boy meets failing girl. His parents hire a hit man to off failing girl, getting their golden boy back. Was that a realistic scenario? Carson seemed genuinely distraught over losing Liza. It was hard to imagine that any parents would deliberately cause their son so much pain.

"Seems harsh. Were you able to learn anything else about the Starks?"

"Just the stuff we found online. Things are pretty tight lipped about them."

"What about the friend Lisa was going to meet? Did she ever make the suspect list?"

A long uncomfortable silence filled the phone.

"Mr. Paladoski, are you still there?"

"Yes. I just...Yes and no. Madelyn Price made our suspect list, but she was quickly removed."

"Because you and Cole cleared her, or did the brass tell you to remove her?"

Another pause before he said, "We removed her because there wasn't anything there. She's not terribly forthcoming, but that has nothing to do with her guilt or innocence. Just seems to be who she is."

I caught a hint of defensiveness in his voice. Perhaps he had developed a fondness for Madelyn Price. What was it with this lady? She seemed to be able to cast a spell on men.

"Mr. Paladoski, this is a bit of a personal question, and I understand if you don't want to answer it, but why did you leave the force?"

This time he answered as soon as the question was out of my mouth.

"DPD was not what my dad and his buddies told me it was. I wanted to fight for justice. Not politics and corruption. There are a lot of people doing a lot of good outside of the force. This case just got things all twisted and it was hard to see straight. I decided I'd had enough of the city and DPD. I quit and headed west. Got a little farm out here. Get to go surfing often-just decided I'd had enough. You know how it is."

"Organic farming. That's quite a change."

"It is. A necessary change."

"Anything else you want to tell me?"

"Just...Don't mess up anything you don't have to mess

up. If you stumble on something good, even if it is strange, let it be."

"I'm sure that will mean something in time. Thanks for taking the time to speak with me."

"Sure thing. Just keep my name out of things."

"Yes. I promise to do that."

THE PHONE CALL with Archie Paladoski didn't expand any of my working theories. The gang angle was interesting, but since Carson had hired me, it didn't make any sense. Not to mention, there still was no evidence of Liza having an affair-except for Abigail's assumptions. There did seem to be some type of gang connection, based on the picture Peter Abernathy had given me. I stayed up half the night wondering about a myriad of possibilities before falling asleep on the couch. The next morning, I headed out to meet Detective Cole.

We met at a tiny café in Redford Township. Cole had deep bags under his eyes and his striped tie was crooked. He looked disheveled.

"Hey. Rough night?"

"You have no idea. Archie might've had the right idea. Pull up stakes, quit this job and move west. Speaking of Arch, I heard he called you."

"Yeah, he did. I appreciate you passing on the message. He had a few cryptic tips that will probably mean something later."

"Everything means something eventually. No coincidences in this world. If this job has taught me anything, it's that. Nothing is a coincidence."

"What can you tell me about Demario Masters," I asked. Shifting gears.

"I recommend that you reconsider working this case. You've stumbled upon a member of one of the most notorious crime families in Detroit," Detective Cole told me.

"Really? Tell me more."

Cole shook his head and fished a small envelope out of his back pocket.

"I can tell you he's a dirty bastard. Born into a low-grade crime family, but the Masters are crafty. They make money, but they blow it on stupid things, which is why I call them a low-grade crime family. The Masters have been killing and selling dope since the late sixties. None of them have ever done time for either one of those offenses, and only Demario has done hard time. Demario's father was a supplier of heroin at an automotive plant, his brother has served time for identity theft, and his pseudo brother-in-law allegedly killed his dad. The Masters are Detroit at its worst."

Cole dumped the contents of the envelope onto the table and spread out pictures of a tall, wiry man with long, smooth braids cascading down his back—the same man who was in the pictures Peter had given me. In one photo, the man was posing with a sawed-off shotgun. In another, he was flanked by a man and a woman— his siblings presumably, based on the matching high cheekbones and slanted eyes. The trio held up wads of cash as proof of the family fortune.

"This dude is smart. Almost won his most recent appeal, but he's insane—that's what lost it for him. The prosecutor exposed his psychopathic tendencies; proved that he was just as unstable as we'd speculated. Generally, he had been unable to hold down a job, was a known abuser of women and children, and he came off as calculating to the jury. There was no way he could have been innocent in the jury's eyes. And it's a good thing that they felt that way: this guy is a pariah."

"I think he might be tied to the Stark case I'm working."

"We didn't find any evidence of that."

"I believe he had a child with one of the character witnesses—Madelyn Price."

"Really? The yoga teacher? No way! She was not his type."

"Yes. Apparently, there was a bit of a love triangle. This Demario Masters is tied to both Liza and Madelyn. In the nineties, Liza lived literally around the corner from Madelyn, their boyfriends were friends, and Liza's body was found in the alley between the two streets where they lived."

"The murder was in 2011. How do you think that fits?"

"I'm not sure. I just think it's too much of a coincidence that Madelyn Price and Liza both lived in that neighborhood, and that they were involved with the same thug."

"You have a point, but Masters has been in jail for a while. He wasn't free during the time of the murder."

"Yeah, but I think Masters may have known a guy who was dating Liza at the time."

"And you think the murder in 2011 was a revenge plot?"

It all sounded so far-fetched, but street life and poverty were fueled by necessity. The dealers never made enough to elevate themselves from the neighborhood, and the hits they carried out were usually determined by desperation. What I couldn't figure out was why someone would come back and kill Liza after more than a decade had passed.

"I just want a little info before I drive out to the state prison to talk to this guy. What's his Achilles heel?"

Cole shook his head and smirked.

"You really think there's something there, don't you?"

"Yeah. Just have a feeling."

"Okay. Well, like I told you, this guy, he's smart. He knows how to manipulate, but he was abused as a child. The pain and suffering from his childhood really makes him long for normalcy. Underneath all the violence, all he ever wanted was what we all want: love, money, family a place to belong. He was just too sick to make it all work out."

"If he's a psychopath, he can't feel empathy."

"No, but he's a high-functioning psychopath. He knows that he's different. He'd never admit that the difference is the reason he is not able to function, but he's aware of it. Play his game—that's how you'll get info out of him."

Coldness. I'm not unfamiliar with it, nor am I above using it as a tactic. Some people become savvy criminals; others go into law enforcement.

"Anything else?"

"Yeah. Did you talk to the sister-in-law?"

"Yes. She gave me some information. The Starks are in construction, and the Abernathys are in real estate. Liza was going to be added to her father's will and the brother didn't like that."

Cole's eyes lit up. I watched a nervous hand grip the edge of his non-fat soy latte.

"What?"

Cole swirled his drink in a circle. A possible attempt to further mix his fancy coffee, or a show of nervous energy?

"The chief wasn't too keen on the case. Just be careful."

"Why?"

"Well, some people thought that she got exactly what she deserved. Women don't get the benefit of the doubt when they're out cheating."

"What evidence was there that she was cheating?"

"Location, location, location."

"You don't think there could be any other explanation?

"You got a better reason why she was sniffing around Brightmoor?" Cole asked.

"I work infidelity cases and this thing feels different. I think something from the past came back to haunt Liza. Her friend is tied up in this thing too. I just have to figure out how."

"Maybe we missed something. Like I said, no one wanted us to dig too deep."

"I know how that goes. Any last-minute advice for my visit with Masters?"

"When you go to see this guy, you need to make him think that you respect his intelligence, and treat him like you would an old friend, or something like that. He is huge on respect. Oh, and take some Twinkies and Mountain Dew with you. The guys around the precinct told me he loves that stuff."

"Respect. Okay—I can do that. Disgusting pop and sugar filled sponges masquerading as food...Any other tips?"

"Don't ask him about the crime he committed. He's adamant that he didn't do it. The sexual abuse he experienced as a child really scarred him, and I think it drives him crazy to know that he has caused a child the same type of pain he experienced."

"I don't have any power to wheel or deal. Better do some recon before I drive two and a half hours."

"He has family in the area. You might want to talk to them first. They'll know more about him than I do. I just know what we saw in the courtroom."

I thanked Cole and went back to the office to conduct more research on Masters and his family. The summary of Demario Masters' life looked dismal, even on paper. He was number four of five children. One sister was deceased, one lived in California, and one lived in Brightmoor. There wasn't a current address for Demario's brother, but there was a number for Sara Quick, the sister in California, and an address for his other sister, Alyssa Masters.

Masters only had two siblings who had avoided the criminal justice system—the half-sister, Sara Quick, who was fifteen years older than the next sibling, and Daria, the deceased sibling who had been three years older than Demario. Alyssa Masters had a mugshot online, plus a list of petty offenses. Sara Quick, by all appearances, was doing well: she was a psychiatric nurse with three sons of her own, living in southern California. Sara's social media pages presented her as being single, and all her pictures included one or more of her three, curly-haired boys. Her sons looked to be in their twenties, and each one had inherited her mysterious hazel eyes. They were quite a lovely family. I hated to bother them, but just as in Peter's case, no one dishes like a sibling. Perhaps the geographical separation was in place for a reason.

The phone rang once before the call connected.

"This is Sara Quick," said the woman on the other end of the phone in a monotonous voice.

"Hello, Miss Quick. My name is Sylvia Wilcox. I'm a private investigator reviewing the murder of Liza Abernathy, a woman I've been told dated your brother at one time."

Brief silence was followed by a frustrated sigh.

"I remember Liza. She was trash, but so was my brother. Just trashy people. I'm sorry that she was murdered, but she wasn't the best person."

"Would you mind telling me what you remember about your brother Demario and his relationship with Liza Abernathy?"

"My brother is just like his father, Albert Masters: a cheater, dishonest, and not fit for society. The difference was that Albert was smart enough to stay out of prison, but my brothers didn't inherit his cunning ways. They are both stupid criminals."

Dead air followed a short pause. I waited for more information.

"Liza Abernathy wasn't a good person. She was like *my* father. My mother, who was also a swindling, criminal-minded individual, met my father Oliver Quick, got pregnant, and the man never showed his face again. Liza was like him. She went slumming for a while, found the worst man she could locate, and then ran away one night. She left her first-born child with a criminal."

A child? This was the first I'd heard of a child outside of Liza's marriage. The pictures of her, Demario Masters, and the baby flashed through my mind.

"Liza had a child with your brother?"

"Yes. They had a little girl and she left her with my brother. Don't you think that's trashy?"

I ignored the question and asked, "Do you know where the daughter is?"

"Not off-hand."

"Do you think that Demario would have gotten in touch with Liza before her murder?"

"Possibly. I haven't spoken to my brother or my other siblings in a few years. I send cards for the holidays, but that is the extent of our connection these days. I moved to California to get away from my family. They were constantly asking for money, and we're just halves—none of them are whole siblings—so I packed my bags and moved as far as possible away from them."

I was sketching a rough family tree for the Abernathys

and the Masters while I listened to Sara Quick. Her bitterness was thick and harsh. Once again, an angry sibling was ready to talk.

"What happened to your niece?"

"No idea. She could be dead, or she could be in the juvenile justice system by now. The Masters have bad blood. I tried my best to keep my boys away from them."

"Do you know Madelyn Price?"

"Yes. My brother had a baby with her as well, but Madelyn was smart. She just made a mistake when she was young, but after a short time with Demario, she got wise and left him. I don't think he ever saw her little girl again. Sounds bad, but it was definitely for the best."

"Liza Abernathy abandoned her child to Demario? I know you haven't had contact with her in a while, but do you remember her name?"

"Danica. She was a cute little thing; deserved something better than those two losers. I haven't had much contact, but I'm willing to bet she is in a terrible place if she's made it this far."

The accounts of Liza's life continued to take sad turns. I'd never met Liza, but I couldn't help but feel sorry for the way her life had worked out. Distant parents, angry brother...at least she had Carson and Abigail. I took a small comfort in the idea that Liza had a few people in her life who truly knew and loved her.

"Thank you so much for speaking with me. Is there anything else you can think of?"

"Liza was probably seeing some guy in Brightmoor. She was obsessed with my brother. It didn't matter what he did, she fought to be with him."

"Do you recall when they met?"

"Let's see...He was incarcerated between the ages of

fifteen and nineteen, so he would have gotten out in January 1996. He met Madelyn, who was just a kid, and got her pregnant, but she was always too smart for him. Cunning and crafty, but not the worst person in the world. We knew she would leave him sooner or later. Liza gave birth not too long after Madelyn's baby turned a year old. That was when Madelyn decided to leave him."

I had stopped drawing the family tree. Madelyn Price had a child by Demario Masters. I thought of the calm, quiet yoga teacher living in the converted farmhouse on the outskirts of Ann Arbor. In theory, there was no way she had ever been connected to a thug, but the proof was overwhelming that she, in fact, had been involved with Demario Masters. But what was even more shocking, was that Liza had a child with Demario and this was the first I was hearing of her. It was unbelievable.

"Miss Quick, I just want to be sure that I have this straight."

"Okay."

"Liza Abernathy and Madelyn Price both have children by Demario Masters? They were caught in a love triangle that resulted in two children, correct?"

"Yes."

"Liza and Madelyn were enemies, or at least rivals?"

"Correct."

My brain almost refused to accept what I was being told. Then I started analyzing the conversation I'd had with Madelyn. She and Liza had met when they were living a "different kind of life". Their boyfriends hadn't been friends. Instead, the two women had been involved with the same man.

"Miss Quick, thank you so much for the information."

"You're welcome."

"I appreciate your time."

I grabbed my pen and started writing down the suspected timeline. Madelyn had given birth to a baby in December 1996, and Liza's baby had been born in April of 1998. The timeline was remarkably short. Demario and Liza would have been living in Brightmoor around that time, and somehow, Madelyn had neglected to bring up this curious connection she shared with Liza. In so doing, Madelyn Price had just moved into the number one murder suspect spot.

## 9

Charles sent me a text that evening about meeting with his informant, Don. He'd set it up for 10:00 the next morning at Lucy's Coney Island in Brightmoor. After my run, Martin came over and I informed him of what I'd learned.

"Madelyn Price is our suspect?" he asked.

"Yes. She lied about how she met Liza, and she was also part of a love triangle between her, Demario, and Liza. Revenge—maybe a little jealousy or envy. I don't know, but she's number one and I need anything you can find on her. Anything."

"Okay."

"I have to meet up with an informant in Brightmoor. I'll call you when we're done."

The freeways were kind and I arrived at Lucy's Coney Island around 9:45 a.m. A tall man in a black hoodie and dark glasses stood out front. Don was lanky and rough around the edges, but you could see that he had once been attractive. His dark skin showed the wear and tear of short stints in jail, and a life spent in poverty. He was standing in front of the restaurant smoking a cigarette when I pulled up. Charles must have told him what I looked like, because he stomped out his smoke, pulled a pair of sunglasses out of his pocket, and slipped them on.

"Don?"

"I guess you must be Sylvia," he said, holding out his hand.

He gave my hand a vigorous shake before opening the door to the restaurant and following me to a booth in the back. As we sat down, I told him to order anything he wanted.

"THANKS so much for meeting with me."

"No thang," he said, removing his sunglasses.

"I'm looking for information on a woman named Madelyn Price. She would have lived on Dolphin Street between '96 and '98. She was sixteen when she moved there, and she had a child named Kara."

Don scratched his bald head and pulled a menu out of the carousel at the end of the table.

"You talkin' 'bout old times. I think I smoked away anythang from the nineties. I was just a kid then."

I dug a printout of Madelyn's high school yearbook picture out of my purse and laid it in front of him.

"Super-smart girl; she wasn't from these parts."

Don picked up the picture and studied it. His eyebrows creased. I could see the wheels turning. Ah yes, the agony of a pothead who strives to remember...

"That Stripe girl."

"Who?"

"Stripe. He was this badass used to run with a gang. I wasn't never into gang stuff, but I know Stripe because he tried to roll for a while. He was lazy, tho. Couldn't leave him up in a spot if you wanted anything to get done."

"I'm guessing that his real name was not Stripe?"

"Probably not. Didn't know him too well. Just smoked wit 'im every now and then. Had a lot of hair. Wore it in braids most of the time. Would puff it out every now and then."

An afro. Reminded me of what Peter Abernathy had told me about the man Liza had brought home for the holidays.

"What else can you tell me?" I asked, pulling out my notepad.

"He 'bout the same height as me. Some called 'im D. Used to be skinny, always pissed off, and ready to fight at a moment's notice. Had a kid or two. One might be this lady's baby. I don't know."

Procreating with someone who called himself Stripe— that didn't sound like the little prim and proper Madelyn Price I knew.

"Do you remember a girl named Liza?" I asked, pulling one of the photos out of my purse Peter had given me, and setting it on the table.

Don looked at the picture, squinting his eyes and scratching his brow.

"Yeah. I remember her. She was Stripe's girl too. Once there was like a showdown between the two. It was wild."

"Can you tell me anything else about Liza?"

"Not really. I didn't know her, but I remember the drama."

"What can you tell me about the drama?"

"Two girls fightin' over a dude who didn't care nothing for neither one of them. Don't know much about it. Just know it was the gossip throughout the hood."

I asked a few more questions that didn't net answers, told Don to order, paid his tab, and left.

That night, I stayed at home and restricted myself from looking at any information about the case. Instead of working overtime, I seared a tenderloin, steamed asparagus, poured a glass of merlot, and had a quiet dinner at the long pine table in the living room. I'd decorated the house with quaint antique furniture from thrift stores and estate sales. People were always throwing out old pieces of furniture because it wasn't new. I admired the past and spent my free time restoring the items I picked up. After dinner, I climbed into the bronze claw-foot tub in the master bathroom and soaked. My life wasn't perfect, but I had never had the type of pain and suffering Liza must have experienced. A sense of gratitude warmed my heart.

"I'm lucky," I muttered, and smiled before getting out of the tub, drying off, and sliding under the soft, cool bamboo sheets.

THE NEXT MORNING, Martin stopped by as I was finishing breakfast. I fixed him a plate of leftovers, two slices of bacon, and scrambled eggs, and brewed a fresh pot of coffee. He looked disheveled and exhausted.

"Long night?" I asked.

"Not too bad. I guess I'm just struggling to see any decent angles in this case."

I felt a tinge of pain for pulling Martin into this murder case. We'd been working on infidelity cases for well over a year. Initially, I wasn't open to any cases that involved missing children or murder, because those are the two types of cases that get personal for me. One of the reasons

I'd allowed my brother-in-law to be my assistant was because I thought it would be a good way to keep him safe. There was a certain amount of guilt in my heart over Derek's death. Keeping Martin safe and mentally healthy were priorities.

"Well, this is a tough case. Not really one I should have taken, and it's getting dangerous. I think you should stand down. I can handle this one."

"What's dangerous about it?"

"I believe Madelyn killed Liza, but Madelyn and Liza were both involved with a gang member. I'm headed to the prison in Muskegon to visit Demario Masters. He's gang-affiliated, and he comes from a criminal family."

"Are you going to forfeit the case?"

A smarter woman would've given up the case and gone back to easier, safer work, but I knew what it was like to have a dead spouse and no answers. I knew what it was like to have an explanation that didn't make sense. Discovering the truth about Derek's death had been the most painful experience of my life, but now I could sleep at night. I wanted the same for Carson, and anyone else who'd lost a loved one under mysterious circumstances.

"No. I'm headed to Muskegon to talk with Liza and Madelyn's ex-boyfriend. I need to meet with Madelyn as well. She's a liar, by the way."

"You think this ex-boyfriend is related to the case?"

"I need more information on both Liza and Madelyn. Since Madelyn is my number one suspect, I need a motive for her hatred of Liza. Who better to get the info from than a gang-member ex-boyfriend?"

I set a cup of coffee in front of Martin and gathered my notes from the table.

"Good point. He might be able to pinpoint a moment

that may have spurred the revenge. But do you really think Madelyn did this?"

"No idea, but she's the best suspect I have. Carson just doesn't look plausible. Oh yeah, Liza also has a daughter with the thug—and guess who else has a child with him?"

"No!"

"Yes. Madelyn and Liza have daughters who are half-sisters."

"That's huge! What the hell is going on?"

"No clue, but I'm going to figure it out. I'm headed to the prison. Why don't you try to find Liza's kid? Her name is Danica Masters."

"Got it. I'm on it."

"Get an address, phone number, whatever you can. Normally I wouldn't tell you this, but if you have to...catfish. Pretend I didn't say that."

I was out the door before Martin could answer. I stopped at the gas station and picked up the Mountain Dew and Twinkies before topping off my tank. The drive to the correctional facility in Muskegon was uneventful. I went through the pat-down and shoe check and was led into a large visiting room. I sat at a table and waited. Initially, I had been hesitant to visit the convict, but since he wasn't the person who'd killed Liza, and he was in prison, perhaps he would be willing to talk a bit about their relationship. What did he have to lose?

Demario was a little over six feet tall, but he walked with a slightly bent "gangsta gait." His hair, which was in silky black cornrows with streaks of gray, ran down his back. Slanted dark-brown eyes darted around the room, as if he was checking to see if there was a way out. His face looked eager and full of impulsivity.

"Mr. Masters," I said, holding out my hand. Demario

ignored my palm and slipped into the chair on the other side of the table.

"Call me D."

"Okay. My name is Sylvia Wilcox, and I'm here because I'm investigating the murder of Liza Abernathy Stark."

"What? Liza?"

The convict's brow creased with concern, an unexpected expression.

"Yes. I'm sorry to tell you that Liza was shot five times behind a store in Brightmoor about two years ago."

How could he not know that Liza was dead? Demario Masters diverted his eyes to the floor, and for a minute, I thought they might brim over.

"I ain't got nothing to do with that. What you want from me?" he asked.

"She had kids and a husband. I've been hired to find out what happened to her."

"Why you here? If she died a while ago, it couldn't be me. I was in here. Why you here?"

Good question. I didn't want to show all my cards. I would stay on the conservative side with the questions and answers.

"Liza's murder may have had something to do with her past."

"Why you think that?"

"Brightmoor. The two of you lived there once, correct?"

"Yeah."

"Well, she was murdered in Brightmoor. She had to have been there for some reason, and nothing in her current life would have led her there."

Demario nodded, caught up in nostalgia.

"She never liked it there. Just played the game to be with me."

"How did you two meet?"

"She was friends with this chick I knew."

"Madelyn Price?"

"You already know everything. Why you here?"

"How did you two break up?"

Silence.

"D, how did you two break up?"

"She left me. We were down in New Orleans. Had just moved to try something new. My momma was down there visiting and we were getting thangs straight, but then she ran away on New Year's Eve. Threw a drink in my face and booked."

The mysterious move to New Orleans was proving once again to be intriguing.

"How long did you live in New Orleans?"

"I stayed there for about two years. Liza left after two or three months."

"Do you know why she left?"

"Not really, but I think it was all about Daddy's money. As long as she was wit' me, she couldn't have Daddy's money. She had to work for thangs. I think she left because she wanted to be on Easy Street. I know she went on and married a doctor after she got back to Michigan. Gold-digger."

"Did you talk with her once she returned to Michigan?"

"Nope. Well, not for a long time. A few years later, after I'd moved back to Michigan, she tried taking me to court."

"For what?"

"Just thangs we had between us. She wanted them returned."

"Material things?"

"Something like that."

"What happened?"

"She had a little addiction problem at the time. It was real hush-hush, but the judge threw out the case."

"How do you know she had a drug problem?"

"Didn't say drugs. She was addicted to me." He chuckled and smirked with satisfaction. "The girl was a good actress."

"Weren't you angry that she was having sex with you and taking you to court?"

Demario shrugged his shoulders.

"Didn't make me no difference. She wasn't going to get far with none of that. We both knew it."

A young white woman challenging a black guy with a lengthy criminal history in court? Why wouldn't the case go far?

"What makes you say that?"

Demario leaned across the table and whispered, "Because Liza never really wanted what she said she wanted. That's probably why she was in Brightmoor. She was looking for someone like me, not her husband."

It was odd, the way that Demario didn't hate Liza. He was a child-molester, an abusive person, and a convict with a long rap sheet, but he didn't hate this woman who had abandoned him and taken him to court. Why was he still sweet on her?

"You and Liza had a child. What happened to her?"

"She died."

"When?"

Demario pushed back from the table.

"I don't wanna talk about that."

"This could be helpful."

"How is a dead child helpful? Look, lady, that don't make no sense, and I'm done."

"I know you still care about Liza. Don't you want her to have justice?"

"Nope. She dead. That's all the justice she need. She got Jesus now."

The passive-aggressiveness piqued my interest. It was clear that Demario was affected by Liza's death, and the death of their child. Although it seemed far-fetched, I was still convinced he knew something about Liza's murder.

"Okay. I have a question about Madelyn Price."

"What about her?" Demario asked, in a curious, somewhat friendly tone. I could see why both Liza and Madelyn had been attracted to him. He was gregarious, attractive, and smarter than he looked.

"What was Madelyn Price like when you knew her?"

"That bitch? Now she know *exactly* what she want. She's a scheming bitch. What do you want to know about her?"

"You dated her?"

"She's my baby momma."

"I heard that rumor."

"We got a kid together. I ain't seen my little girl since she was about eight months, but I know she out there. What Madelyn got to do with all of this?"

"She was Liza's best friend."

Demario stood up from the table.

"Now you in here lying! They ain't never been friends!"

"Are you sure?" I dug out one of the photos Carson had given me. Liza and Madelyn were standing arm-in-arm in front of a Christmas tree, smiles all around.

Demario looked at the picture before tossing it across the room. The thin photo floated and landed gently on the edge of the table.

"What the hell is going on? You lying to me!" Demario screamed, his cheeks hot with anger.

My heartbeat increased as I watched the man slam his

fist into the wall. A guard appeared at the door. I nodded to let him know things were okay.

"Yeah. Apparently, they were good friends before Liza died. In fact, Madelyn was the last person to talk with Liza before she was killed."

"Wait, lady. Just wait, okay? This don't make no sense. I need you to wait a minute."

The convict sat back down at the table and placed his head in his hands. I felt a little bit guilty for rocking his world.

"I know this is a lot, but I think you want to see Liza's killer caught."

I'm just trippin'. Tell me the truth. What is this all about?"

"I don't know, D. That's why I'm here. Tell me about you and Madelyn, and Liza and Madelyn. What happened?"

Demario provided me with a review of what I already knew, but also added some details I hadn't been aware of. The two women had caught him in lies, and Madelyn had broken up with him. After Liza's baby was born, they moved to New Orleans to start a new life. She ran off on New Year's Eve of 1999, and he didn't see her again for a few years. Madelyn had never filed for child support, so he hadn't been able to find Kara. He told me that the baby he'd had with Liza had tragically died soon after Liza left New Orleans-something I knew was a blatant lie.

"How did the baby die?"

Once again Demario refused to talk about his lost child, which I figured was because he didn't have time to make up a believable lie. I figured that I had gotten enough information from him for the day, but since he'd lied to me-no Mountain Dew or Twinkies would be left for him. I thanked Demario for his time, and called for the guard. I placed a quick call to Martin before hitting the road.

"Marty, I need you to do me a favor."

"Sure."

"Find court records for a civil case: Liza Abernathy vs. Demario Masters. Apparently, Liza took him to court for belongings or something after he returned from New Orleans."

"Any idea what year and county?"

"Check years 2000 to 2002 in Wayne County. Liza lived in Livonia with her parents when she returned."

"On it. Did you learn anything else?"

"Yeah. Masters still has a thing for Liza."

"No way!"

"Yes! He was a little hurt to hear that she was dead. I think it threw him off a bit which may explain why he lied about Danica dying when she was a baby. Also, he seemed kind of indifferent about Liza taking him to court. He didn't have a lot of bad things to say about her, but he did say that Liza never really wanted what she said she wanted."

"Hmm. What do you think that means?"

"I think it means that Liza's death definitely had something to do with a secret she was keeping. You might be right about the cheating."

"Ah-ha! Rookie sleuth no more!"

"Now, now, don't get carried away. I just said I'm willing to entertain the idea. No cigars yet, Kemosabe."

"Why do you think he lied about Danica?"

"I don't know. Maybe he's just trying to protect her."

"Or maybe she decided to get revenge on a mother who abandoned her."

"Ugh. I hope we aren't dealing with matricide, but we'd be negligent to not look into it."

"Rookie sleuth strikes again!" Martin yelled into the phone.

I hung up and headed for the highway.

TRAFFIC WAS sparse until I got within an hour of Metro Detroit. The drive home took an additional twenty minutes, pushing the clock beyond working hours. Martin sent a text informing me that he was heading to my house. Sometimes, when days were long, he'd slip over to my place and take a nap. It usually meant that he had good information that couldn't wait until the next day.

The house was quiet and still when I arrived. Martin was stretched across the blue sofa in the living room. Notes were scattered across the floor and his laptop was open at the foot of the sofa. I let him sleep while I headed into the kitchen, prepped a meatloaf, and threw it into the oven with two red potatoes. After that I took a long, hot shower before slipping into sweats and one of Derek's old white t-shirts. I set the table for two and poured myself a glass of Shiraz. Why were Madelyn and Liza still in touch with one another when everything in their pasts indicated that they should be enemies? My brain started ticking through the people I thought could give me insight into the women's complex relationship. Once again, siblings might be the best way to go.

I wrote the name of Demario's three living siblings and Peter's name on a slip of paper. I had already spoken to Demario's half-sister in California, but the other siblings were in Detroit. They probably had a better grasp of their brother's relationships. I grabbed Martin's laptop and typed each name into a search engine. After a few clicks, I pulled up the address of Demario's sister, Alyssa, who was living on the outskirts of Brightmoor. A number was attached to Alyssa profile. I called the number, listened to series of rings, and left a message when the voicemail came on. Next, I looked up his brother who lived in the Cass Corridor section of Detroit. As far as Liza's brother went, I thought it might be a good idea to talk to Peter and his wife together. Of course, the recent divorce might make the meeting awkward, but I had a feeling that Abigail Abernathy could pull off the meeting without much trouble. I was asking a lot, but justice for Liza was worth it. I called Abigail Abernathy and asked, in the kindest voice possible, if she would be willing to meet with me one more time, and if we could ask Peter to join us.

"You must think you have something, then. We will meet with ya. Peter's here now. Can you stop by tomorrow morning?"

"Sure thing. What time?"

"Nineish? After we drop off the kids at school."

I programmed the meeting into my phone and pulled dinner out of the oven. Martin was still snoring on the couch. I debated whether I should wake him up. One glance at his bony arm flopped over the edge of the couch made the decision for me. He needed a good meal. I called his name until he rolled over and opened his eyes.

"Sorry, buddy, but it's dinner time."

"That's okay. I'm hungry," Martin said as he twisted into a full body stretch.

"Hey, guess what?"

"What?"

"The court case you told me to research—guess what it was for?"

"What?"

"Liza took Demario to court for custody of their daughter. She started the case, but abruptly dropped it for some reason."

"What? Really?"

"Looks that way."

"Did you run a search for her?"

"Sure did. Couldn't find anything.

"Did you look for a death date? Just in case."

"Yeah. Nothing there. I'm pretty sure she's alive."

"We have to find her. I'm meeting with Peter and Abigail Abernathy tomorrow, and I might try to squeeze in a meeting with Alyssa Masters-if I can reach her. This is an interesting development. Did you check social media?"

"Yeah. Didn't find anything, but then again, some of the younger crowd like to use an alias for those accounts."

"Good point. She's a teen, so I'm sure she has one or two. They're probably under some ridiculous moniker."

"Yeah. It looks like Liza took Demario Masters to court for custody of their daughter. It got a little ugly, and one of the things that came out was the idea that Liza didn't have any familial support. Demario had sisters, older nieces and nephews, and his mother to help with the kid. To be honest, the way it was going, I think Liza would have lost."

"Really? The man I just met doesn't scream father of the year."

"Right, but if he had support and she didn't, he would appear to be the better choice. And it seems like she was completely unfit. After all, she left the kid with him."

"Abigail Abernathy, and everyone else I've talked to about Liza, except for Carson, has portrayed her as being a little bit off. Common sense, from what I've heard, wasn't her strong suit."

"Here's the thing about the court case: the daughter,

Danica, was almost three when all of that was taking place. Do you think she knows about it?"

Children are typically more aware than adults realize. In a complicated family, information might leak out in front of children. They may not know exactly what is going on, but there was a chance that Liza's daughter was somewhere out there with these memories of the mother who abandoned her, tried to get custody later on, but eventually decided it wasn't worth it.

"Danica needs to go on the suspect list."

"She's pretty young, isn't she?"

"If she was with Demario and his family, then she grew up in Brightmoor, which means she's much older than her birth certificate states. She was barely a teen when Liza was killed, but that's old enough to be a killer."

"Okay, so we're going with Madelyn as our number one, and Danica as our number two?"

Martin looked a bit confused. It was hard to imagine a child murdering her mother, but it wasn't that far-fetched.

"I know. It's not what we want to see, but think about how maddening it would be to have a parent who abandoned you, then went on to have additional children and live in a mini-mansion. Meanwhile, Danica was left to the wolves. Her father is in prison. Who knows where she's been living? My bet is that she's on the street."

"When you put it like that, it kind of makes me root for her."

"Well, yes, in a way, but the law is the law. You can't murder people, even if you feel wronged."

"Have you learned anything else about the Masters?"

"Yes. I think it would be a good idea to track down the remaining siblings, especially the sister that lives in Detroit. She would likely have had more contact with Demario than the others. When I searched their names, I found that she and Demario lived under the same roof a number of times over the years."

"Danica probably lived with them as well."

"Exactly. We definitely need to find her."

## 10

Martin and I ate dinner and talked. There was one subject that always seemed to come up when the shop talk ended.

"So, I've been looking into Derek's death."

I forked a piece of meatloaf into my mouth so that my silence wouldn't seem strange.

"Syl, I don't think he committed suicide."

Chewing and staring off into the distance, I tried to remain cool and calm.

"Are you going to respond?"

"Marty, I don't want to think about that right now."

"But what if there was a cover up and- "

"Martin! Stop! Don't do this to yourself-or me. Okay?"

"I- "

"No! Derek drove into the Huron River-that's it. There weren't any other cars around and he just...He's gone. We need to love and cherish his memory."

Martin shook his head and switched subjects.

"I've been researching Madelyn Price. Do you really see her as a viable suspect?"

I was thankful that he had dropped the idea of investigating his brother's suicide, but I knew he was going to quietly pursue it on his own. I wasn't sure what to do about that, so I didn't bring it up. Instead, I followed Martin's pivot to a new topic.

"She's a possibility, but I see your point. We do need to consider other suspects, like Danica and possibly Peter, but Madelyn has more motive than anyone else we've come across."

"Do you really think she's our killer? She just seems like a little yoga instructor."

"Upstanding, but full of secrets. When I was a cop, sometimes it was the least likely person who committed the crime. I'd have my eyes set on the obvious perpetrator, ready to strike at the first sign of a misstep, and then the upstanding, righteous person would do something that would change the course of the investigation."

"Fair enough, but motive seems to be missing."

"The past could be her motive. Something happened and she decided it was time to strike."

"Like what? What would make her kill Liza after more than a decade of being done with the love triangle?"

Martin was right. Madelyn Price did seem at peace with the world and it was clear that her relationship with Liza was intact at the time of the murder. They may have come together over time, creating some type of alliance against Demario Masters.

"Well, I'll have more information tomorrow. Abigail and Peter Abernathy seem eager to speak with me. Maybe they can shed some light on an alternate suspect. Enough shop talk... I'm going to settle in for the night. You're welcome to stay."

"Thanks, but I better get home."

I considered prying and asking if home was still a rented room in the basement of his old college roommate's house, but I refrained. He was a grown man, free to do what he pleased without an overbearing sister-in-law monitoring his life choices.

"Okay. I'll see you in the morning." I pushed back from the table and gathered our dinner plates.

"My mom is back."

The plates on my forearm wobbled a bit. A fork went crashing to the floor.

"Oh, I see."

"I don't want you to worry. She's been okay this time. I really think she wants to have me in her life now."

"Of course. I just...I'm happy to hear that." I wasn't, but what else could I say?

"I better get going," Martin said, slowly backing away from the table, but maintaining eye contact. He wanted my approval. It mattered to him, so I did my best to smooth out the worry lines in my brow and smile.

"Alright, kiddo. Have a good night."

"You too. Thanks for dinner, Syl."

I PULLED into Abigail Abernathy's driveway just after 9:00 a.m. the next morning. The doorbell echoed through the hallway and I listened to Abigail lumbering through the foyer. She was smiling when she opened the door. Peter was standing in the background with his hands in his pockets. He nodded and forced a shy smirk onto his face.

"C'mon in. We're ready. Want some tea or coffee? We've got some pastries on the table too."

"Coffee would be great," I said, climbing onto one of the bistro chairs around the red, diner-style table.

While Abigail was in the kitchen, Peter came and sat at the table.

"Mr. Abernathy, thank you so much for agreeing to do this. I think—"

"I want you to find 'im."

"Yes, I want to—"

"Mrs. Wilcox, my youngest kid had a birthday the other day. My sister's kids were there, but my sister...She couldn't be there, and she'll never be there. Really hit me, ya know? Because someone took her life, she's gone. Find this son of a bitch, Mrs. Wilcox. Whatever you need from us, we're willing to do."

"Thank you, Mr. Abernathy—I really appreciate the help. I would like to talk with you and your wife about what I've learned over the past few days."

Abigail set a cup of piping hot coffee in front of me. I thanked her as she wiggled onto one of the bistro chairs.

"Okay. We're ready for it. Tell us," Abigail said.

"Peter, did you know that Madelyn and Liza both dated Demario Masters, the man in the picture you gave me?"

Peter frowned and shook his head. "No way. Madelyn is a good girl. She wouldn't have nothing to do with a jerk like that."

I decided not to force the issue. Peter obviously had some warm feelings for Madelyn. If I pushed too hard, he'd probably shut down.

"Who is Demario Masters?" Abigail asked.

"A man that Liza dated a long time ago."

"Hmm...Interesting," she said.

"Mr. Abernathy, I need you to think about when Liza lived out of state. Did you have any contact with her?"

"No. I didn't know that she had lived out of state, but then again, like I told you, we haven't ever been close."

"She lived in New Orleans for a few months."

"Really? I never knew that. Did she go there with that dude?"

"Yes. Liza moved back to Michigan in early 2000, leaving her daughter behind with Demario and his mother."

"Daughter? What?"

"Liza and Demario had a child in 1998, right before they moved to New Orleans. It looks like Liza may have left both Demario and the baby in New Orleans. When did you say that she reconciled with your parents?"

"Uh, I'm not sure on exact dates, but she was definitely around in 2000. I remember coming home from state and being shocked when she pulled open the door. She didn't move back in until 2001, but she was around a little before that."

"Do you recall her mentioning the name Danica?"

"Never. Who is that?"

"Danica Masters is her daughter."

"What happened to her?"

"Well, initially, I thought she had died as an infant— sudden infant death, an infection, something like that—but I can't find anything that indicates she is deceased."

"Oh, no." Abigail sighed.

Peter ran his hands through his spiked hair.

"I can't believe this," he muttered. "I have a niece out there that I don't know? Liza left her with that loser's family? How old is she now?"

"About fifteen. I haven't had any luck tracking her down, but just because there aren't clear records of her doesn't mean she's not out there. If she was left with the Masters, there's no way to know how she was raised, or if she was taken to school. There is one curious court case from twelve years ago."

"What is the case about?"

"Custody. Liza fought for custody."

"She never told us."

For the first time, Peter looked sad. His forehead creased, and he sat silent for a moment.

"Listen, I know we probably sound like the most dysfunctional family ever, but you have to understand. Mom was always trying to put on this show, and if we didn't go along with it, she tried to force it. You know what I mean?"

"Why don't you explain it to me. Just to be sure I understand," I said, gently encouraging Peter to open up and share more information.

"Mom wanted this perfect little family, and we weren't that. She wasn't willing to accept that we were human, so she forced us to do a lot of things that we didn't want to do. Some of which weren't good for us. Liza had to take all these ridiculous classes and extracurricular things because the other girls on our block were taking them. My sister was different. She needed more guidance than most, but my mom treated her like she had superstar intelligence, you know what I mean?"

"I don't want to assume anything," I said, avoiding agreement so that Peter would continue.

"Okay, well, I guess what I'm trying to say is that Liza was a little behind the curve. At times, she needed someone to remind her to bathe, eat, wash her hands, and there was no way she was going to complete her homework without a massive amount of help. She wasn't someone who did well on her own. My mom couldn't handle that. She refused to accept that Liza had a few screws loose."

Loose screws? I wasn't sure if Peter was telling me that

Liza was intellectually challenged, or if she had experienced some type of mental illness. Whatever the case, it sounded like Mrs. Abernathy had been disappointed in her.

"I know Carson isn't your favorite person, but I'm wondering how he and Liza got together. You said that Liza had some challenges, but Carson is a surgeon. How did those two get together?"

"I don't know if it will be relevant, but they hooked up when Liza worked at a hospital for a while. I think she was a CNA or something like that. At one time, she had thought of becoming a nurse, but the coursework was too rigorous. She never passed the test for her teacher certification either. The girl wasn't good with academics, but from what I've heard, she really took to the CNA thing. Carson met her at the hospital, so he would have seen her in her best light."

"Liza was a Certified Nurse Assistant at the hospital, and that's how she met Carson?"

"Well, she volunteered at the hospital for a while before she worked there. Liza had a good heart. She could be very frustrating at times, but she always liked to help people if she could. By the time she met Carson, she'd been at our parents' house for a while. Since she wasn't working full-time, she decided to volunteer to fill up her free time. Mom suggested that she might want to become a nurse, Liza said okay, became a CNA and enrolled in night school. The coursework was hard for her, and after working as a CNA for a while, she quit school and started thinking about other stuff she could do. She'd been around Carson for a while by then, so he probably mentioned that teaching was a noble profession, or something like that. He just happened to be Catholic, and I think that inspired her to want to teach at the Catholic school. We're Lutheran, so I think she took the teaching job to impress Carson."

I knew that Peter wouldn't be privy to major details about their courtship, but I was curious as to whether he knew one not-so-intimate detail.

"What did you think of Carson when you first met him?"

"I thought he was okay. I mean, he wasn't really that bad at first. It seemed like he was really into Liza, so I liked him in the beginning."

"What changed?"

Peter rubbed his hands through his hair again. This time, he dropped his head and shook it from side to side.

"Mrs. Wilcox, I have to be honest here. I know I told you that I hated Carson, and that I thought he was responsible for Liza's death, but you must understand. For the past several years, I've hated everyone. Carson ain't my kind of person, but I think he genuinely loved my sister. He was gentle with her. It was like he understood her and loved her just the way she was. They were...happy."

Abigail ran her hand along Peter's arm and gave it a squeeze. Peter Abernathy's gnarled face had softened and relaxed. He looked closer to his age, and his faded blue eyes glistened with emotion. The man had loved his sister.

"Thank you for being honest, Mr. Abernathy," I said, taking a pause before asking, "So, if it wasn't Carson, who would you say would be most likely to kill your sister?"

"That's a good question. The only person I can think of is that Masters dude. I could see him having a grudge of some sort against her. If he'd married her, he would have moved up several socioeconomic levels. Their break-up was intense, and if there was a kid involved, I could see him being extremely bitter."

"Well, I thought that as well, but Demario Masters was in prison at the time of Liza's murder. Mr. Abernathy, I have an angle that you might not like, but I have a reason for thinking this is a possibility."

"Oh, go on. We want to know what you know," Abigail said.

I prepared for my theory to be rejected.

"I think Madelyn Price may have something to do with Liza's murder."

Peter leaned forward, ready to protest, but Abigail held his arm, squeezing it again. He closed his mouth and waited.

"Why do ya think that, Mrs. Wilcox?" Abigail asked.

"Madelyn and Liza were dating Demario Masters at the same time. It was a love triangle. Madelyn was first, and Demario is the father of her daughter. Liza gave birth to Danica around Madelyn's child's first birthday. Madelyn left Demario, but not before having a confrontation with Liza."

"A woman scorned," Abigail muttered.

"Yes. So, my first question is: how close were Liza and Madelyn? My second question is: why were they close if they had that type of history, and why is Madelyn tied to the place where Liza was found? She lived a block away, Liza was going to meet her when she was killed, and even though everyone has told me that they were great friends, Madelyn described Liza as a 'student' when I interviewed her."

"That doesn't sound good for Madelyn," Peter said.

"Ms. Price hasn't been forthcoming in interviews, and I'm looking for any information you have about her. I just have a feeling that she is connected to Liza's murder in some way."

Abigail looked like she was contemplating whether what she had to say was relevant. After a few minutes of painful silence, she spoke.

"Well, she is always out of town. It's strange. Liza would go with her sometimes, but like I told you, they didn't seem that close to me. It was strange that they would take trips together."

"Okay. Good. Thank you for sharing that. Anything else?"

"She's really strange when it comes to her kid. She doesn't even like people to know her name. It's like, she's got this awesome kid stashed away at a fancy school, doing all types of great things, but she don't talk about her. I'm a mom, and I couldn't imagine not talking about my kids. That's weird."

"Did you participate in any of the girls' nights that Liza and Madelyn had?"

"Well, like I said before, they weren't really girls' nights out. They weren't much fun when they were together. Liza and Madelyn didn't have anything in common and it showed when they hung out."

Except for Demario Masters. Why would they be friends?

I asked if they could think of anything else, but neither of them had much to share. They told me they'd call if anything else came to mind. Not exactly an illuminating interview, but they'd reinforced some of the strange observations I'd made about Madelyn. I left the Abernathy's and headed for the office.

## 11

"She had to have been having an affair," Martin said. "I'm not getting that vibe. We also don't have any evidence to support that idea."

After the string of new clues, the case had gone cold. Martin and I had been having the same conversation for days. As the time passed without any developments or clarity, I'd started to get discouraged. Martin had hit a wall with his research and once again we were sitting in the office, stuck.

"Okay, how do we get out of this rut?" Martin asked.

"I don't know where to go with this. Liza was murdered because of something that happened years ago, but then again, it might be because of some secret life she was living right before she died. But we have no proof that she was having an affair or doing anything else, so what the heck was she doing in Brightmoor?"

"Yeah, that about sums it up. Nothing makes sense."

"Maybe we need to try something different."

"Like what? What did you do when you got stuck on a case when you were a police officer?"

I thought for a moment. What did I do when I was a cop? Usually, I would run some off-the-wall theory by my partner or draw a diagram with the evidence and create a hypothesis. This time, I felt like there were too many missing links for either scenario.

"We need more evidence."

"I know, Marty, but I'm not sure where to get it. I've talked to—" I stopped mid-sentence. Yes, I had talked to everyone I could reach, but maybe talk was cheap in this case. Maybe I needed to be watching instead of talking. I'd watched Madelyn's place one evening over the past few weeks, but without additional evidence, the pursuit had seemed futile. But Madelyn was a patient, intelligent woman. If she had something to hide, she would be incredibly elusive.

I grabbed my phone, computer, and notepad.

"Where ya going?" Martin asked.

"To watch Madelyn Price."

SURVEILLANCE IS NOT ALWAYS EFFECTIVE, but when I have a good hunch, I will subject myself to hours upon hours of wasted time in a car. When I first started watching Madelyn, she appeared to be a creature of habit. Her yoga classes ran from 8:00 a.m. to 12:00 noon on Mondays, Wednesdays, and Fridays, 1:00 to 4:00 in the afternoon on Tuesdays and Thursdays, and 12:00 to 3:00 p.m. on Saturdays. She taught a course at the U on Tuesdays and Thursday mornings, and the rest of her time was spent meeting friends for lunch or dinner. She observed Sunday as a day of rest, which included church attendance. The first Sunday, I trailed her to St. Mary's Preparatory campus, where she attended Mass with her daughter, followed by lunch. Then, after three weeks of watching Madelyn go through the exact same routine, I gave up and decided to stop watching her.

"Why aren't you watching her anymore?" Martin asked.

"Because she's just a yoga teacher who happened to be casual friends with Liza. I'm not seeing the connection between them, or any indication that she had something to do with the murder."

"But you had a hunch. Aren't detectives supposed to go with their hunches?"

"Yes, but some detectives have better hunches than others. I really have no reason to follow her other than the fact that I have nothing better to do."

"At least it's something. Speaking of which, I have been thinking about the convict's sister, the one that won't call you back. What's her name?"

"Alyssa Masters. What about her?"

"Well, what if she knows something about the murder and that's why she isn't calling you back?"

"Yeah, that's probably the case. What's your point?"

"Hear me out. She lives in Brightmoor and her brother is locked up in prison. What if he had her kill Liza?"

It was an interesting angle, but unlikely. Demario Masters had plenty of time to kill Liza before he went to prison. Why wait and then have your sister do the dirty work? He also had seemed genuinely shocked when he found out that Liza had been murdered.

"I don't know that I see the connection there. I'm assuming that she still lives in Brightmoor because she's poor and her family has a footprint there."

"But she and Liza knew each other. Isn't it possible that they were in contact?"

"Yes. It actually is possible. Okay. We don't have anything

else. Maybe this will go somewhere. Let's flesh it out a bit more. So, we have Liza in Brightmoor several times before her death. Alyssa Masters lives there. Demario Masters has obviously been out of contact with Liza for many years, but there is a familial connection."

"Danica."

"Yes, Danica. She may have fallen into the foster care system, but she could also have been taken in by one of Demario's siblings. His younger brother is sick, according to the oldest sister, and one sister is dead, so Alyssa would be the only one Danica could be living with-if she's with a close family member."

"Which might make her skittish about calling you back."

"She would want to shield her niece. The kid has already lost both parents—one to prison and the other to murder. Okay, Marty, I like it. Today I want you to find out everything you can about Alyssa Masters—where she works, her schedule, and any other interesting tidbits you happen to come across."

"I'm on it."

"Okay. I'll be out today."

"Where ya going?"

"I have a hunch," I said, winking at Martin before heading out the door.

The kid was right. I had a hunch and I should follow it. So what if Madelyn had not changed her routine in three weeks? She was stealthy and private. Maybe she even had an inclination that she was being followed. Now that I'd laid off for a day or so, any suspicion she might have had could be gone. My hunch was far-fetched, but I didn't have anything else to go on, so why not stick with it and see it through to the end? After all, Carson Stark was paying me a small fortune to find out what happened to his wife. Even if

Madelyn didn't have anything to do with Liza's death, I was sure she knew more than she'd told me.

Madelyn's routine schedule dragged on for two more weeks, but just as I was about to drop the surveillance gig for a second time, things got interesting. Madalyn left the house around 6:15 one evening, just as dusk took over. She climbed into her Honda Accord and took off. A late winter storm had blanketed the Huron Valley in several inches of snow, which made tracking Madelyn more difficult. I trailed her through the back roads, almost losing her on Geddes. She made a sharp turn that caused me to hesitate. I couldn't follow her, but I knew if I went back and turned left on Geddes Road, I'd find another road that would take me close to that area. I drove past the road, waited, and doubled back, pacing myself and letting a few other cars turn onto Prospect.

The snow-covered fields and desolate two-lane road never saw much traffic, and even less at night. A dirt road in a winter storm isn't a popular means of transportation. I had to wait quite a while before another car turned. About seven minutes after Madelyn had gone down the road, I crept up behind a blue Mustang that was struggling to get traction in the heavy snow. Madelyn's car was nowhere in sight, but there weren't many places to turn off the road. I figured that she had to be at the end of whatever this thoroughfare was.

While twisting through Ann Arbor's outer reaches, I noticed that the snow had thickened. I drove through the blanket of white, hoping that Madelyn wasn't somewhere by the side of the road listening to my tires crunching on the snow and ice. In the distance, I spotted a building with smokestacks puffing pollution into the air. I could see a few cars parked in front of it, but the last illumination of the day was fading. I quickly scanned the scene for Madelyn's car, but came up with nothing.

I continued to creep along the road, edging closer to the building, which looked like a small factory of some sort. There were tire tracks on a secluded road to the right of the structure. Proceeding could mean running the risk of being caught or getting stuck in the snow. If I parked on the far side of the factory, my car would appear to be just another employee vehicle. I pulled into a parking stall, bundled up in my down-filled coat, and headed out. The snow-covered brush was thick, and the large, fluffy flakes reduced visibility. A pair of ski goggles shielded my eyes, but I still had trouble making out much of anything. I noticed a path of crushed snow that led deeper into the forest. I followed it for what seemed like a lifetime, but in reality, was only about ten minutes before I spotted a cottage sitting far back from the road. The small house could easily be missed if you didn't know what you were looking for. I walked over to the edge of the road, kneeled behind a thicket of bushes, and pulled out my binoculars.

The cottage was hidden behind tangled branches and snowdrifts. I crept closer and focused the binoculars on the window blinds. Between the cracks, I could see that several young women and children were inside. I observed what I thought was probably the serving of dinner. Three women were working in the kitchen, two women were setting places at the long wooden dinner table, and a few children milled about. Madelyn was working underneath the kitchen sink and appeared to be fixing a pipe. A leak, perhaps? From what I could tell, there wasn't much in the way of conversation. It wasn't a friendly scene. This was business.

After Madelyn had finished under the sink, she seemed to instruct the women on what to do and how to set the table. I watched a cold and unfeeling dinner unfold. Madelyn stayed and ate with the others, but this was not a cordial gathering of friends. There was a crisp and formal feel to this meeting. The eyes of the women were dull and downcast, and their mouths silent. I scanned the group, noticing the somber looks. A very strange social setting. I put the binoculars back in the case and headed back to the car. My moccasin boots slipping on the fresh, hard powder as I made my way to the car.

"Okay, this isn't much, but it's a little odd."

"What?" Martin asked. I had called him the moment I walked in the door.

"I trailed Madelyn to this place, and she appeared to be freelancing as a plumber of some sort. She went to a cottage that was full of women and children, and it didn't look like a friendly get together. Madelyn fixed a pipe and had dinner, but I didn't see any chatting or smiles. I can't really figure out what the connection was between her and the other people there."

"Tell me more."

"Well, she fixed something under the sink, directed traffic in the house, and had dinner with the group. There wasn't much in the way of conversation or anything like that. Didn't really seem like a friendly scene."

"Hmm. What do you think is going on?"

"Not sure. They could just be some associates."

"Do you think this has anything to do with Liza's murder?"

"That's hard to say. It just seems weird to head out to a

secluded cottage, fix a pipe and have dinner in a little cottage that is packed with women and children."

"That is odd. Guess what I found out about Danica?"

"What?"

"She's been in and out of foster care, just like you thought, and you were also right about her living with Alyssa. She did live with her for about a year. I don't know what happened, but I don't think she's there anymore. She's going to Cody High on the other side of town."

"How'd you find that out?"

"Spent a little time in Brightmoor. Why are there so many kids out during the day in that neighborhood?"

"Truancy is their thing. How many kids did you talk with?"

"Three. They were standing around in a huddle in front of a burned-out house. Didn't look like they were drug dealers, or anything like that, so I decided to talk with them. They know Danica. She's around sometimes—knows gang members, but she isn't part of the gang. Her dad is in prison, as you know, and she drifts in and out of the neighborhood. Sometimes she stays at a shelter in the area, other times she lives with friends, or finds a way to get by. Alyssa does something in medial field, and she might be going to school."

"Good job, Marty! This is great info. Now we know that we just have to be on the lookout for her. Maybe we should switch details. I can go to Brightmoor and you can watch Madelyn. I thought you'd search for info online."

"You don't think I'm tough enough for Brightmoor?"

"It's not about being tough enough. I just don't want you to get hurt."

I was happy to have the information, but the idea of Martin hanging out around Brightmoor gave me chills.

"I can handle it," Martin said, an edge in his voice.

"I know. Thank you for all of your hard work," I said, while simultaneously wondering how I could get Martin out of the detective business.

THE NEXT MORNING, I drank two cups of strong coffee and headed out for an early morning run. Along the way, I recalled the strange scene I'd encountered the night before. How many women had been there? At least twelve. How many children? Five? No, maybe seven. Nothing nefarious seemed to be going on, but something was off. What did it all mean?

Strange fruit, but at least I had something new to ponder. The yoga instructor/abnormally calm "best friend" had a secret of some kind. I wasn't sure what the secret meant, but being tucked away in a little cottage half a mile from the road, indicated that Madelyn might have something to hide. Whatever it was, I intended to find out.

After the run, I hopped in the shower, got dressed, and headed to the office. The winter thaw was beginning, making the stroll to the office rather pleasant. Martin arrived a few minutes after nine.

"What's the plan for today," Martin asked.

"We need to figure out what's happening at that cottage in the woods. I'll show you where it's located this evening. I want you to watch and see who comes and goes."

"Will I be able to sit in the car, or will I have to freeze outside?"

"Well, if you park far enough away, you can stay in the car. Take some binoculars and you'll be fine."

"What about this morning?"

"I'm going to see what else I can find out about Madelyn.

Why don't you print off all our information, organize it, and stick it in a binder?"

"Easy enough," Martin said, grabbing his laptop and heading to the printer.

I sat down at my desk and began researching Madelyn Price again. After some math and guesstimating, I found Madelyn's college graduation photo. There wasn't much information about her, but the blurb stated that she had attended U of M on a scholarship. During her time at the U, she was a straight-A student and the leader of several clubs, including a single mothers' group. It seemed that she was a natural leader and stood out from the crowd.

The one thing that didn't seem to be included in Madelyn's life was a romantic interest. Her Internet presence was minimal, but her daughter's social media pictures included several images of Madelyn. She was by herself of with her daughter Kara, in all of the pictures. Based on what I'd observed, and the information I found online, Madelyn seemed to be focused on keeping the yoga studio running, and ensuring that her daughter received the best of everything. With that in mind, I decided to look at the yoga studio. Surprisingly, there was not a website for the yoga studio. How had Madelyn built the business and kept it running while maintaining such a low profile?

The yoga studio didn't have a name per se. Madelyn had given her business a vague, uneventful title. If you looked up "yoga studio," the address came up, but there was no name attached to the establishment. I was sure that she had a business license, but to have one, she had to have given a name of some sort. It was odd not to have specific information online. How did people find the studio? The best way to figure that out would be to talk to one of Madelyn's patrons. I decided to switch the focus of the surveillance.

What I needed was an in. The only way to get that would be to get in touch with someone from Madelyn's inner circle. My guess was that Madelyn's patrons had other ties to her, and that was the way she acquired customers. Yoga classes that only took women, no official name for the studio...it was all so covert. The only way to learn more was to infiltrate.

After a day of online sleuthing, Martin followed me to the cottage on the edge of Ann Arbor Township. We parked at the little factory and I led Martin through the trees and showed him the little house. Large snowflakes were falling that evening, creating a certain level of camouflage.

"Stay out of sight, okay?"

"Will do."

"You can sit in your car and wait to see if anyone drives down the road. If they do, try to follow them. Just don't get caught."

"Don't worry. I've got this," he said. Slight irritation slipping into his voice.

"All right, kiddo. See you soon. Call me if you need anything."

Martin nodded and I headed back to my car. He didn't seem to suspect that I'd given him this job because it was safe.

DAYS TURNED into weeks without leads. Nothing was happening and each time Carson called asking to meet, I would make up an excuse as to why I was unavailable. I try to remain honest in my dealings with others, and I don't like to bring innocent people into the mix when researching a case. Unfortunately, I was at the point where I felt like I didn't have a choice. I needed information from an insider-someone in Madelyn's world. I chose an early spring day at the end of March to put my plan into action. Parked at the edge of Madelyn's driveway, tucked away behind the barren branches of winter-beaten trees, I waited until someone turned onto the main road. An hour passed before any cars emerged, but just as I felt my head start to nod with sleepy boredom, I heard the rattle and hum of a vehicle. An early 1980s blue Volkswagen Beetle crept along the bumpy dirt road, twisting and coughing before steadying itself on the black top. I waited two minutes for the Bug to climb the small hill that sat a few hundred yards from Madelyn's driveway before pulling onto the roadway.

The blue Bug chugged along Whitmore Lake Road, on the edges of rural Ann Arbor Township, until it came to Barton Drive. It snaked along to Plymouth Road and eventually stopped at Mocha's on Main, a tiny coffee shop on Main Street. A young woman climbed out of the car and grabbed an apron from the backseat before heading into the coffee shop. I wrote down the license plate number of her car, and the address of the coffee shop before heading home to change. If I was going to chat up a barista, I needed to look the part.

I CALLED Mochas on Main as soon as I got home. The first time I called, a man with a deep, trombone voice answered the phone. I hung up and called ten minutes later. This time, a woman with a soft, southern drawl purred into the phone.

"It's a great day at Mocha's on Main, this is Lacresha. How can I help you?"

"Hello. What are your hours today?"

"We're open 'til ten tonight."

"Thank you," I said before hanging up.

Lacresha. Okay, so now I had a name. It was a like having one drop of water in a pond, but it was something. I typed in Lacresha, Mocha's on Main, and Ann Arbor into a search engine. The combination pulled up hundreds of results. Switching to a social media site reduced the results to twelve. I sifted through each result, ruling out the ones with pictures immediately, and concentrating on the five that didn't have pictures. In the end, I settled on the account with the posts that contained what I thought was southern dialect. The data was sparse, but it led me to believe that the profile I was looking at belonged to the girl I'd spoken to at the coffee shop. Ann Arbor and New Orleans were both mentioned, and the few pictures she had posted were of downtown Ann Arbor. I decided to head to the coffee shop.

Lacresha Newman enhanced the charm of the dark, dank, but somewhat quaint hole-in-the-wall named Mocha's on Main. The café was a tiny storefront sandwiched between a used book store and a small-plates restaurant. I gave the heavy oak doors a yank and entered a dimly lit room with small, cheap tables and old, sagging couches along the wall. There was also a bar with stools at the front of the café. I spotted Lacresha Newman behind the counter. I headed for the last stool at the end of the bar.

Lacresha was soft-spoken, with a southern drawl and big, brown, sad eyes. She wore a tie-dyed, purple, baby-doll shirt and inexpensive skinny jeans that were just shy of being too small. It was clear that she had once been petite—perhaps the yoga class was part of her quest to improve the fit of the jeans. A nametag dangled on her shirt, just south of her chin. I waited patiently for her to blend a coffee drink for the hipster in front of me.

To fit the part, I'd taken my hair out of the bun and fluffed it out in a carefree, tamed afro. I'd thrown on capris, a tank top, Birkenstocks, and a backpack. Yes, it was still chilly out, but that never stopped anyone in Ann Arbor from dressing like it was mid-June. I'd added glasses and a hippie charm necklace I'd worn in college. It was still winter, but a warm spell had given us temps in the high forties, so I'd thrown on a vintage jean jacket. It may have been a little overkill, but I blended in well with the eclectic Ann Arbor scene. I ordered a non-fat mocha and sat at the front counter for a while, watching Lacresha work. Nervous, shaky hands led to sincere apologetic whispers, but she was doing better than she thought. A caring manager encouraged her. I almost felt bad for what I was about to do, but there was no getting out of it. I needed information.

"This mocha is great."

"Glad you like it."

"Are you new?" I asked casually.

"Yes."

"Welcome. I love this place. Best mochas in A2."

No response.

"Is that an accent I hear?"

"Yeah."

"Where ya from?"

"New Orleans."

"Nice. I love that city. You a student?"

"No, I just moved here with my son. He's two. We're starting over, fresh and new."

Her smile was genuine and hopeful. Starting over could mean a lot of things. After Hurricane Katrina, fleeing the Gulf Coast was not uncommon, but that disaster was well in the past now. Perhaps she had left Louisiana for another reason.

"So, what made you choose Michigan?"

"Got a few good friends here. They helping me get things in order. My life was messed up back home. After Katrina, it was just too hard to get things together. I was just a kid when it struck, but nothing was ever the same after that. No more struggling. I'm ready to make it big in this life."

She was working hard to hide her accent and vernacular, but she kept slipping into her southern drawl.

"Do you plan on going to school?"

"Eventually, but my friend says she goin' help me get thangs together and git me in a program. She owns a daycare, so I don't gotta worry 'bout nothin'."

"That's so cool. Well, welcome to A2."

"Thanks."

"What do you think of the city?"

"Haven't seen much, but I like what I've seen."

"It's a great place. A2 is unique. I think you'll like it."

"Me too. I don't miss Louisiana as much as I thought I would. Would you like some key lime pie? Maybe lemon cake. It's all made in house."

I considered the lemon cake but decided against it.

"No, I'm just tanking up on coffee for lab tonight."

"What you taking?"

"Chemistry."

"Oh man, I couldn't handle that."

"It's challenging, but I like it. Nothing worthwhile is easy, right?"

"Amen," she said, before flipping on a blender to mix a drink.

"So, did you come here to visit and decide to stay?"

"Naw. It was more like a leap of faith. I hadn't been here before I moved."

"Really? How did you make friends?" I asked.

She hesitated and looked at the ceiling before answering.

"Well, they kind of found me. Thank God they found me," she said in a serene voice.

I spent the next few minutes making small talk and working to pry any small details from her. Lacresha was nice and eager to tell parts of her story, but she kept the major points to herself. I felt guilty taking advantage of the young girl's optimism and naivety, but over the next week, I continued to stop by for mochas and lattes.

On day six, I took Martin with me. Sneakiness comes easily to him, so when I told him the plan, he was excited and ready to help. I took him in and introduced him as my chem. lab partner.

"Hey," Lacresha said.

"Hello," Martin said, his eyes sparkling with admiration.

Today, Lacresha's hair was swept up into a bun, and her dark skin held a new glow. She had now mastered her job, and must have been getting used to Ann Arbor, because her southern hospitality was on full display. She talked freely with Martin, who I think genuinely liked her. He maintained eye contact and the two of them ignored my comments the way potential lovers ignore the third wheel. Towards the end of our stay, I got up and went to the bathroom. Standing at the mirror, I fluffed my unruly locks, washed my hands, and pulled out my phone to check invisible text messages. I counted to thirty before returning to my seat. Martin winked at me the moment I sat down. We stayed for a few more minutes, and then made our excuses and left. Chem. lab was waiting.

We made our way to the car, cool, calm, and collective. Once we were pulling out of the parking space, Martin began to talk.

"She told me she'd had a hard time, wasn't ready for anything new. Said her last boyfriend had not been 'nice' to her. She stuttered a bit, looked down when she said it. I think you were right. Something's up with her."

"What do you think that something might be?"

"No idea."

"Where is she living?"

"She didn't give me an exact address, but it sounds like she might live with Madelyn. She said she's staying with a friend."

"What else did you find out?"

"Sounds like she was in an abusive relationship. I asked about yoga and she mentioned that her yoga teacher is amazing. Maybe Madelyn Price is a good lady?"

I listened as we cruised through Ann Arbor. Was I exploiting a young single mom and my lonely brother-in-law? A twinge of guilt welled up in my throat.

"You really liked her, didn't you?"

Martin shifted in the passenger seat. We let the silence linger for a few minutes, and then I spoke.

"You liked her. Martin, I shouldn't have involved you in this. I won't ask you to do anything like that again. It was unfair."

"It's okay. I'm always asking for more responsibility. Well, you gave it to me. I did kind of like her. She's so pretty."

"Well, maybe you'll go back and visit her after all this is over. Madelyn doesn't know who you are, so there's no reason for you to be connected to this debacle. Afterwards, go back and ask for her number again. She might be a nice girl to get to know."

Martin was visibly uncomfortable now. The faint hue of a blush crept onto his cheeks. He looked like a schoolboy in love.

"How old is she?"

"Twenty-three."

"Maybe she likes younger men."

"Sylvia!"

"Just saying." I laughed and slugged him in the arm.

"Whatever. Let's stay on topic," he said, stifling a laugh.

"How'd she find the yoga studio?"

"Didn't say, but she did say she'd met the friend she's staying with in New Orleans. Madelyn has some ties there, right?"

"Yes. So did Liza."

"You're thinking Lacresha met Madelyn in the Big Easy, kept in touch, and moved in with her?"

"Sounds like it. That would lead to knowledge of the yoga studio."

"Wonder how they met. Lacresha is quite a bit younger than Madelyn."

"Maybe a yoga conference? They have that in common."

"Okay, I guess that works, but the bigger question is, what does it have to do with Liza's murder?" Martin asked.

"No clue."

"Madelyn may have instructed others to kill Liza— maybe for money, or just for fun.

"But what would be the motive?"

"That's the thing. There isn't a motive. Madelyn isn't moving in on Carson, she didn't have financial ties, and the yoga studio has nothing to do with Liza."

"Do you think we're missing something?"

"Have to be. I just don't know what it is...yet."

## 12

T he rest of the work week stretched on without revealing much information about Liza's murder. I spent Thursday and Friday on the computer, typing in various combinations of words I thought might bring up valuable clues. Saturday is generally my day off, but I spent six hours searching through old deeds and newspaper clippings at the library. That night, I passed out before having dinner and didn't wake up until a little after six a.m. the next day.

I keep the Sabbath as much as I can. There are times when I need to work, but I almost always keep my standing date of 6:30 a.m. Mass. That Sunday morning, I put on a suit and headed to St. John's as usual. By 7:15 a.m., I was normally on my way back home.

That Sunday, I waved to the familiar faces—most topped with white hair—before sliding into the second-to-last pew at the back of the church. Mass started at 6:29 a.m. and lasted forty minutes. Father Keegan gave a gentle homily encouraging us to welcome the stranger, regardless of who the stranger happened to be. After the procession from the sanctuary was complete, I slipped out of the pew, genu-flected toward the altar, and finished the solemn event with a holy-water-laced cross on my forehead.

Generally, after Mass I keep my head down, wave at a few acquaintances, and share a brief chat with Father Keegan, who has been my priest since the beginning of time, and head home. On this particular Sunday, however, he held my hand after our cordial handshake and quietly asked, "May I have a moment of your time?"

Father Keegan and I have known one another for decades. He was the priest at the Catholic school I attended as a child. At the time, he'd been a spry young man eager to save young souls. Now he was slightly less spry, but still an excellent priest. He had helped me navigate the emotional waters around Derek's death.

In answer to his question, I said, "Sure, Father Keegan."

"I'll be in the social hall in a few minutes. Do you have time to wait?"

"Absolutely." I grabbed a cup of coffee, waved to several elderly parishioners, and received a few kisses from blue-haired ladies. Ten minutes later, Father Keegan pulled up a chair at my solitary table.

"How are you doing, my friend?"

"Doing well. Is everything okay?"

"Well, I don't know. Are you working any cases?"

Generally, I don't answer that question for anyone who doesn't need to know, but Father, being my priest and a confidant, was in a gray area, so I told him yes.

"I see. Someone came here asking questions about you."

"Really? Did he or she leave their name?"

"No. The woman wasn't very friendly, and she refused to leave her name. She was small, petite, and her hair was pulled back into a bun. The questions she asked were intrusive. I guess she thought an old priest would just fold and answer them."

A mistake indeed. Father Keegan had been a priest in the heart of Detroit for several decades before moving to a suburban parish; he knew how to handle intruders, and kept a Glock handy.

"I'm working on a high-profile case. Do you remember the story about the woman who was killed in Brightmoor? It was a about two years ago. She was a Northville stay-at-home mom, married to a doctor."

"Oh, yes. I remember that."

"Her husband asked me to find her killer."

"Oh, Sylvia, why do you always want to make things hard on yourself? I thought you usually refused murder cases. You're a PI—this could be dangerous."

"Don't worry. I will be careful. What did this woman ask you?"

"She wanted to know where you lived and which Mass you attended. I told her I was not at liberty to disclose any information. It was disturbing that she knew that you attended this parish. She wasn't friendly, Sylvia. I don't know if she's dangerous or not, but you should be careful."

Madelyn Price was obviously investigating me. It was very strange that she wanted to know about my church habits and where I lived.

"Will you try to snap a picture of the woman if she comes back? She's very sly and coy. If I confront her without any definitive evidence, she'll deny everything."

"I will use my fancy phone to snap a picture, but keep in mind that you don't know who she is yet."

"No, but I have a good idea that it is my number one suspect. Her name is Madelyn Price. Throw her name out if she comes back; see if she reacts."

"Do you really think she's a murderer?"

"Part of the reason she's my number one suspect is because she was so reluctant during my interview with her, and I think this murder is rooted in the past. She didn't want to answer questions and, like you said, she's not friendly."

"Sylvia, have you considered getting out of law enforcement? Derek was so proud of you. He wouldn't mind if you went a different way."

It was true: Derek wouldn't care what I did. He'd always been my biggest fan.

"Thank you for saying that. I know it's true, but I feel an urge to do this work, so I'll be in law enforcement until it doesn't inspire me anymore."

"It's not your fault, the thing that happened. You don't have to make up for something that isn't your fault, Sylvia."

"Father, I do this because I feel called to do it. You know what it's like to be called to something, right?"

He nodded. "You've got me there. Just be careful, Sylvia."

"No worries. I'm always careful."

"Well, I hope that this case is solved soon. It's not comforting to know that someone is snooping around trying to get information about you."

I wondered if Madelyn knew she was my number one suspect. I felt a little violated, but recognized how hypocritical that thought was. We were both suspicious of each other and searching for answers.

"Don't worry, I'm a crack shot," I said, winking and getting up to leave.

"See you next week!" Father Keegan called after me.

∾

ON THE WALK HOME, I pondered the meaning behind Madelyn's questioning of my priest. She'd asked about my faith when I interviewed her. Had she been on a fact-finding mission too? We were both playing the same game. Back at home, I checked my messages. One of Carson's coworkers had left me a voicemail.

"Mrs. Wilcox, I know you called me a few months ago, but I have been so busy, I've just now had a chance to get back to you. If you are free, please stop by the hospital this evening. I will be able to chat about Liza and Carson."

The coworker's name was Dr. Breanna Freeman, but I didn't remember calling her. In fact, I was sure that I hadn't called her because I was satisfied with the conclusion the police had come to. Carson wasn't a viable suspect. Even so, I was curious about what this woman wanted to tell me, so I decided to play along and go to the hospital. I waited until after 8:00 p.m. that evening, hoping that the doctor might have a lull in the action.

I waited for half an hour before Dr. Freeman could get away and speak with me. She stood almost six feet tall, slender and agile. I watched her bounce through the hallway of the hospital with speed and grace, her close-cropped curly gray hair dancing in the air.

"I suppose you are Mrs. Wilcox," she said, towering over me, giving my hand a firm shake.

"Yes. Thank you for agreeing to meet with me."

"Of course. Anything to help find Liza's killer. Let's head to the lounge downstairs and chat a bit."

I grabbed my briefcase and followed her to the stairwell.

Dr. Freeman took the two flights of stairs with a fierce fit of energy. I raced to keep up with her. She was a tall woman with a confident stride. The lab coat flowed behind her as her long legs moved over the stairs.

"I never use the elevator. Keeps me young."

In the cafeteria, Dr. Freeman grabbed a plastic cup of peaches and an apple. I went for a bottle of grapefruit juice and followed her to a booth at the far end. We sat opposite one another, the doctor struggling to fold her long legs beneath the table.

"So, you want to know about Carson and Liza?" she said.

"Yes," I said pulling a pen and notepad out of the briefcase.

"Well, Liza was a sweetie: nice, simple, and quiet. She was always present for her shifts, smiled and did what you asked her to, but she wasn't a go-getter."

"How so?"

"She didn't want anything else in life. Most of the girls come through here as CNAs because they want to be nurses or doctors someday. Liza was one of the few who never planned to advance beyond a CNA—that's like the worst job you can have here. They deal with all the stuff no one else wants to."

"Did she like the job?"

"I don't think so. I think she liked working here, but she wasn't enthusiastic about that job. It was like, 'I'm here, I'll work, but if you need anyone to go home...' She wasn't the person to call if you were short-staffed."

Lazy, I thought, in between scribbling notes. This description was a bit contradictory to what Peter had told me. He had speculated that Liza impressed Carson in the workplace.

"So, what can you tell me about Carson and Liza's relationship?"

"I think it was love at first sight. Carson is so gentle. He's always kind and warm with the patients; he was the same way with Liza. In fact, it was after a doctor got nasty with

Liza that they started dating. Liza was just cowering in the corner while a doctor berated her about changing out sheets in one of the emergency rooms, and Carson stepped in to defend her. He was still smooth and calm, but he let the other doctor know that it wasn't okay for him to talk to anyone like that. That was how it all started."

"So, Carson isn't a 'Type A' person?"

"Well, I wouldn't go that far. What I will say is that he is a very kind and warm person. He still has some of the tendencies of a Type A person, but not like what you see on TV. He's gentle, and he was especially gentle with Liza."

"What about since Liza's death? Is he the same?"

Dr. Freeman shook her head. "Sadly, he isn't the same man. Misses his wife so much."

I nodded and waited for more. I wasn't sure why Dr. Freeman had called me, but it wasn't because I'd called her, so she obviously wanted to tell me something.

"I'm sorry to hear that," I said. The conversation felt awkward, and I wasn't sure how to extract the information I desired.

"Do you have any suspects?" Dr. Freeman asked.

Before I answered, I made a mental note that Dr. Freeman's eyes were anxious and eager. Was she just a close friend of Carson's, or was something else going on?

"Well, as you know, anyone can be a suspect."

"But some people are likelier suspects than others."

She didn't have anything to tell me. Instead, she was digging for information.

"I'll keep that in mind, Dr. Freeman. Thank you for meeting with me," I said, standing up to indicate I was leaving. She continued to sit at the cafeteria table.

"I'm happy to help in any way I can," she said, waiting for more.

I nodded, thanked her again, and headed for the parking garage. I wasn't sure what to think about the interview. She was pumping me for information, but I wasn't sure why. Carson hadn't been on my suspect list, and I didn't think that Dr. Freeman had contacted me at his request. Did she really think I wasn't smart enough to remember that I hadn't called her?

I was putting different scenarios together as I headed to my car. The click of my black pumps echoed throughout the parking garage. I was still wearing my church clothes and the eerie quiet of the evening caused the hairs on the back of my neck to stand up. Clutching the briefcase against my leg, I slid my other hand over the butt of my gun. I got the feeling that someone was watching me. A glance around the parking lot didn't reveal anything out of order, but there seemed to be a double echo. Click, click, click, clunk. The clunk was not from my heels. I stopped and scanned the parking garage, remaining silent and looking for any abnormalities. My eyes fell on some movement at the north end of the garage. I spotted a return gaze in the darkness for a split second, but then it disappeared. I ran toward the dark corner.

No one seemed to be there, but a slow scan of the parking stalls by the exit revealed a person dressed in black from head to toe.

"Hey!" I screamed before taking off in an awkward sprint. After stumbling a few feet, I paused and kicked off my shoes before continuing to run toward the figure.

The person turned and began to run into the darkness, and out of the garage. I didn't think I could catch him or her, but I needed to mentally record the person's appearance as best I could. The figure was small in stature—stood about five foot one—and was clearly female. My bare feet were hurting as I pounded against the cold pavement. After a five-minute pursuit, I stopped running and allowed the shadowy figure to disappear into the night. It was now certain: someone was watching my movements. I circled back to the parking garage, located my shoes, and headed home.

MY HOUSE IS EQUIPPED with an alarm system and cameras on all sides. After I got home, I spent some time watching the cameras and loading my shotgun. Coming to my house would be a big mistake, but this person was bold. I had to be ready. Martin called at around 10:00 p.m. to see what the plan was for Monday morning.

"Marty, someone followed me today."

"What?"

"Yes, someone followed me into the parking garage at the hospital. I chased them for a short while but couldn't catch up."

"I'm on my way." Martin hung up before I could tell him that wasn't necessary.

Was Madelyn hunting me? It seemed so far-fetched, but clearly someone was tracking me. It was late, but I decided to call her. She didn't answer, which made me wonder if she was watching me from some secluded spot on the block. I would go by her house first thing in the morning.

Martin showed up that evening and camped out on my couch. I slept for just under six hours and got out of bed around 4:30 a.m. I started the day by reviewing paperwork and brewing coffee. After the first cup, I threw on sweats and a t-shirt and headed out for my run. The morning air was crisp and brutal, and a light mist left little crystals on my cheeks. Riverside Park was still and abandoned; the gurgle of frigid water harmonized with my footfalls. I thought about what I was going to say to Madelyn. If she was following me, she'd be expecting me this morning. That could give her time to prepare. I decided to surprise her by showing up just after dawn. Rude, but hey, it might be the only chance I had.

The red converted barn sat quiet and still. No cars were visible, and a quick check of the mailbox showed that the mail had not been collected for many days. I tapped on the front door, noticing that the "We're Open" sign was still posted. I tried the door and pushed it open with ease. It was 6:00 a.m., but a sunrise yoga session was not unheard of.

"Ms. Price," I called, pushing open the door. The yoga studio was empty and spotless, and Madelyn's office was in perfect order—no sign of a struggle. Was Madelyn Price missing, or had she taken leave of her own accord? I wasn't sure, but the howl of the wind and the isolation gave me the creeps. Even so, curiosity outweighed my sense of self-preservation, and I found myself searching the house. The house seemed to be empty. I was sure that Madelyn had been following me, but she could also be in danger.

A stack of letters was on her desk. As I got closer, I realized that they weren't letters—they were utility bills for various houses around the state. I took a peek at the bills and realized that the addresses were different. Interesting. As a landlord, it would be wise to pass some of the cost of the utilities on to tenants, but Madelyn had not done that, which meant that she probably wasn't a landlord, at least not in the traditional sense of the word. I pulled open the bottom drawer of the desk and found detailed files on Madelyn's clients. Each folder had demographic information, pictures, and what appeared to be short biographies. I closed the drawer and headed to the back of the yoga studio, where a bunch of mats was piled up in front of a door.

After shoving the mats out of the way, I tried the door, which was locked. Something in the back of my mind clicked. As a civilian, I had to be careful—even if I still had a badge, there was no reason to believe that Madelyn was missing or in danger. I shouldn't be in her residence. I left the house and headed home.

AFTER THE THIRD day of not being able to get an answer at the yoga studio, or catch Madelyn while she was home, I decided that she might be missing for a reason. Of course, someone with properties around the state could always get away. Maybe she had decided to flee because we'd picked up the scent and knew she had probably killed her best friend. Or maybe she was on a hiatus. I decided to get in touch with Carson.

"Mr. Stark, have you heard from Madelyn?"

"Not in the past few days. Why?"

"I haven't been able to get in touch with her. I have some questions, but it seems like she has gone out of town."

"Oh yeah, she's probably out of town—not a big deal. I bet she'll be back in the next few days. Any new info?"

I considered telling Carson about the leads we'd been chasing, but realized that we weren't any closer to finding out who killed Liza than we had been on the day we took the case.

"I will update you at the end of the week."

"Okay. Thanks."

I thought about what the update for Carson might sound like. Mr. Stark, I have discovered that your wife's best friend was probably involved in her murder, but I really don't have any concrete evidence. Oh, and your wife has a child that she abandoned, and she might be the killer. So, basically, I don't have anything concrete to share, but the hypotheticals are highly disturbing. Thanks! Defeat was sinking into my soul when the phone rang.

"Hello?"

"This is Alyssa Masters. I'm returning a call from Sylvia Wilcox."

I held my breath for a minute. Finally! A call back from Demario's sister who lived in Brightmoor.

"Thank you for calling me back, Ms. Masters. I'm investigating a crime and—"

"My brother is in jail, but he probably did it before he got locked up." Her voice was sorrowful.

"Actually, I would like to talk with you about some people that your brother knows. May I stop by?"

"I guess so."

She gave me her address, which matched one of the numerous listings I'd found online. Currently, Alyssa Masters lived on Rockdale, two streets away from where Liza's body had been found. The vinyl-sided house was in a state of disrepair, but it looked much better than many of the other neighboring houses. I parked on the street, checked my surroundings, and headed for the front door. When I knocked, Demario's sister was in the middle of cooking. She pulled the door open and nodded for me to come in. Without saying a word, she moved back into the kitchen. I stood by a small hutch just inside the door, holding my breath, trying to avoid the billowing smoke from the stove. Alyssa was frying a huge mound of bacon, and children were everywhere. I couldn't help but wonder how many kids she had.

"Have to make these kids dinner. You can come in here."
She spoke without turning to see if I was following her.

A boy who was probably fifteen or sixteen was sitting on a beanbag with earbuds attached to a cell phone. A younger boy of five or six was playing with Legos on the dirty beige carpet. A little girl, who couldn't have been more than two, was standing by the front window playing with the frayed yellow curtains. A voice erupted from the bedroom just before a tiny young woman stormed out, booming with anger. I caught a glimpse of her burning green eyes as she tossed stuffed animals out of her way. An explosive, child-verging-on-woman sporting a red bandana and a long pony-tail, she was clearly startled by my presence. I recognized her as one of the thugs I'd seen at Ali Mansu's party store. The only difference was that she was much thinner now. Alyssa Masters met the girl's gaze and the young woman calmed down.

"Roe, I'm takin' care of business," Alyssa said, as she lined a plate with paper towels.

"Sorry, Momma," the girl said, before heading back into the bedroom.

The house was extremely modest, but its cleanliness made it look nice. The wood paneling was old, but clean and intact. Dull, faded brown tile ran throughout the kitchen and there was a small makeshift bathroom in the back corner of the house. From what I could see, the house only had one bedroom. Where did all the children sleep?

"Thank you for taking the time to talk with me," I said.

"Yep. What you want to know?"

"So, tell me about Demario, Liza Abernathy, and Madelyn Price."

Demario's sister was barely five feet tall and she had sad brown eyes, and an almond-shaped face. Her hair was pulled into a ponytail that flowed to the middle of her back, and she was dressed in scrubs.

"I'm working on becoming a nurse. It's tough with all the kids, but we're doing okay."

"Congratulations. Are all the kids yours?"

She looked at me.

"Yes. All seven."

"Thank you for meeting with me," I said a second time, hoping to move the interview forward. I held out my hand. Alyssa stuck her hand in mine and gave it a limp shake.

"You're welcome. Thought about saying no, but Liza was a decent girl. Not smart, but she meant well. I'm sad to hear that she was murdered."

I hadn't expected that reaction.

"Yes, it is sad indeed. So, what can you tell me about Liza?"

"Well, in the beginning, she was a sweet kid that my brother brought home one day. We were surprised, because Demario never liked school. He was too old to be there anyway, so we knew he was up to no good. His plan was to meet some woman who would take care of him. He was always lazy; always looking for a free ride. I don't think Liza's family was rich, but they had money."

"Liza was murdered not too far from here."

"Yeah. I remember hearing 'bout that. Didn't recognize the name at first."

"She was shot here in Brightmoor. Do you find that curious?"

"Yep. She musta found another one like my brother. Liza was nice, but not smart. My brother is sick, but he always really got into the girls he dated. Liza started playing a game with him after a while, but I don't think she could help it. A rich white girl wasn't going to be with him. She was always going to run back to her parents. Everybody knew it."

"Do you know if your brother kept in contact with Liza after they broke up?"

"I don't think so, but he did a lot of things I never knew about."

"You knew about Liza's death, but Demario didn't."

"We aren't close. Couldn't stay in touch with him because of the kids."

"Demario couldn't be around children?"

"Yeah. And I know you know why," she said, an edge in her voice.

"What else can you tell me about your brother?"

"Demario has always been unmotivated and disturbed. He never held a job longer than a few weeks. No woman, especially one who likes money, was going to stay with him —that's just common sense. Liza left the kid with him, so he was satisfied. Didn't really care that she was gone."

Alyssa Masters distributed bacon onto the paper towels.

"Kids! It's ready!" she yelled. Recognizing that Alyssa wasn't open to discussing the reason Demario couldn't be around the children, I asked a different question.

"Why did Demario have trouble holding down a job?"

Alyssa rolled her eyes. "My mother treated him like a golden calf. She worshipped that boy. Anything that he wanted was his. We all knew that was going to lead to trouble, but she just kept on babying him."

"What did your father think of this?"

"He was too busy with his other women to worry about us, or the way Momma was bringing us up. My father was in and out of the house, and it was understood that he was cheating on Momma. She seemed to accept it as a way of life. I never once heard her complain about all the women in his life. By the time I was sixteen, we'd met my dad's full-time mistress. Momma accepted his behavior. It was a terrible example to set for us., My brother and sisters, have fallen into similar patterns."

"So, Demario hasn't been a part of your life for a decade?"

"Correct. He has a daughter who I think he molested. I reported my suspicions to social services. Eventually, I gained custody of Danica, but she was a handful. I have five children of my own, so when Demario wanted her back, I let her go. Seven years ago, Demario and his daughter were living with my brother. Demario had a girlfriend who also had a child, and out of the three adults, she was the only one bringing in any money. At that point, the household had deteriorated into a full-fledged, welfare fraud haven. I wanted nothing to do with it, so I cut ties and moved on with my life."

I made a mental note of the discrepancy in the number of children she said she had. First it was seven, not it was five.

"How many siblings do you have?"

"Started out with five of us, but we're down to three and a half at this point. My other brother, Raymond, will be dead soon."

It was a sad, but common Detroit story.

"Do you think Demario would hold a grudge against Liza?"

"I think Demario would use any excuse to kill anyone, but I don't see how he would have a grudge against Liza. He always told her that the only way he would kill her was if she took their child. I'm sure that is why she made the difficult decision to leave the child when she left him. She wasn't being callous. She just knew it was the only way Demario would let her live."

"Demario was fine with the break-up because he got what he wanted?"

"Yep—he is all about control. If he can control the situation and hurt the person he is dealing with, he's happy. Liza made the ultimate sacrifice, and I'm sure he was extremely pleased."

"What can you tell me about their daughter?"

"Danica? Such a shame. A pretty little thing, but she never had a chance. She was born into a family that had no hope of ever being normal. My parents made sure that we were good and screwed up, and we passed that on to our children. That little girl experienced hunger, abuse, and neglect during her young life. I'm not sure what type of young woman she has grown into, but I'm sure she's struggling. I've looked for her from time to time, but I don't know what the past seven years have been like. Before that, I know that she was always frowning. Her eyes were blank and dull."

"How old would she be now?"

"About fifteen."

"And you don't have any way of getting in contact with her?"

"Not really. My kids tell me that they see her around the neighborhood, but I haven't come across her. You might want to check the new shelter they built on Grand River and Lasher. I've heard that she spends a lot of time there."

"Ms. Masters, what can you tell me about Madelyn Price?"

Alyssa's eyes narrowed.

"Poor Maddie. Of all the girls my brother could have screwed over, she was the worst choice."

"Why is that?"

"She was a sweet, brilliant girl who had everything going for her. He pulled her into his world and almost messed things up for her, but Maddie was smart: she got away from him."

"Were Maddie and Liza acquainted?"

"My brother was seeing both of them. My oldest sister told Madelyn, and she confronted Liza. The two had a fight, but Maddie was done. She moved away, taking my niece with her. I don't hold it against her. She made the right choice."

"Do you ever hear from Madelyn's daughter?"

"Nope. Never."

"Did Liza ever attempt to contact Danica?"

"She didn't want her. She was...well, she was black, and Liza's parents weren't too keen on that. It was easier for Liza to just leave her behind."

"Did Danica remember Liza?"

"No. The last time she saw her was during the custody hearing. She was only about three, so I doubt that she'd remember that. Liza didn't ever try to contact her after that."

"So, you remember hearing about Liza being murdered behind the party store?"

"Yeah. I remember hearing about it and not giving it much thought at first. Like I told you, I didn't know it was her for a few weeks. After seeing her face all over the news, I recognized her."

A child I hadn't seen before emerged from the basement. She looked to be about ten years old. Her face was almond-shaped, like her mother's.

"Ma, can we eat now?" the pre-teen asked.

Alyssa Masters looked at the empty plate where the bacon had been.

"You'll have to excuse us, Mrs. Wilcox. I gotta find something else for the rest of them to eat," Alyssa told me. A half smile crossed her lips. She looked old and tired.

"You've been a big help. I appreciate your candidness." I shook Alyssa Masters' limp hand and headed for the car.

I stopped by Madelyn's house again on my way home. My knocks went unanswered, and the door was still unlocked. Yes, it was possible that Madelyn was out of town, but why would she leave the door unlocked? What if something had happened to her and I was the only one who knew she was missing? I decided that was reason enough to enter without permission.

I went back to the door that presumably led to the cellar. After shoving the yoga mats out of the way, I pulled on the door handle again. It was still locked tight. Should I pry it open? No. What if Madelyn had been kidnapped or worse? It would be a bad idea to have my fingerprints on the door. I wiped the handle clean, looked around, and noticed that it was getting dark outside. Perhaps this wasn't the best idea. Madelyn had been avoiding me before she vanished, so maybe she hadn't vanished at all. I headed back to the car and watched the motionless house for another hour. As dusk set in, I pulled out of the driveway and headed home. Where was Madelyn Price?

## 13

The weather began to deteriorate during the drive home. It was early April and winter was fighting off spring's advances. That night, a chilly rain began to fall in the early evening, and by the time I got home, the temperature had dipped below forty degrees. As I pulled into the driveway, sleet began to materialize. I'd stopped by the grocery store for a few provisions on my way home and was reviewing a taco recipe in my head as I gathered the bags from the passenger seat. To avoid multiple trips, I lined my arms with the six bags and sprinted for the house. After a slight fumble with my keys, I opened the door and rushed into the darkness, setting the bags on the floor in front of the refrigerator. A slight creak sent my intruder radar into overdrive. As I came back to an upright position, I grabbed my gun and spun around to face the door.

"Don't move!" I yelled.

Madelyn Price was standing just inside the door, soaked and distraught. Her chest was heaving up and down, and her bun was uncharacteristically wild and out of place.

"Please! Mrs. Wilcox, I'm in danger! I need help!"

Unwilling to remove my hands from the gun, I slid my elbow along the edge of the wall and pushed the light switch.

"Come in."

Madelyn began to drop her arms to her sides.

"Keep your hands up!" I commanded. She obliged.

"Close the door and apply the deadbolt. After that, get a chair from the living room and set it in the middle of the kitchen floor."

Madelyn followed my instructions, walking carefully into the living room, and slowly picking up a chair. She brought it into the kitchen.

"Okay. Sit down, nice and slow."

The gun remained trained on Madelyn's chest. It was still possible that Madelyn had killed Liza; I couldn't take any chances.

"I'm going to put the gun away. Then you're going to tell me why you put yourself in danger by sneaking to my place."

"I didn't know where else to go," Madelyn responded, tears mixing with the raindrops on her face.

"What happened to you? Are you hurt?" I reached for her shoulder, but she pulled away. Her face had a look of pure terror, as if she'd seen a ghost.

"I'm ready."

I knew what she meant-finally, she would tell me the truth.

"Okay. Come into the living room. You're shivering and it's warmer in there."

I put my gun away and pulled one of the afghans out of the hall closet. Madelyn eased into a chair, pulling the blanket round her as tightly as she could. She looked like a terrified child.

"You're safe here. If they come here, they won't be leaving, and they won't have time to hurt you."

"You don't understand! He could order someone to hurt anyone and they would do it! He knows so much and he—" She stopped mid-sentence and began to sob.

"Calm down. I'll put on some tea," I said before heading into the kitchen. I took my time putting the kettle on the stove and getting cups out of the cupboard-giving her time to cry it out. By the time I had returned with two cups of ginger tea, she was calm. I set down the cups and threw a few logs into the fireplace. It only took a couple of minutes to get a nice fire going.

"We're going to need more than one cup."

I nodded and climbed into my leather recliner.

"You can have as much tea as you need. I think you came here to tell me something."

Madelyn nodded and sighed, took the cup of tea, and started from what I assumed was the beginning.

"At first, we were brutal enemies. We would face off from time to time with silly catfights that always began with, 'You stole my man!'" Madelyn dropped her head and laughed. It was in that second of reminiscing that she looked close to her age.

"Demario was a looker who turned out to be a dangerous person—a psychopath. He was abusive and relentless. Liza once ran to the Upper Peninsula to get away from him. You might think, 'Wow, she overreacted', but Demario truly was a monster. He'd done such horrible things to Liza. After she moved to New Orleans, she sent me an anonymous letter. It was five pages long, and it could have passed for junk mail. I don't even remember why I opened it. I was haunted by the letter. It was a cry for help, but I had no idea who had sent it."

"How did you know it was from Liza?"

"I didn't, until a month later when she sent me an email. All it said was, 'It was me.' After that, I decided to help."

"Why?"

"I don't know. I guess I felt some connection to Liza. Kara came first, but Liza had her baby, another girl, about a year later She was too scared to tell her parents. Instead, she left the baby with Demario's sister and went back home."

"So, she abandoned the baby. Did you ever hear what happened to the little girl?"

Madelyn shook her head. I noted that this story was slightly different from what Alyssa Masters had told me had happened to Demario and Liza's child. I was fed up with Madelyn's lies.

"Okay, I need to hear the whole story; don't lie to me. Start from the beginning, and don't leave anything out."

The kettle whistled again. I retrieved it and refilled our cups. As I was handing the tea to Madelyn, I noticed how small and scared she looked—nothing like the woman I'd met with several times at the yoga studio.

"You don't need to know everything."

"Yes, I do. I need to know everything because you never know what's relevant until it's revealed," I said, getting frustrated with the game Madelyn was trying to play.

"I know if information is relevant or—"

"Do you want the cops involved? You can deal with them instead of me. Your whole secret life will be out in the open. Is that what you want?"

"You don't understand! There are so many lives in

danger! Exposing me would harm so many young, innocent women."

"I know about the cottage and the little group with the women and children, or whatever the hell you're running. I don't really care what you do in your free time, but I want to know what happened to Liza Stark."

"Okay, okay. I'll start from the beginning, but I need your word that you won't hurt the innocent people involved."

"If they're innocent, there's no reason to worry. Start talking."

She sighed and paused before beginning.

"It started when I was in high school. Demario began beating me after we moved in together. I was an honor student, doing well in life, but when I met him, I thought I was in love. He was older, attractive, and interesting. When I got pregnant, my parents wanted nothing to do with me. They told me I couldn't live with them anymore, so Demario encouraged me to get on public assistance. Once I had that, a social worker helped me find a house in Brightmoor. There was a family that owned houses there and they wanted to help young single mothers."

"Let me guess—the Abernathys."

Madelyn nodded.

"Yes. They were my landlords."

That explained why they had such a high opinion of Madelyn. She'd come a long way from being a teenage mom.

"Keep talking," I said.

"At one of my prenatal appointments, the doctor noticed bruises on my arms and neck. She gave me the number of a women's shelter, but they had stipulations. I wanted freedom without the psychobabble, the labels, and the sad reality that I was weak. What I wanted was an escape—a fresh start with my baby. I hesitated for a while, but after Kara was born, it was clear that Demario wasn't going to change. I stayed in the relationship too long, but as soon as I graduated, I was ready to go. Liza was getting ready to have her baby, and I just wanted out of the situation."

"How did you get away from Demario?"

"I was struggling to finish high school; I was still with Demario, and we had a child. He was beating the hell out of me, and I also knew that he had corrupted my landlord's daughter. She was pregnant and living around the corner. I couldn't get away without help, but at the time, I didn't have anyone. I started going to this church called Precious Blood, and I met an elderly couple, Sharon and Raymond Carter. They took to me and the baby instantly. It was like they knew I was hurting. They ran a safe house for young women who had run away from home, were pregnant, or were being abused."

"So, they took you in," I interjected.

"Well, they tried—twice— but both times, Demario found me. That put all the girls in danger, so the Carters had to turn me away. Sharon tried to convince Raymond that they could ensure the safety of all of us, but he knew that wasn't true. One Sunday after church, Raymond slipped me a piece of paper with a phone number. I asked whose number it was, because there wasn't a name. He told me to just call the number. They were expecting me."

"The number was to a group that would help you escape and leave the state."

"Yes. I called the number the next day. The person who picked up on the other end didn't go into detail, she just paused for a second before saying, 'Meet me at the old train station. Come alone. Bring your baby.' When I got there, I climbed into the car with Kara, and the person behind the wheel told me I was never going back."

"It's an organization for battered women and children, an underground railroad."

"Something like that. There were people who wanted to help, and I knew that I was indebted to them for what was done for me. After I was back on my feet, I figured I should give back. I wasn't sure how, until I received this anonymous letter. Before that, I just volunteered with a shelter, but those places have so many rules and stipulations; I wanted to do something more. Anyway, the letter Liza sent detailed horrific abuse, but it wasn't signed. It haunted me for months, but I had no way of finding out who sent it. Eventually, I received the email from Liza."

"Liza was the inspiration for your organization?"

"No. I had already been working with organizations that helped battered women, but I wanted my own thing. Over time, I found that I didn't like all the stipulations. Some groups require group therapy, labels, etc. I wanted to start something because I'd been one of those girls, and I wanted an organization that was a bit more empowering for women. I started with girls from Brightmoor. Liza was the first out-of-state rescue."

"You've been doing this for years? How can you afford to take care of all the women and children?"

"The women are free to stay with us without worrying about anything for the first three months. After that, they pay one hundred dollars a month for utilities, rent, etc. There are very strict rules: they don't leave the safe house, and they aren't allowed to have any communication with outsiders. After three months, they're able to go out and find a job. We give them aliases, and we have a few employers in town that we work with. They know very little about the operation, but they know me, so they're willing to take a chance. They forge the necessary paperwork, but I provide proof that the women are eligible to work in this country. They need to be untraceable for a while. We take twenty percent off the top to keep the operation functioning, and the women can keep the rest of their money. Most of the time there is a surplus, and we use the excess to fund the resettlement of the women."

"That sounds good, but I doubt that you're able to pay for everything these women need—the houses, food, clothes, etc.—with just twenty percent of their incomes."

"Income from the yoga studio supplements that."

"And your salary. That's why you pick up the therapy sessions every now and then, isn't it?"

Madelyn refused to confirm or deny the allegations. There was a great sense of selflessness in her. Was it inspired by altruism, or guilt?

"You haven't had any trouble with the ladies not complying?"

"They are helpless by the time they think that they need a drastic escape plan, so they are very compliant. A few have had trouble with the structure, but after a couple of weeks, they comply. Let's face it: refusal to comply means you're on your own, which generally means going back to the abuser."

"How long do they stay?"

"Most of the girls have enough money to get their own place within six months."

"Do most of them leave after six months?"

"Most stay at least a year."

"Because you're good to them."

Madelyn pulled the afghan tighter and shook her head. "I owe debts that can never be repaid. Helping these girls is the least I can do."

"So, walk me through this. How do they find you?"

"Chatrooms, college cafeterias, or—and I'm not proud of this—even on the dark web. I know there's a stigma, but think about it: all the criminals are on the dark web. Some of the victims are on there as well."

"Really? What are the victims doing on there?"

"They stumble upon it—young women, teenagers curious about what they can find on there. They get sucked in, but if they come across one of my forum spies, they can be saved. Well, at least some of them."

The dark web, Michigan, Louisiana—where else did Madelyn have a presence? I started to realize that I was dealing with something much bigger than a former abused woman gone rogue. I was dealing with a highly organized, far-reaching organization. Madelyn Price wasn't the person I thought she was. Archie Paladoski's words echoed in my head. It was all very fascinating, but I felt my number one suspect slipping away.

"Did you stop by to see my priest?"

Madelyn tilted her head and wrinkled her brow. "What? No. Why would I go to see your priest?"

"Someone fitting your description stopped by my church to ask questions about me. My priest described a small, black woman with her hair in a bun. I assumed it was you."

"Why would I do that?"

"I have no idea why—I just suspected it was you." If it wasn't her, who was it? "Did you follow me to the hospital when I met with Dr. Freeman?"

Madelyn hesitated before answering.

"Dr. Freeman is a friend. She helps with things, and we knew you were getting close to finding out what we do. She —well, we were nervous, and we thought that if we helped you understand that this was just a random act of violence, you would stop digging into my past."

That explained Dr. Freeman's lie about returning a phone call, but it didn't clear up why someone had stopped by to see Father Keegan. Madelyn was the only person I could think of, but realistically, it would be stupid for her to stop by and talk with my priest. Everyone knows that a priest is not going to tell a stranger something about one of his parishioners unless he has their permission. But apparently, there was someone out there who didn't know that.

"You think Liza's murder was a random act of violence?"

"Yes. She was careless at times."

"Okay. Explain how she was careless."

"Well, sometimes we would go to help a girl in another state, and Liza would make 'friends' with strange men. She wasn't necessarily cheating on Carson, but she liked to flirt and get attention from other men."

I thought about the conversation I'd had with Abigail Abernathy. She thought Liza was having an affair before she was murdered. Perhaps Madelyn had been in on the affair, and that was why the lady behind the counter at Mickelson's had recognized Liza's picture.

"Did you and Liza spend time at Mickelson's?"

"No. Liza always refused to go there, even if we were helping a girl in the area. I've been there many times, but never with Liza."

It was hard to tell if Madelyn was being completely honest. It seemed like she was still hiding information, but I needed to find out more about why she had shown up on my doorstep.

"Why did you come here?"

"I need help. Someone has been following me and leaving threatening notes. I don't know why this is happening now, but I think it has something to do with Demario Masters."

"Demario Masters is in prison and has been for years. Why do you suspect that he's after you?"

"I took his child away. The one thing he always said was that I could go, but his daughter couldn't. I took his child; his family hated me for it. I think he has told them to find me."

Madelyn seemed to be delusional about Demario. No love lost, but Demario didn't seem to have enough venom to stalk and kill Madelyn, and Alyssa Masters even seemed to have a slight affinity for her.

"What about one of the husbands or boyfriends of the women you've helped? Couldn't one of them be after you?"

"It's possible, but I've been doing this for years and nothing has happened. I'm very careful. Think about it. You thought we were in a cult or something like that. There isn't much evidence to connect me to the women."

It was true: Madelyn's operation was covert and impressive, but I still wasn't sure how this fit into Liza's demise.

"Ms. Price, how was Liza involved in all of this, and what do you think it has to do with her murder?"

Madelyn sighed. "That one situation—the way that we got her out—is something I regret. If I could just have those moments back, I would change so much."

"You think she was murdered because of her past?"

"Yes."

I nodded before heading into the kitchen to boil another kettle of water. When I returned, I pulled my chair closer to Madelyn.

"Start from the beginning; do not leave anything out."

❦

NEW ORLEANS, *Louisiana – New Year's Eve, 1999*

NEW ORLEANS SAT in a thick cloud of haze. The causeway was packed with commuters and early partygoers enthralled by the Y2K storyline. What would happen when the clock struck twelve? Would the world fall into mass chaos? Even though New Year's Day had come and gone without a hitch on the other side of the world, the partygoers allowed the lure of Y2K to heighten their passions. On New Year's Eve 1999, the Big Easy offered more sleaze than usual.

Liza Abernathy was eagerly awaiting the massive shutdown of the city at midnight, but not because she wanted to party. Instead, Liza wanted the chaos of Bourbon Street at midnight because her life depended on it. Of course, to save herself, she would be sacrificing an innocent, and for that, she was truly sorry, but what else could she do?

"You can't panic. The moment you get the chance, do it. After that, you run like hell to the corner of Canal and Bourbon. Canal and Bourbon Streets are where all the festivities start, so by that time, the crowds will be moving toward Esplanade. We'll have the benefit of the crowd, and no one will be paying attention to the alleys. We're armed, so we won't have to worry about the dopers and prostitutes. If we lock the doors and keep the guns handy, we'll be fine. Once you're in the van, you're safe. You hear that, Liza? Once you're in the van, you are safe, so just get to the van. If you don't make it to the van by 12:45 a.m., we're leaving."

The black Ford Econoline van would be idling in the alley. They knew traffic would be terrible, but that was okay. As long as Demario didn't see her get into the van, it didn't matter how long they were stuck in traffic, or if they were able to get out of town that night.

"We'll camp a few days in Fontainebleau State Park. Hotels are easy, and all the information is traceable, but staying in a park will buy us time. On January 4th, we'll hit the highway and head back to Michigan, but you have to change your address to the safe house in the French Quarter before we leave. Got it?"

The team would head north but leave a trail that led to the French Quarter. Liza Abernathy would be listed as living with Madelyn Price in a small two-bedroom apartment on Dumaine Street. If Demario went looking for them, he'd search in Louisiana.

Liza listened to the rapid-fire instructions with great trepidation. Clearly, Madelyn had done this before— perhaps a million times—but this was her maiden voyage.

"He's crazy, so we can't take any chances. There won't be any time for goodbyes or anything like that. In fact, I must insist that you don't tell anyone here or back at home what we're doing. Just run like hell. We will take care of the rest."

Liza nodded.

"I need a firm commitment. My life could be on the line as well. I'm willing to take the risk if that means you will be free, but I have to know that you're ready to make the commitment."

Madelyn spoke and moved like a soldier. Her eyes were intent and focused, and her words clear and precise. Directions and actions were given without emotion.

"You want to go back to Michigan, which is fine, but you will need to stay at the safe house for three months before you let your family know you're safe and in town."

"I don't have much money saved. How will—?"

"You will stay at the safe house in Cheboygan for three months. During that time, Demario will try to track you down. First, he'll find out you've rented a place here, which will be false. Next, he will look for you in Detroit and Livonia. He thinks you're weak and stupid, and that you only know to run back to your parents."

"What if he continues to look for me after three months?"

"By the time he finds you—and he will—you will be in control of your life. You also will not be living in Detroit. That is another stipulation. If you want to deter him, live in the suburbs. If he shows up in Northville Township, Novi, Farmington Hills, etc. he'll have to be on his best behavior. He's black. The police will already be watching him because they know he doesn't belong."

Liza bristled at the insinuation that covert racism could save her life. Madelyn noticed.

"In this case, the unfortunate stereotypes are protecting you. It is what it is. No need to feel one way or another about it. Besides, he's a monster. Do not feel sorry for him."

"Why aren't we leaving New Orleans immediately?"

"If you're running, no one expects you to stay in the place you're running from. It also gives you time to understand the weight of what we're doing. Demario will look for you around town, but not in a park. He's a city boy; he'll assume you're in the city. He'll contact any friends or family of yours he knows back in Michigan, and since they don't know anything, and you've been estranged from them, they won't act. Demario is an arrogant criminal. He's not going to walk into a police station and file a missing person report."

Liza already knew the answer, but she decided it was worth asking anyway.

"Madelyn, what about Danica? Is there no way we can get her? Maybe we can stop by and get her before heading back to Michigan. I—"

Madelyn slammed her fist against the side of the van.

"We've been through this. You know the plan. Do not deviate from the plan!"

"But she's my baby. I need to—"

"Demario Masters is lazy. He won't find work, and after a few months, he'll be back in Michigan. In a year, once you're on your feet, you find him, take him to court, and get your child back. That's the way it has to be."

## 14

M adelyn had told me the tale wearing a blank, nondescript expression, but I could see the pain and regret in her eyes. She hadn't made a mistake—her actions had been deliberate, and there was no way to undo them.

"What would you change about that situation?" I asked.

"The lies. I wouldn't have told them. We could have gotten both of them out. I was younger then, and stupid. After I left Demario, I was angry. I blamed Liza for the end of my relationship with Demario. Of course, that was a godsend, but as a young woman, I didn't see it like that. I wanted her to pay for what she'd done. Even though I was over Demario, I wasn't over how she snuck in the back door and took what I considered to be mine."

"Why did she reach out to you?"

"I don't know. I guess she knew I would understand. She had left her entire life behind. Her parents were distraught, but the best they could do was rent her a tiny frame house in Brightmoor. She kept running away, and they just wanted her safe. So, they rented her a house, but they didn't have anything to do with her. She mailed the rent check and never saw them. They had no idea how bad things were. They didn't like how she was living, so they stayed away. I don't even think they knew she was in Louisiana."

"Why did you agree to help her?"

"She needed help."

"And you knew how bad it was because you'd been with him."

Madelyn nodded.

"He was extremely violent; I knew that. Liza tracked me down because she wanted to know what I'd done to get out. All she wanted was to get out, and I forced her to leave her daughter. It was a blind jealousy. I didn't even know that was what it was back then. I would do anything now to change it."

It wasn't the story I'd expected to hear, but it made sense: everything is about love or money. This time, love, or at least a relationship that had been carried out under the guise of love, had spurred something nasty. Now, I just needed to find out if all of this figured into Liza's murder.

"What happened after Liza came back to Michigan?"

"After we got Liza out, she was so grateful that she wanted to repay us by helping. That was great, because she could reach a certain demographic that didn't respond to me. Liza knew all the former cheerleader-turned-alcoholic abused wives who lived in the suburbs. I knew all the college girls who hid their pain in the silence of dorm rooms. Over the years, we've helped more than sixty women get out of abusive relationships."

"You mentioned that Liza was careless with men. Why are you so sure she wasn't having an affair?

"She was more of a tease—just liked the attention. We weren't best friends, but we had to be open about secrets because of what we were doing. I would have known if she was having an affair."

"What were you meeting about the day Liza was murdered?"

"She wanted to talk to me about something; said there had been a development of some kind. We were always careful about what we said on the telephone. We didn't think our phones were tapped, but we'd learned the best way to transmit delicate information is in person."

I had a feeling that Madelyn knew exactly what Liza wanted to talk to her about. Even so, I held my tongue. She had given me more than enough information to research. Now, I just needed to find out who was upset about Liza and Madelyn's underground network.

"How many people know what you're doing?"

"Just those of us who work to get the girls out. Others know that we help women, but they don't know the particulars."

"Tell me why you think someone is after you."

"Someone has been leaving notes and trailing me. Tonight, I was followed from the parking garage at the U to my house."

"Do you have the notes?"

"Yes." Madelyn pulled two half sheets of loose-leaf paper from her jacket pocket. Both notes were scribbled in erratic, angry print. The letters appeared to have been carved into the paper with great force. The ink marks penetrated the faded blue lines. The first note said, "Live by the sword, die by the sword." The second note said, "Sins of the father."

"These are clichés—nothing personal. Someone feels like you've wronged them, but they don't know you well enough for personal attacks. As for a sword...Who have you cut down?"

"Are you thinking that this is some type of metaphor or symbolic message? That might be over-thinking it a bit."

"Well, if someone simply wanted to scare you, the messages would be more ominous. These messages are meant to shame and remind you of something. Someone feels you participated in an injustice."

"I haven't wronged anyone."

I considered pointing out the tale Madelyn had just shared, but thought better of it. Instead, I said, "You may not have wronged anyone in your eyes. I'm not saying you did anything to deserve this, but perception is subjective. Someone out there feels like you did something to them."

"That can't be it," Madelyn said with finality.

I needed Madelyn out of my hair. She'd come to me for help, but engaging in a debate was futile. I needed time, and the freedom to work.

"Ms. Price, you have houses around the state. You need to go to one that is outside of this area. Stay there for a while. I'll send my assistant with you. Before we do that, do you think you were followed here?"

"I don't think so. The car I think is following me is an old, reddish-brown Cutlass. It's probably a 1984 or '85, in great shape. I lost them by sneaking into the shed out back and riding my four-wheeler away from the house. There's another safe house about two miles from my place. I picked up my other car once I got there."

An old Cutlass wouldn't stand out if it was in good shape. People love their cars in Michigan, and cherished classics are seen on a regular basis. "Okay. Well, I'm going to call my assistant and have him stay with you at one of your houses. Do you have anything outside of this area? Perhaps something on the other side of Detroit?"

She nodded but didn't elaborate, which was fine. I didn't

need to know at this point, and Martin would tell me later. I called Martin and asked him to come to my place as soon as possible.

Martin and Madelyn left for parts unknown and I headed to my home office in the basement. The messages from the notes ran through my head. 'Sins of the father'; 'live by the sword, die by the sword'—someone was sending a message. It sounded like revenge, which gave some credibility to the idea that Demario Masters was involved, but he was in prison. The younger brother was living on borrowed time in Cass Corridor, one sister was caring for a bundle of kids, and the other sister lived across the country. Of course, there was also the chance that Madelyn was simply trying to shift the focus. Her story was curious. It was understandable why she hadn't originally told me about her undercover efforts to help battered women, but due to the nature of her endeavors, the perpetrator could be anyone—an ex-husband, or even a battered woman who held Madelyn responsible for her life after leaving the abusive relationship. But if either of those were true, what did it have to do with Liza Abernathy's death? Why did Liza want to meet with Madelyn the day she died? Who was the person Liza had told Abigail Abernathy about? Madelyn had said that Liza wasn't "careful" with men. According to Madelyn, Liza liked attention, but wasn't a cheater.

The Masters had to be the missing link. Demario was locked up, but his two sisters, brother, daughter, and several nieces and nephews were out in the world. Perhaps someone was carrying out an order from Demario. It wouldn't have been the first time someone in prison had ordered a hit. It was late in Michigan, but the evening was just getting under way in California. I decided to call Sara Quick a second time.

She answered on the third ring.

"Mrs. Quick, I need to find your niece, Danica. Any information you have that will help me do that would be helpful."

Sara sighed and waited before speaking.

"Mrs. Wilcox, I don't want to open a can of worms I can't close. I keep my distance for a reason."

"I understand, but I need to speak with Danica. Please, if there is anything you can do to help, I would appreciate it."

A long, tense silence filled the phone. After a few minutes of nothing, I was getting ready to bid Sara Quick goodbye when she said, "She's at Alyssa's house. I checked after we spoke."

"Are you sure?" I asked, refraining from telling Sara that I had just visited Alyssa's house and there had been no mention of Danica being there. I thought back to the kids in the house. The boy on his cell phone, the toddler, the elementary-school-aged kids from the basement, and...the angry girl with the green eyes.

"Thank you, Mrs. Quick. You've been very helpful."

I would stop by Alyssa's house early in the morning and wait for Danica to leave. She may or may not attend school, but it looked like Alyssa was at least trying to do the right thing for the kids. I decided to give her the benefit of the doubt. Maybe she really was working hard to keep the kids on the straight and narrow. In the meantime, I would see what else I could find out about the Masters family.

The Masters family didn't have a major web presence. Demario's brother, Raymond, had a few social media accounts that he hadn't used in several years. The posts he'd created were inarticulate and sparse. His face was thin and worn, showing the signs of his illness. The last address listed for Raymond Masters was in Cass Corridor, a section of Detroit where I had no desire to venture. I couldn't see a reason to talk with Raymond, but another visit to the prison might be in order. First, I would try to track down Danica. Why would Alyssa Masters lie about knowing where her niece lived? The obvious answer was to protect her, but I had no idea what she needed protection from. A murder conviction? A plethora of bad memoires? I couldn't deduce what was going on from the interview with Alyssa. I needed another perspective.

I needed to run all of this by someone. Martin was busy, so I decided to call my old friend. Father Keegan had been my confidant for several decades. As a child, after my brother was abducted, my parents went into a permanent state of mourning. The inexplicable loss of a child and the constant search for answers made them aloof. It had been painful, but as I'd aged, I understood that irrevocable harm had been done to our family. When I'd been younger and bitter, Father Keegan had helped me to keep from becoming a terrible person.

He was accustomed to my late-night phone calls and inquiries outside of his realm of expertise. It was a little after midnight when I decided to give him a call.

"Father Keegan, can you talk?"

"Hi, Sylvia. I'm at the hospital. Is everything okay?"

"Yeah. I just wanted to talk, but it sounds like you're busy."

The hustle and bustle of a hospital wing raged on in the background. He must have been anointing someone, or administering the Last Rites.

"I am not too busy. I'm all done for the night."

Father Keegan was always very careful about what he told me. He considered his duties as a priest sacred and private. He could tell me who he'd seen in the hospital, but he had a knack for only revealing what was necessary. That was one reason why he was such a great confidant: I knew that whatever I told him wouldn't find its way to anyone else.

"Father Keegan, I'm having trouble pinpointing deception. That woman who came to see you was here tonight. Claims that someone is after her, but I don't know if she is just trying to throw me off the trail, or if there really is someone after her."

"Meet me at Chauncey's in twenty minutes. I need a pint."

Chauncey's is a dank little pub two blocks over from my house and four blocks from the church. I arrived at 12:45 a.m. and headed for a pair of stools at the end of the dimly lit bar. I had a pint of Guinness waiting when Father Keegan arrived. His wispy white hair crept out from underneath a black skullcap and his brown eyes showed exhaustion. I felt bad for disturbing my elderly friend at such a late hour.

"Father, I'm sorry for keeping you awake. I had to send Martin on a job and—"

He waved off my apology and picked up his pint, holding it in mid-air, motioning for a toast.

"I know how it is to be lonely, to be the person that everyone turns to—not that I am having these issues. I'm just saying that I understand."

Life had been lonely since Derek's death. Initially, I hadn't thought of my call to Father Keegan as a cry for help, but maybe it was in a way. I needed someone.

"Thanks for understanding," I said, lifting my glass and clinking it against Father Keegan's.

"So, what has you stumped?"

"I don't know if this woman is guilty or if she's trying to throw me off the scent. She was my number one suspect, but now she is telling me that someone is after her. Perhaps it is the same killer, but why wait so long to strike?"

"Well, maybe it's not so black and white. Maybe the woman is protecting something or someone. She might be afraid of what will happen if you find out the truth, but she may not have had anything to do with the murder itself."

"She's protecting someone because..."

"Because she thought they were justified—something like a killing in the name of righting a wrong. Yes, killing is still wrong, but there's more to it. It's like the amount of culpability in a crime."

"Like sin?"

"Yes, like sin. There are venial and mortal sins, but the severity of a mortal sin can be reduced by the circumstances surrounding the situation."

"As in killing someone in self-defense."

"Exactly. It sounds like you remember that lesson."

"I definitely remember "Revisiting Confession". You gave us fifth graders that handout with a million pages. I never thought I'd read that thing, but I did read it; it stills sticks in my mind."

I took a drink and reminisced about elementary school. My brother had been gone for only a few months at that time. I remember being so angry with him. So resentful and full of hate that I hadn't been able to miss him. At times, it seemed like things were so easy back then, but nothing was —or ever had been—easy. Funny how our minds try to convince us that the past was better than it was.

"Sylvia, you aren't necessarily looking for deception. You could be looking for mercy—misguided mercy perhaps, but someone is looking out for another person who didn't deserve what happened to them. Or, maybe you've got the wrong suspect."

I thought of Madelyn Price. She'd been cagey, but maybe she was hiding something other than the fact that she was a murderer. Maybe she was protecting something, or someone else. Yes, she and Liza had a shaky past, but they had clearly moved past all of that. Why wait so long to strike? The rationale didn't make sense.

"Misguided mercy," I repeated. "Interesting. I guess my suspect could be protecting someone else, or I could just have the wrong suspect. I hadn't really looked at it from that angle."

"I don't know exactly what you're dealing with, but think of what the suspect cares about. What does the person hold dear?"

"She's an activist of some kind. She's really doing good in the world, but she does it in a covert manner. Very few people know what she's doing."

"She doesn't want to be a hero. Well, that tells you that the opposite of the obvious is probably what's going on. Sounds like a puzzle, but I bet you'll figure it out. You've always been one smart cookie." Father Keegan turned his glass up and guzzled the last of the beer. I did the same before tossing a twenty-dollar bill onto the bar.

## 15

The next morning, I slept in a bit, waiting until after 5:00 a.m. to rise. After two cups of coffee, I ran my usual route, showered, and was dressed by 6:15. Whether or not Danica was attending school was debatable, but many of the folks in Brightmoor were underemployed, and sending kids out to school was often a reprieve from being surrounded by children. When I was a cop, we'd run into scores of teenagers roaming the streets during school hours, most likely taking part in petty drug deals. Parents in Brightmoor sent their children out into the world every morning, but school was not the landing place for many teens. Alyssa had a house full of children; sending them to school would be her only relief.

Even though it was early in the day, young people could be seen scattered throughout the neighborhood. I made it to Brightmoor by 7:00 a.m. and parked down the street from Alyssa Masters' house. Some of the younger children emerged from the house and headed down the street I stayed near the end of the street and watched the house for almost two hours before the teenage girl I'd seen the other day came out the front door. She was wearing baggy blue jeans that hung loose on her hips, and a red-and-black flannel shirt. I knew what that meant: gang affiliation, or a wannabee. Either way, it told me a bit about her mentality. Her thick, curly hair was pulled back into a bun and restrained under a red bandana. A tattered brown backpack hung from her shoulder, and her face was pushed close to a cell phone screen. I started the car and cruised down the street, following her at a steady speed. She appeared to be headed to Fenkell, probably to a bus stop. I considered stopping her, but decided it would be more interesting to find out where she was going.

The girl stopped on Fenkell Avenue and waited at a bus stop that was shrouded in litter and early spring grass. The backpack hung from her left shoulder. She was intently focused on her cell phone, fingers moving swiftly across the screen. I waited at the corner of the street for ten minutes and watched her get on the bus. I lagged under the speed limit, following three car-lengths back, waiting to see if she got off the bus. Surprisingly, she seemed to be going to school. After the closure of Redford High, most Brightmoor students ended up at Cody High School, which required a somewhat lengthy bus ride. I drove ahead and took a chance, parking on a side street adjacent to the school and waiting for the bus to arrive.

As I heard the bus roaring down the street, I got out of the car and stood near the small shelter near the bus stop.

"Danica," I said, as the girl stepped off the bus. She turned and looked, her thick, dark hair concealing the side of her face. As soon as my face registered, she took off running. She was in full flight, running north of the school into a neighborhood of burnt-out houses, but the forty-five strapped to my ankle provided some comfort. I hadn't expected to venture into a Detroit neighborhood. Proceed with caution, I reminded myself as I closed in on the girl. Her backpack and purse flapped against her back. She was fast, but after a block, she slowed down, tripped, and fell to the ground. I grabbed hold of her backpack.

"Calm down. I just have a few questions," I said, holding on to the squirming teen.

"I ain't saying nothin'!"

"Listen, I'm going to let go of your backpack. Do not try to run, okay?" I waited until she nodded her head in agreement.

Danica Masters was short in stature, and her face had been weathered by years of living in uncertainty. Her body was swimming under her oversized clothes.

"Danica, I just want to solve a murder. A woman was murdered in cold blood, and I just want to know why."

"How would I know anything?"

"I just want to question anyone who is connected to the deceased. I assume that you know why I want to talk to you."

Danica nodded, but didn't speak. She folded her arms and tried to look tough, but failed miserably. Underneath the thuggish exterior was a scared little girl.

"I'm here to ask some questions about your parents."

She tried to look uninterested, but I saw a slight gleam of interest in her eyes.

"Do you know this woman?" I slid a picture of Liza out of my pocket. Danica looked at the photo. There was no recognition in her eyes. She shook her head—no. Next, I pulled out a picture of Madelyn Price and showed it to her.

"Do you know this woman?" Danica's eyes lit up.

"I don't know her, but I seen her around."

"Where?"

"Brightmoor. She come around every now and then. Sometimes she go to that fish place, and she drive through every now and then."

"What else can you tell me about her?"

I stalled, feeling guilty about the next line of questioning. The poor girl didn't recognize a picture of her own mother.

"Wait." Danica raised her head and looked me in the eye for the first time.

"Was that...my ma?"

Suddenly the rough-and-tumble street thug looked like a small child. I hesitated before responding.

"Yes. That was a picture of your mother."

"Can I see it again?"

I handed her the picture. Danica ran her fingers over the photo, as if she was trying to touch her mother. This wasn't quite what I had expected. A cloud of shame came over me as I recognized that I was putting her through the pain of reminiscing about the abandonment.

"Do you ever see your father?"

She looked up from the picture. "Yeah. When we had a car, Auntie would drive me up there. Our car been in the shop, so we ain't been up in a while. But we write, me and my dad."

"So you know about your mother, correct?"

"Yeah."

"Did you have any contact with your mother?"

"No, but I know she sent money to whoever was taking care of me. It still come."

A stipend for anyone who would care for Danica. Sad, but interesting. It was also interesting that it was still being sent. Who was sending money? Carson?

"How long have you lived with your aunt?"

"'Bout a month. Foster parents got tired of me; sent me back."

"Why were you calling your aunt 'Mom'?"

"'Cause she all the momma I ever known! What you think?"

Strange—she'd only been there for a month. Even so, I felt guilty for torturing Danica with questions.

"Okay, so you've seen the lady in the second photo. Can you tell me exactly where you've seen her, besides the fish place?"

"Around. Usually Dacosta, Dolphin—those streets by the fish place. She must know people 'round there."

I thought about Martin stashed away with Madelyn. Was he safe? I wondered if I had set him up to protect a murderer.

"Okay. Make sure that you head to school. If you don't, I'll report you for truancy." An idle threat, but maybe she would think that it was a possibility and actually head to school. I let go of Danica's backpack and headed back to the car. Danica took off fast in the opposite direction. I considered following her, but decided that she was probably just skipping school. Not to mention, I had a bone to pick with Alyssa Masters. Why had she lied to me? Why agree to meet, but not tell me that Danica was living with her?

I needed to check on Martin. The longer he was with Madelyn, the more uneasy I felt. I called him when I got back into the car.

"How are things going?"

"Fine, but I'm not sure Madelyn is in danger at this point. We're really off the beaten path."

"Yeah, I was just thinking that. How far are you from the office?

"'Bout two hours away."

"There's been a development. Meet me at the office in two and a half."

"So, Demario and Liza's daughter is alive, and she lives with her aunt. This makes me think that the husband should be added back to the suspect list," Martin said.

"Why is that?"

"Think about it. Liza is dead; Carson and his children inherit everything unless there is another child: one in need. She lives in Brightmoor, and they live in Northville Township."

"Someone's paying a stipend for Danica."

"Well, maybe it was rage. Carson killed Liza because he discovered Danica existed. What if Liza was sending money to the girl behind his back? What if he had no idea Danica existed until a few years ago, right before Liza was murdered?"

It was an interesting angle, but Carson didn't really need money, and a small stipend didn't seem like something he would flip out over. He had been wealthy long before he met Liza, and her death hadn't changed his financial situation, but what if he had found out that Liza had a child by another man? A secret child? What would his reaction have been? Money is one thing, but finding out that your wife had neglected to tell you she had an illegitimate child might be a bit much.

"Let's look at Carson again. I wonder if he knew about Danica."

"He could have been completely in the dark about her,

but if he found out, I doubt that he would like the fact that his wife lied to him. Does he seem violent?"

"No. In fact, he is rather gentle with the children and the housekeeper. He seems to be a Type A personality, but he's mild in that sense, and he doesn't give off the vibe of a murderer."

"So, what's our next move?" Martin asked.

There were avenues to explore, but just because there were secrets, I couldn't draw the conclusion that all secrets were related to the crime. Some people keep secrets to protect those they love; I knew that all too well.

"I'll interview Carson once more. You're coming with me this time. Watch for his reaction when I bring up Danica. I also need to talk with the Abernathys again. They have a granddaughter out there they might not know about, but if they do know about her, I'm curious about why they didn't mention her. Alyssa Masters deserves another visit as well. She conveniently forgot to tell me that Danica lived with her, and the two pretended to be mother and daughter."

"What's the angle there?"

"Alyssa could just be protecting Danica, but I don't know why. Is she protecting her because she's guilty of a crime? Or because she's a child who has already experienced so much pain?"

"What are you hoping to learn from the Abernathys?"

"The Abernathys' daughter was murdered, and I'm trying to find the murderer. My hope is that they will be inspired to share whatever they know with me. All information is pertinent until it isn't. They have a granddaughter who has been left on various doorsteps, and their daughter is dead. What is going on there? Did Demario get angry about this abandonment? Is Danica seething with hatred and resentment for being left to poverty-stricken relatives when her mother was living in the lap of luxury?"

"Liza didn't just burn bridges, she set eternal fires."

"Right. She altered the lives of several people; the grudges could run deep."

"What do you want me to do with Madelyn?"

I had almost forgotten about her.

"Have you talked with her much?"

"Not really. She seems nervous and cagey. If Carson didn't kill his wife, this Madelyn lady did. She's so odd."

"Being odd doesn't mean she's a killer. Go back and spend a couple more hours with her. Talk to her about Liza and see how she reacts. I'm heading to the Abernathys' first and Alyssa's after that. We'll touch base this evening."

I arrived at the Abernathys' house around noon. Once again, Mrs. Abernathy pulled the front door open before I could knock. She was dressed in pale blue Capri pants and a flower print tunic. Her hair was swept up into a hair clip. A few shining blonde strands fell freely over the seashell adornment at the back of her head.

"Mrs. Wilcox. How can I help you?"

"Mrs. Abernathy, there have been some developments. Would you mind if I asked you a few more questions?"

I remembered the emotional outburst that had taken place last time we'd talked. My heart was beating in my throat, but I kept my voice soft and calm, as if it didn't matter whether she agreed to talk with me or not. I watched her eyes go from suspicious to curious and sad. No matter how crazy she was, the motherly instinct, the need to know what had happened to her daughter, caused her creased brow to smooth out and her head to tilt.

"I don't have much time, but you can come in," Mrs.

Abernathy said, stepping back and allowing me to enter the house.

The information I had to share wouldn't be pleasant. I knew it was a risk, but I had to resurrect the past if I hoped to solve the case.

"Would you like tea?"

"No, thank you, Mrs. Abernathy."

"I'm going to get my husband. If you have news about Liza, he'll want to hear it."

I followed her into the living room, took a seat, and waited. Mrs. Abernathy headed upstairs and, after what sounded like a muffled argument, the couple emerged. Mr. Abernathy's hair was ruffled, and his eyes were red. It looked like he had been taking a nap.

"Mrs. Wilcox. My wife says you have information about Liza. If that's true, I think we should fire all the police in Detroit and have you solve the city's cold cases," Mr. Abernathy said in a sarcastic, but jovial voice.

"Well, I do have some information. First, I'm wondering if you knew that Liza had a child while living in Brightmoor. Since she was living in a house you owned, I assume that you know about Danica."

Mrs. Abernathy stood up and left the room. Mr. Abernathy watched her leave, but didn't say anything.

"I've learned that you own houses in Brightmoor. You rented a house to Liza and Demario Masters, correct?"

My question was greeted with silence and a blank look.

"Mr. Abernathy, I'm not here to judge you or your family...I just need to know what happened when Liza was living in Brightmoor. Now, this may come as a shock, but I think that Madelyn Price might have something to do with your daughter's murder."

"When she was a teen, Liza ran away and did what she

wanted. We were disturbed by it, but we didn't want her in the system. We let it ride itself out."

"You thought setting her up in a house of her own was best?"

"We rented a house to Liza because we wanted her to be safe. You must understand: she was a disappointment at the time, but we never abandoned her. We didn't want to condone her behavior, but we wanted her safe. Over the years, we've made a habit of renting those places to young single mothers, but Liza was an exception. It was just her and that man, but we thought, well, why not? At least we know where she is."

"Did you visit her?"

"Never. We told her to come home when she was ready. We weren't going to accept her lifestyle, but we loved her. Mrs. Wilcox, you have to believe that we loved her."

"Did you know about Danica?"

He waited, parted his lips, but didn't speak.

"Did you know about Danica?" I repeated.

"We told her to have an abortion. We assumed she'd done that, but eventually, we found out that she'd had the child and left it with the Masters. It sounds callous, but we thought it was for the best. After all, we didn't know much about those types of children, so we thought it was best that the girl be with her people."

Disgusted by his inability to recognize that Danica was one of "his people," I moved on to Madelyn.

"You rented to Madelyn Price. Tell me how she fits into all of this."

"Madelyn was a good girl—one of my business associate's daughters. Great grades, stable home. Somehow, she got mixed up with this Demario Masters character. Within a few months, she was pregnant. Her parents were outraged and wanted nothing to do with her after that. We'd met Madelyn a few times and had tried to forge a bond between the girls because we were looking for good influences for Liza. It was a total shock when Madelyn got pregnant. The two didn't get along well, but after Liza went to visit Madelyn a few times, the girls seemed to have a friendship. Then the truth came out—it was Madelyn's boyfriend who had caught Liza's attention."

These women had a history of familiarity, but not necessarily friendship. How deep did the deception run?

"Liza ended up starting a thing with Madelyn's boyfriend?"

"Yes. She started running away, skipping school, and not listening to a thing we said. We had no idea what to do with her. Eventually, we compromised. We set her up with a house in Brightmoor because that was where she wanted to be."

"How did Madelyn feel about Liza taking her boyfriend?"

"Obviously, there was trouble between the two girls. Madelyn was angry, but she got over it real fast. Within a year of leaving that guy alone, she had graduated and was doing well. Eventually, she ended up getting an internship at my company, and kind of became like our surrogate daughter. During that time, sadly, we lost touch with Liza. She always mailed the rent check, so we never had to go over to collect. It's sad and shameful, but we just couldn't stand what she was doing."

Rivals. Liza and Madelyn had not only competed for Demario, they had also vied for the Abernathys' affection. The prodigal daughter hadn't been accepted back into the fold as easily as she'd been expelled. If a friend took my place in my family, we would no longer be friends, I thought to myself.

"Madelyn Price was the person Liza was going to meet when she was murdered. What do you think about that? Surely, doubts about Madelyn's alibi must have come up. She's the last person to speak to your daughter, the person that first noticed she was missing, and the person Liza was going to meet."

Mr. Abernathy was quiet while he ran the information through his head.

"Mrs. Wilcox, I can't think of Madelyn in those terms."

"Why is that?"

"Because it would be like losing another daughter!"

That made sense, but I needed to know what he really thought about all the coincidences involving Madelyn.

"Mr. Abernathy, Madelyn Price is connected to your daughter's last moment on this planet. I need you to think about what that really means. Realistically, she has to be the number one suspect."

"I have thought about it at times. It is strange that Madelyn is connected to Liza's last hours of life, but I don't believe that she killed my daughter."

"Think about it: Liza stole her boyfriend years ago, but Liza goes on to marry a rich man. She doesn't get stuck with single motherhood because she abandons her kid, and Madelyn ends up raising a kid by herself. Madelyn doesn't get a Prince Charming—imagine how the resentment festered. There all those years of pretending to be friends when in reality, neither of them was thrilled to be connected."

Mr. Abernathy folded his hands in front of his face. He appeared to be considering that Madelyn Price could possibly be someone other than who he thought she was.

"It does seem odd, but if you knew Madelyn the way we do, you would understand that she couldn't have done this. She's such a special soul."

I tried to imagine what had given Mr. Abernathy this impression of Madelyn. There had to be a missing piece to the puzzle. I could admit that she had the yoga culture running through her veins, but it was clear that she had been something other than that to them at one point. If the Abernathys had rented a house to her, they knew about her past. Why wouldn't they take that into account?

"Mr. Abernathy—Liza and Madelyn had a fight over Demario Masters. It's something that the neighbors remember. Their rivalry wasn't just a silly schoolgirl thing."

"Mrs. Wilcox, I think we're just about done here. If you want to waste your time pursuing this avenue, feel free, but I don't have anything to add to your suspicions. We love Maddie, and she was good for Liza."

I decided to let go of that angle.

"What can you tell me about Liza and Carson?"

"I think we've told you everything we know about that situation."

"Why were they together?"

"Well, I guess there must have been a love between them. I—"

"Mr. Abernathy, this is your baby girl. She's dead; gone. And someone stole her from you. Just tell me why they were together. A surgeon marries a girl who isn't getting along too well in life. How did that happen?"

The words must have stung. Mr. Abernathy shook his head. A somber look came over his face before he said, "They'd always had a thing for one another. We knew the Starks from business deals in the past. Over time, we became friends; our kids played together. Peter never liked

Carson, but Carson and Liza always had a bond. The Starks didn't want them together. Neither did we, but they ended up together."

Now it made sense. The connection had been cemented in childhood, much like myself and Derek. The childhood memories, those moments in life when you are free to be yourself—a young, fresh, innocent person—had been at the root of Liza and Carson's love. It was poetic and bittersweet. Carson Stark, Type A personality, superstar surgeon and rich guy, never forgot his first love.

"So, they were friends as children?"

"Yes. They played together as children. For a while, they were best friends. Then, around the time Liza was seven, we cut off contact."

"Why?"

"Liza wasn't the type of girl Carson was supposed to marry."

I kept my composure as I listened to Liza and Carson's love story.

"Why is this such a big secret? Why not tell me that you've always known Carson?"

"His father and I had some bad experiences. A lot of money was involved and we had a falling out. We haven't spoken since then, even after Liza and Carson were married."

"Is there anything else you can think of that might help the investigation?"

"No, but I want you to understand something: we loved Liza so much. Mistakes were made, but we loved her."

"One more question..."

"Okay."

"Are you supplementing Danica's caretakers?"

"What?"

"Someone is sending money to Danica's aunt. Is it you?"

"No. Like I said, mistakes were made, but we wouldn't do something stupid like that. There'd be no way to know that the money was being used for the girl."

"Thanks for your time, Mr. Abernathy," I said, standing up and shaking his hand. Once again, I let myself out.

## 16

The Abernathys had frustrated me with their need to keep up appearances. As I pulled out of the driveway, I reviewed other leads. Now I had another avenue to consider. There was much more to Liza and Carson's story. Why hadn't Carson told me they'd been childhood friends? I would contact him and schedule a meeting, but before I did that, I wanted to head back to the office and give myself time to digest the information.

Martin was in the office when I got back, searching for information about the Abernathys.

"Hey. How'd things go?"

"Martin, you're not going to believe what I found out, but before we get into that, let's put our suspects on the board."

"What about the Abernathys? Anything important come from them?"

"Yes."

"What?"

"Madelyn and Liza were always competing, so much so that the Abernathys aren't willing to consider that Madelyn could be involved in the murder because she's like a daughter to them— possibly the favorite daughter. Also, Carson and Liza were childhood sweethearts, but the Abernathys cut off contact between them when they were young."

"What? Why didn't Carson tell you that he and Liza were childhood sweethearts? That's kind of weird."

"Right, so I think there is something we've missed. Let's go through it together."

I clicked a few buttons on my computer, sending a file of pictures of our potential suspects to the printer.

Martin grabbed the pictures as the machine spit them out and started taping them to the whiteboard.

"First, we have Madelyn Price," I said. "Yoga instructor, last person to talk with Liza, frenemy."

"Who's next? Carson?"

"No. Danica."

"You want the kid on the suspect list?"

Danica had seemed sweet and soft when I'd trailed her that day, but that didn't mean she couldn't have killed her mother, especially considering that her mom had abandoned her to a life of poverty while Liza and her half-siblings lived in luxury. Also, she was in Brightmoor—that meant she probably knew gang members and would have had access to opportunities to join.

"Yes. Think about it. You know what Carson's neighborhood is like, and you know what Brightmoor looks like. Imagine being left with a child-molesting felon and seeing that your mother had moved and had a new family."

"Good point—I guess she is a viable suspect. It would just be sad if she's the one who pulled the trigger."

"Still, she has to be on there."

Martin added Danica to the suspect board.

"Madelyn is the number one suspect, but Danica is a close number two."

"Any others?"

"Sure. Carson Stark: husband, doctor, wealthy—seemed to love his wife but was not aware of wife's past; remembers the little girl he knew before she took a stroll down thug lane. But Carson could have found out some of this stuff about Liza and reacted very strongly."

"Are the Abernathys Danica's benefactors?"

"Mr. Abernathy claims that they aren't."

"Do you think Carson loved Liza?"

"I do get the sense that he loved her, but Liza's past is rather surprising. Carson has a good reputation to protect. Finding out that Liza had been a single mom who had gone slumming in Detroit would have been shocking. It could have been too much."

"Do you think he is the benefactor?"

"Possibly, but he might also be angry about the whole situation. We'll keep him up there. Next, we have Peter Abernathy. Liza's bitter brother is the only other heir to the Abernathy money, and he seems to despise his sister. He was softer when I talked with him and Abigail, but the first meeting left a bad taste in my mouth. Also, money is a motivator for many crimes. We don't know how much money, but we know they're into real estate, so probably a decent amount."

"But the parents are in good health, right?" Martin asked.

"Yes, but Liza wasn't in the will until she rejoined the family."

"Why wait to kill Liza?"

"I don't know, but we need to leave him on the list."

Martin picked up the blank piece of paper.

"What's this for?"

"The mystery Brightmoor boyfriend."

"What do we know about him?"

"Well, lives in Brightmoor, so he's poor; let's also assume he's black because ninety percent of the population in that area is, and let's say he is a drug dealer."

"That's a lot of speculation," Martin said.

"Sure, but he's my suspect to create," I said, winking at him.

"Any other suspects?"

I tried to think of any other people to add to the list.

"I don't think so."

"What about a random killer?"

"Random killers are always a possibility, but I don't think so."

"Why not?"

"Because Liza was murdered in Brightmoor. She drove herself there, had been seen hanging around in the previous weeks, and she was shot five times. Something was pulling her to that place, and whoever shot her made it personal. Also, she wasn't robbed: her diamond ring, money, purse, and truck were left behind."

"What do you think about the ex-con guy she lived with?"

"He could have had a minion kill her, but it would be odd because of the time lapse. That's the only thing about that scenario—it doesn't make sense."

"Okay, then we really only have three good suspects, and only two are really viable, right?"

I sighed and shook my head. As uncomfortable as Peter had made me feel during the first meeting, he didn't feel like a good suspect.

"Let's fill out the reports for the suspects, file them, and go home. Also, I think you can tell Madelyn it's okay to go home. I don't think she's really in any danger. We've had enough for today."

We copied the information from the whiteboard into files for each, put them away, and closed up shop. I told Martin to meet me at the office at 9:00 a.m. the next day and headed home.

The house was too quiet and still that night. I put on Vivaldi's "Winter", found some kale, spinach, and garlic in the refrigerator, and began chopping the trio. Once everything was chopped, I tossed it in the blender, added basil, parmesan, and olive oil, and blended the combination. Eventually, I sat down with a bowl of Fettuccini with pesto for dinner. As I forked savory, green-coated pasta into my mouth, I considered who would be the most viable suspect. Madelyn had been the best lead, but the more I thought about it, the more I liked the idea of the Masters family being behind Liza's murder. Carson Stark would be calling for an update soon. I would confront him about not telling me that he and Liza knew one another as children. That would shift the focus of our conversation. I finished my pasta and headed for my home office.

I was piecing together a timeline of Liza's life when the phone rang. I stuck another clue on the whiteboard before answering.

"Hello?"

"You're not looking in the right places." A dry, scratchy voice croaked into the phone.

"Hello? Who is this?"

"You're looking for something that isn't there. A generation that didn't care went and followed the ultimate dare. You won't find tracks to trust, but building a case is a must. The past holds the clues that lead to the truth."

The voice was raspy, scratching my eardrums. A chill ran down my spine.

It was close to midnight and my eyes had begun to burn with exhaustion. Even so, I stumbled around the office searching for a pen and paper. A pen pierced the palm of my hand, but I shook off the pain as I struggled to find a slip of paper to write on. I ripped a piece of paper out of a notebook and began writing down what I had heard.

"The past holds the clues that lead to the truth. What else do you want to tell me?" I muttered into the phone, to keep the person on the other end talking. The voice was carefully crafted to sound male, but I could hear a hint of femininity behind the riddle. I jotted down the strange message.

"Yes. A generation that didn't care went and followed the ultimate dare."

'A generation that didn't care'...Was this a reference to Liza? She hadn't cared about her family's past. The fact was that they were well-off, white, and not interested in mingling with people outside of their immediate social sphere.

"Who is this?" I asked in vain.

"A friend who cared, but couldn't stay there to see her die inside."

The voice was creepy and weird, and the phone call was just plain annoying. If this person knew who had killed Liza, why not just spill the beans, for goodness sake?

I repeated the words as I wrote them down.

"A friend who cared? Who did the friend care about? Liza Abernathy?"

"No," the voice snapped, harsh and cold.

"Madelyn Price?"

"No." Another snap.

"Then who?" I asked.

No response.

"I'm listening. What do you want to tell me?" I asked.

The phone disconnected. I tried to remember the voice. Had I heard it before? The riddles were similar to the messages Madelyn had received. I didn't think I'd heard the voice before, but because it was disguised, I couldn't be sure. What did the riddle mean? I racked my brain for the next hour or so, trying to figure out what the caller wanted and who they were. Eventually, I had to admit that I had no idea who the caller was. I went to bed and suffered through a night of restless sleep.

"I'm looking for Mrs. Sylvia Wilcox."

The phone had rung seven times before I picked up. My brain was searching for clarity as I held the phone to my ear.

"Hello? Is this Mrs. Sylvia Wilcox?" The voice was high-pitched but masculine, and the caller had a slight lisp.

"Yes, this is Sylvia Wilcox."

Silence.

"Are you there?" I asked.

"My name is Raymond Masters and I need to see you."

Raymond Masters was Demario's younger brother. I was stunned. Glancing at my cell phone, I saw that it was 6:30 a.m. I had overslept.

"Mr. Masters, I would be happy to meet with you. Tell me when and where."

"I can meet you at your office in an hour."

"Okay."

"I'll be there in an hour," he said, hanging up. No need for the address.

I jumped out of bed. My heart was racing. Perhaps the prison hit had some validity. Maybe Demario Masters had set up Liza and had her killed by one of the gang members on the outside.

After a quick shower and a cup of coffee, I rushed to the office. I wasn't sure how Raymond had found me or why he had called, but I was eager to hear what he had to say. He arrived within the hour. I was standing at the door when he rang the bell.

"Hello, Mr. Masters. Thank you for coming," I said, opening the door and holding out my hand.

A small, emaciated man wrapped his skeletal fingers around my hand and gave a weak squeeze. His face was aged beyond its years, but there were hints of how handsome he'd been. His eyebrows had been plucked and shaped, and a heavy layer of foundation was covering the cracks and wrinkles on his face.

"I had to come," Raymond Masters said, stepping through the door with a feminine sway.

"Okay. I'm ready to hear whatever you have to say." I led him to the comfortable chairs by the desk and motioned for him to sit down.

"I know what happened," Raymond blurted out as soon as he sat down.

"Great. Tell me."

"First, you gotta understand that my brother is crazy. He was abused as a child and he went on to abuse me and his daughter, and probably others."

"What type of abuse are we talking about?"

Raymond's eyes shifted to the floor. I nodded my head to show that I understood.

"I am sorry you had to go through that. Did you know Liza Abernathy or Madelyn Price?"

"Both. Liza was okay, just not too smart. Madelyn was smart and nice. I always felt sorry for her. We tried to warn

Madelyn about Demario; she just didn't listen. Before she could get away from him, she was pregnant. Her parents were married, and I think she was young enough to think that she was going to be able to marry Demario.

"Danica was tortured by my brother. She's spent time in treatment centers and when she found out that her mother was living the high life, she just exploded. At first, she wanted to get to know her and the other children, but Liza didn't want that. She was okay with meeting Danica, but she wanted her to be a dirty little secret."

That explained why Liza had been in Brightmoor: it was the only place she was willing to meet with Danica because no one she knew would be there. It was hard to imagine Danica as the killer, but the more I heard about how Liza had treated her, the more I felt like Danica was a likely suspect.

"Are you telling me that Danica killed Liza?"

Raymond looked down at his hands.

"Yes."

"Did she tell you that she killed Liza?"

"I know she did this, and she's not done. That's why I'm here."

"What do you mean, she's not done?"

"Liza abandoned Danica, but not all by herself: Madelyn encouraged her. I tried to be a friend to both."

A friend...The soft, scratchy voice from the phone call the night before had mentioned being a friend. Raymond Masters had been the prank caller.

"You think Danica is going to hurt Madelyn?"

There was logic to that assumption. Liza may not have abandoned Danica if she hadn't been encouraged. Then again, if the situation was desperate, which it seemed to be, it was hard to judge Liza.

"I think you need to find her."

The tricky thing about being a PI is that you can't make an arrest. You investigate, and if you have solid evidence, you head to the police station. After you share your information with the officers, they decided whether you've done your job. The next step is the prosecutor's office. By that time, your suspects may have skipped town. If Danica was Liza's killer, I had to be careful how I approached her—before I took the information to the police.

"Mr. Masters, I am a private detective. I can't do anything with this information until I have something definitive to take to the police. Why did you come to me instead of going to the police?"

He pondered the question for a few minutes, then reached a skeletal hand up to his temple. The interview was clearly draining his strength.

"Mrs. Wilcox, I used to live the same life that my brother and sisters did. I ran credit card scams, smoked dope, and prostituted myself. There was a time when I thought I was doing all of that because I liked it. Danica is seventeen years younger than I am. I've watched her grow up in the same dysfunctional way that I did. And I know that if she could do something different, she would, but it's all she knows, and the police don't always get that. I think you get that."

It was strange. What had Raymond Masters heard about me?

"If she killed Liza, I want to see her do time for it. You understand that, right?"

"Yes, and I agree. That's the right thing. Mrs. Wilcox, the doctors told me that I don't have long. I waited until it was too late to go to the doctor and get started on the treatments. By the time I got tested, the HIV had turned into AIDS. Now, it won't turn back. Before I die, I want to see as many of my nieces and nephews in as safe a place as possible. Alyssa's mind ain't right, so she can't give them kids what they need—a chance. Danica needs to be away from all of that. If she gets locked up, she might get help, maybe even a high school diploma and college degree. If she stays on the streets, she gonna end up like the rest of us."

I wondered why he thought Alyssa's mind was not right. She was going to school to be a nurse and she was providing the best she could for her family. She was clearly one of the more stable members of the Masters clan, but there was no use telling that to her brother.

"That makes sense, but I can't protect her from what the police might do. The best thing would be for her to turn herself in."

"Yeah, but Demario is her father, and she knows that he would never want her to do that. She gonna run until you catch her. It's gotta be you to catch her."

"Why me?"

"Because you'll hesitate to shoot. You a PI, so you gonna try to do things a different way because you have to."

Raymond Masters knew how it worked. I was a citizen who happened to own guns, but the rights of law enforcement didn't apply to me anymore. He was in my office telling me what his niece had done because I couldn't shoot her unless it was absolutely necessary. Smart.

"Do you know where Danica is now?"

Raymond's eyes filled with tears. He dropped his face into his hands and sobbed.

"I tried to stop her. I tried, but she wouldn't listen. Said she had to finish it; said they deserved it."

"What are you talking about? Mr. Masters, what did you try to stop her from doing?"

"She got a car and some people from the hood. Went out to Ann Arbor late last night..."

I didn't need to hear anything else. Danica had gone to Madelyn's. I hoped I wasn't too late.

"Mr. Masters, I have to ask you to leave," I said, before typing out a text message to Martin and Charles: Meet me in Brightmoor ASAP!

"Please don't hurt her. She's just a kid and she's been through so much," Raymond begged as I ushered him out of the office.

"I will do what I can, but no promises." I thought about the additional charges Danica was racking up. If she had taken Madelyn from her home, she would have a kidnapping charge and, God forbid, an additional murder charge. She would be tried as an adult and her life would essentially be over. Of course, that wasn't unfair if she had taken the lives of two women.

I locked up and rushed down the stairs. Charles called me back as I burst through the double doors and sprinted to the crosswalk.

"What's up, Sylvia?"

"I need you. I think I've got a potential kidnapping on my hands."

"Where?"

"It's in your precinct. Brightmoor. That's why I contacted you."

"Okay. Tell me what happened."

"Liza Stark's daughter killed Liza, and she's out to get revenge on the woman who encouraged her mother to abandon her. It's a long story, but I think we've got something here. We need to get to Brightmoor ASAP."

"Slow down, slow down. First, call the lady you think has been kidnapped. See if you can reach her."

"Yes, yes, you're right. Okay—calling now," I said, just as the light changed and I charged across the street.

The moment I reached the other side, I pulled up Madelyn's number and called. She answered on the second ring.

"Hello?"

"Madelyn?"

"Yes. Who is this?"

"Sylvia Wilcox. Are you still at the safe house?"

"Yes. Why?"

"Have you heard from Danica Masters?"

Silence on the other end.

"Madelyn, this is important. Have you heard from her?"

"No. Why would I hear from her?"

Madelyn was safe. What if Raymond Masters had just told me a bunch of lies?

"Okay. Well, just call me back if anything out of the ordinary happens, okay?"

"Sure. I will do that. Thanks for checking on me."

I slowed my pace and called Charles back.

"False alarm. It appears that I may have been played. Madelyn Price is at home and hasn't noticed anything out of the ordinary. Dammit, Charles, my eyes are starting to cross on this thing. I need help."

"Okay, relax. I'm free this afternoon. Meet me at Mickelson's."

## 17

Mickelson's was sparsely populated. The lunch rush consisted of a group of seniors at a back table chatting and laughing away the afternoon. The same girl I'd spoken to weeks before was working the counter. She took a second look at me when I walked in. There was recognition, but no desire to reminisce. I took a seat at one of the wooden two-tops and waited for Charles. He arrived about ten minutes later.

Charles looked exhausted and ruffled around the edges. His maroon tie was crooked, and his gray suit coat hung unevenly on his oversized arms.

"Long night?" I asked.

"Yeah. Things are kind of crazy at my place. My brother and his family 'surprised' me with a visit. They're all staying at my place. Kids are great, but I'm glad I don't have them."

"Yet," I said.

"Don't jinx me!" Charles said, swinging his arm for a handshake. We sat and waited for the lady at the counter to come over and take our order. Two Famous Fish and Chips, water for me, and a Coke for Charles. After the order was taken, we got down to business.

"Okay. Tell me what I need to know."

"The uncle says that the kid did it."

"Do you believe him?"

"She has a good motive, knows the area well, and who else would Liza go to Brightmoor to meet?"

"The bosses didn't want us doing too much with this case because of the people involved. The Starks are like royalty and the Abernathys are important too. They didn't want to be investigated, but if we'd known about the kid..."

"The kid is a good angle, but she also had a motive to not kill Liza."

"Yeah? Like what?"

"Someone sends money to whoever is caring for her; I'm guessing that someone was Liza. Now that she's gone, the money might keep coming, but there is a chance it will stop. I don't know how much, but life is hard for a kid in Bright-moor. Every dime helps."

"So, the question is whether or not she was angry enough to not care about the money."

"That's one question, the other major question being: why did the uncle come to me? Why give me this informa-tion on his niece? Is it a set-up?"

It was strange that the police had not discovered that Liza had a child, but I knew how politics could shape an investigation.

"Outside forces can really mess up an investigation. Don't think of it as a failure. Now we have something to go on. I just need your help bringing this kid in."

"Okay, but we need evidence before I can step in. The chief doesn't want us working anything that doesn't add up."

"Yeah, I think—" My phone began to vibrate on the table.

"Hello?"

"Kara is missing!"

It was Madelyn Price, sounding frantic.

"Slow down. Start from the beginning."

"The school called. Kara hasn't made it to any of her classes today. She's missing! I think someone has her!"

"Okay. Calm down. Where are you?"

"On my way home! I have to find her!"

"I'm headed to your place, but I'm in Detroit, so it'll take a while for me to get there."

I hung up and filled Charles in on what was happening.

"Let's get lunch packed up," Charles said, catching my wrist as I stood to leave.

He headed to the counter and explained that we had to leave. Our food was delivered in white paper bags with grease stains on the bottom.

"Call me after you talk to her."

"Will do," I said, before getting into the Taurus and heading for I-96.

I drove five over the speed limit and arrived at Madelyn's place thirty-five minutes after leaving Mickelson's. I checked the property, making sure it was secure and free of intruders. Madelyn showed up about forty-five minutes later.

"Mrs. Wilcox, I don't know where to look. Kara is such a good girl. She would never skip school. I just know someone has her!"

"Okay. When was the last time you spoke to Kara?"

"Last night. We talk every evening between six and seven."

"Anything seem off? Did she say anything out of the ordinary?"

Madelyn stared at the floor for a few minutes before looking up.

"Come into my office."

We headed to Madelyn's office and sat down. She opened her desk drawer and pulled out a notepad.

"Obviously, I am always trying to make sure that my child doesn't end up like I did. Last night everything was fine, but last week, Kara said something that caused me to wonder."

Madelyn pushed the notepad across the table. She had scrawled "The Spot?" on the notepad, along with "What does it mean?"

"Kara let it slip that she'd met a new friend. She wouldn't tell me where she met her, but they both enjoyed playing virtual reality games. She mentioned that there was a new club for teens called "The Spot" and her new friend had invited her. I tried looking it up, but couldn't find anything. I know Kara's friends, so it struck me as strange. I asked more questions, but she buttoned up about things."

Back when I was a cop, there was a place the kids in Brightmoor called "The Spot". It was an old factory that had fallen into blight. The building was on the list for demolition, but the city had been slow about tearing it down. I hadn't been there for years, but it was probably still standing.

"Is there anything else you can tell me? Anything else that stood out?"

"No. That was it."

"Okay. I have an idea. I'll be in touch." I pushed the notepad back across the table and headed for the door.

"Mrs. Wilcox! Where are you going? What are you going to do?"

"Just stay here. Lock the door and keep the phone close," I said, closing the door behind me.

I called Martin.

"Hey, what's the next move?"

"I'm headed to Brightmoor. I'm going to text an address to you and Charles. Get there, but don't engage until I call back."

"Okay."

"I've got a hunch."

～

"The Spot" is a small structure that served as a store, café, and pawn shop in the years after the packing factory had ceased production. It sat on the edge of Rouge Park, not far from the Coney Island where I'd met Don, the informant. When I was a cop, it was an unofficial lover's lane during the day, and a haven for rape and drug use at night. The bright street lamps of Rouge Park gave the Spot enough light for criminality without forcing assailants to provide additional illumination. I drove to a parking lot in the park, adjacent from the street where the old, rundown building sat.

I strapped one gun to my ankle and double-checked for the side-mounted Luger. Rouge Park was not a common destination for non-criminals, and the empty parking lot made "The Spot" the perfect place for a crime. I crept along the edge of the aluminum guardrail that separated the park from the former neighborhood. After climbing over the guardrail, I fought through overgrowth and litter, hoping that the crunch of leaves and greenery wasn't as loud as it sounded to me. Inching up against the side of the building, I made sure that I wasn't visible to anyone inside it. I placed my back against the mangled aluminum siding and listened. At first there was nothing, but then I heard the faint sound of a voice. I turned to face the empty window sill and saw Danica Masters holding a small pistol and standing in front of a young woman who was tied to a chair: Kara Price.

"So, you're my sister?" Danica asked as she strolled over to Kara. "Did you know that your mom told my mom to abandon me? Not that I blame your mom, because my mother should have had more of a brain, but that's neither here nor there. My father has told me about your mom— how she was so smart. How she fooled him into thinking that she and Liza were bitter enemies when they were actually running a business together."

Kara looked up, confused.

"Oh, yes. You didn't know? Yeah, our moms helped women leave their husbands and boyfriends and start new lives; it's quite a thing. They have traveled all over the country together. Your mom is the real brains behind it, but my mother was the financial support. Surely your mom told you all of this? No? Well, there's more. Our dad wanted to see you, and develop a relationship, but your mom prevented it. She didn't want you to associate with me or our father. He's languishing in jail, wondering how his eldest daughter is doing. Don't worry, I filled him in, but don't you think it's a shame that a man has to wonder how his child is doing, simply because her mother is a stupid, selfish bitch?"

"Or maybe she's just smart," Kara said.

Danica reached out and smacked Kara across the face, raging into a fit. I took this opportunity to slither through a gaping hole in the wall, and scoot quickly behind a stack of cardboard boxes. The strong stench of excrement hit my nose, forcing me to hold back from gagging. The cardboard prevented me from seeing much, but I couldn't risk peering out over the top of the stack. I looked skyward, asking for strength, before gently lowering myself onto the filthy floor.

"I see you just a stupid bitch too." Danica continued berating her half-sister.

I scanned the room for my next move. There was a beige couch, minus the cushions, opposite the mound of cardboard. If I could get there, I could surprise Danica from behind. I'd just have to wait until she got irate again. In my experience, when criminals were engaged in torturing or ranting at a victim, they missed things. Danica slapped her sister again and pushed her face close to Kara's. While she was screaming, I quickly dug my phone out of my pocket and sent a text message to Charles: The Spot. Hostage situation.

I stayed behind the cardboard, listening and waiting for the right moment to take Danica by surprise. At that point, I had to assume she was a cold and calculating murderer, and her behavior seemed to be escalating. There wasn't time to move to the couch—I would have to act quickly and be ready to shoot. Danica wouldn't have any trouble taking out both me and Kara.

"Your mother was so jealous. A spinster single mother, living a lonely life. She resented my mother. Now there are three kids without a mother. Your mother couldn't stand it, so she took my mother's life. She knew no one would hear a thing. Brightmoor is a ghost town in these parts. We barely have any cops around here anymore."

I eased around the side of the mound of cardboard, catching Kara's eye and holding my index finger against my lips.

"Your mother was weak, but she wasn't a bad person," I said.

"What?"

Danica spun around, pointing her gun in my direction.

"Your mother was weak, but you're more like her than you think."

"What? How so?" I had Danica's full attention now.

"She was just trying to get the best possible outcome for herself, and you're trying to do the same thing. You're hurt, so you are seeking revenge because you think that will make your life easier. Your mother abandoned you because she thought it would make her life easier. You're both wrong. This—what you're doing—is going to make your life worse, and you won't ever be able to fix it. Your mother did the same thing. That's why she was willing to meet with you. Abandoning you left a hole in her life that was unfixable. She thought the pain would go away, just like you think killing Kara—your sister—will make the pain go away. So, you see? You and Liza have a lot in common. Lack of insight, wouldn't you say?"

Danica was angry, but stunned. She stood still, staring at me, while her shoulders began to rise and fall heavily. I saw Kara quietly wriggling out of the ropes. I moved closer to Danica, my gun trained on her forehead.

"You think you know it all, don't you? You don't know shit about me or my mother!"

"I know that your mother fought for you. She wanted custody, but she was too afraid of what her parents would say. They were bankrolling her life, but she would have taken you back. She never wanted to leave you, but your dad was so abusive she just couldn't stay."

A child, no matter how injured or spurned they feel, always wants to know the story behind why their parents abandoned them. I watched Danica's eyes fill with hate before she turned and rushed back to Kara. Sprinting towards her, I caught her ponytail and stomped on her left calf before sticking my gun in the back of her skull.

"I don't want to, but you know I know how to use this," I said. "DPD will be here in a few minutes. You okay, kiddo?" I called to Kara.

I heard Kara's violent crying, but I didn't dare take my eyes off Danica. Sirens screamed in the distance.

# 18

Solving a case always gives your ego a boost. A sense of satisfaction and calm wells up in your soul, and you remember why you do what you do. But that day, I didn't feel a sense of satisfaction; instead, I felt a lump in my throat. Was it possible that Danica Masters had murdered her mom? I remembered the things she had been telling Kara before I interrupted. She thought that Madelyn had killed her mother. The cops thought Danica had killed Liza, but in my mind, something was off.

"She's been talking, but we don't have anything on this kid," Charles said. He'd stopped by my office to fill me in on what was happening with the case.

"I don't think she did it. Not sure who did it or why, but the beef between her and Kara is some weird half-sibling competition, or retaliation against Madelyn."

"Gotta agree with you: there's no proof that Danica had anything to do with her mother's death. In fact, she can't talk about Liza Abernathy without tearing up. She's convinced that Madelyn Price did it, but there's no reason to believe she was involved either."

"I hate that I took this case."

"Why? You've worked it hard. You've done a great job, Syl."

"But there's a man who is waiting for me to tell him that I found his wife's killer. He's expecting me to bring this thing home, and I just can't seem to break the case. I've failed."

Charles sat down opposite me. There was nothing left to say. I had failed. It was time to tell Carson that his wife's killer hadn't been identified, and probably wouldn't ever be found.

"What else has Danica said?"

"Basically, she said that she and Liza had an argument over making their relationship public. Danica wanted to be her daughter all the time, not just when Liza slipped below Eight Mile Road. Well, according to Danica, she was planning on going public and she told Liza that. So, Liza stayed there arguing with her. Eventually, Liza followed her into an alley and the two almost came to blows, but before anything could happen, a black Monte Carlo pulled up. Someone got out, dressed in black, ski mask and all, and they shot Liza five times."

A simple story. Almost too simple—but one thing stood out: the black Monte Carlo. Why was that standing out?

"Black Monte Carlo..." I said.

"Yeah. She claims it was in vintage shape—a shiny, good-looking car."

I only drive it on special occasions.

I could be wrong. I had to be wrong.

"Charles?"

"Yeah, what's wrong? You look panicked."

"I gotta go."

"What do you mean? Where you going?"

I shoved the paperwork aside, jumped up, grabbed my

keys, and ran to the car. If I hurried, I'd make it there before 5:00 p.m. I hit M-14, got stuck in gridlock traffic, and got off the highway at 4:45. I pulled into the parking lot at 4:57. Aileen Stark was walking out of the office, striding confidently in a pinstriped suit. I pulled into a parking stall, threw the car into park, and jumped out. Aileen continued to walk, as if she had not seen my car.

"Mrs. Stark!" I yelled at her back.

Aileen turned around, slipping her sunglasses low on her nose.

"Mrs. Wilcox. I've been expecting you."

"Why is that?"

"You're sharp."

"Are you admitting—?"

"I am very happy that you caught Liza's murderer. She's young; I hope she gets a short sentence. She deserves a second chance."

"How do you know about that?"

"You'd be surprised what I know."

"She's not guilty."

"No? Then why did you have the police arrest her?" she asked sarcastically.

"You're not going to let a fifteen-year-old girl take the fall for you, are you?"

"Mrs. Wilcox, I have no idea what you're talking about."

"Not driving the Monte today? Nice Cutlass."

Aileen smiled and shook her head.

"Remember, I told you I only drive that car on special occasions."

"Like when you go out to kill your daughter-in-law?"

"That's a terrible thing to say.

"Carson loved her."

"He'll love again."

"How could you be so cold?"

"Thanks for stopping by, Mrs. Wilcox but if you don't mind, I have to-"

"You set her up."

"Mrs. Wilcox-"

"You set up a young girl! Your daughter-in-law's child. You were the one who was harassing Madelyn."

"Why would I ever do that?"

"Because you didn't want anyone to know that you murdered Liza, least of all, your son."

Aileen Stark let out a loud, angry laugh before saying, "No one would tell a son that his mother murdered his wife. Think about how horrible that would be."

"There might be one person who thinks it's important for him to know, even if it is painful."

"That same person has too much compassion to do that. Good day, Mrs. Wilcox."

Aileen Stark, Liza Stark's killer, climbed into her car and drove away.

I GAVE all the information I'd gathered to DPD, but I knew there wasn't enough evidence to press charges. Aileen Stark was seventy-seven years old, and rich. The odds of her doing any time in jail were slim to none. The odds that the prosecutor would ever move forward were even less likely. Danica also escaped prosecution for Liza's murder. Because there was no evidence tying her to the crime. She was sentenced to three months in a residential treatment center for what she did to Kara—the short stay a result of Kara and Madelyn advocating for her to receive a lighter sentence.

I put off the inevitable for a few weeks, but eventually, I

had to return Carson's phone calls and set up a meeting. It wasn't satisfying to know who the killer was without being able to do anything about it, but I hadn't taken the case with the idea that it would ever make it to trial. I'd taken it because I wanted to find out the truth for Carson.

"How are you going to tell him," Martin asked.

"I'm not. He's going to figure it out for himself."

"How?"

"By connecting the dots."

"But—"

"Martin, I'm not telling him that his mother killed his wife. He will figure it out. It will be one of those…" I felt emotion well up in my throat. Money was not enough: nothing was enough for a mother to cause her son such pain.

"I guess you're right, but I would want to know the truth, even if it was terrible."

Martin's words struck me. Was knowing the truth always helpful? Was the truth better than hearing a comfortable lie? I didn't have the answers to those questions.

"Carson Stark is a surgeon; he will figure it out."

"Why do you think she did it?"

That was a great question. After running the situation through my head over and over again, I was still confused about it. Why would a mother do this to her son? The alternate answer was even worse.

"There's a chance, a good chance that the bullets weren't meant for Liza."

"What? Why do you think that?"

"If Aileen Stark had wanted to kill Liza, she would have done it before she married Carson. But even more importantly, she wasn't going to have Danica ruining their good name. If Danica made herself known, word would have gotten around. Aileen Stark cares about keeping up appearances and keeping as much money in the family as possible."

"Danica could have demanded money to keep things quiet."

"Exactly—and Aileen Stark wasn't about to let that happen."

"Sick."

"I know. I don't know how Carson is going to react, but I can't stall any longer.

CARSON WAS WAITING at the door with a tall glass of Stolis and orange juice. He offered me a drink, which I declined, before placing my briefcase on the table and pulling out a stack of reports detailing what I'd learned.

"You know who did it?"

"Please sit down."

"Is it that bad?"

"Just...Mr. Stark, just please have a seat. I will read the summary."

There was no softening the blow of the information. Instead of drawing out the details, I raced through the short paragraphs. Carson doubled over and began to cry when I told him about Danica, his eyes searing with the pain of betrayal. I gave him time to cry for a few minutes before I continued. As I started to explain the details surrounding Danica, Carson interrupted.

"Where is Danica now?"

"She's in a treatment center for a few months."

"I want to meet her."

"Okay. I think she'd like that. I can give you her information."

"When did she find Liza?"

"About a year before Liza was murdered. Danica wanted to be a part of her life; she wanted to meet you and the kids, her uncle, aunt, cousins, and grandparents. Liza was afraid you wouldn't accept her, so she kept Danica in the shadows longer than she would have liked. Danica was threatening to show up and expose the secret, which scared Liza. On the day Liza died, she went to meet with Danica. They spent hours arguing in an abandoned building. Eventually, Danica left in anger. Liza didn't want to leave Brightmoor until they had settled things. She looked for Danica and eventually found her by a party store. Danica headed into the alley; Liza followed. Then a car appeared—a black, 1982 Monte Carlo."

Carson looked at me with a blank stare that gave way to eyes full of terror.

"The bullets were meant for Danica, but Liza jumped in front of her. She sacrificed her life for her firstborn."

It was so hard to look Carson in the eye, but I couldn't bring myself to look away. There was nothing else to say or do. Compassionate eye contact was the one thing I could give him.

Having reached an understanding, we sat in comfortable silence. t was the type of quiet you find yourself in when a truth is too true, too bitter. After about ten minutes, I set a sealed envelope of Carson's copy of the paperwork on the table, closed my briefcase, and turned to leave.

"Sylvia," Carson said, catching my shoulder. I turned around and faced him. He'd never used my first name before. "Your payment."

"Carson—" This was the first time I'd slipped up and

called him by his first name, thereby dropping the protective, professional barrier.

"No. Fair is fair. You've more than done your job. I have answers and that was all I wanted." Carson grabbed a checkbook from the table and wrote a check for much more than he owned.

"Carson, this is too much."

"No, no—it's not enough. You don't know what you've done for me."

"I don't—"

"You proved that my wife was a good person; that she loved me, and that she died because she loved her daughter, not because she was seeing someone else. Thank you, Sylvia. Thank you."

He pressed the folded check into my palm. Not knowing what to do with all the emotions, I simply nodded, turned, and swiftly headed for the door. Carson called my name before I could step out.

"I want to meet Danica. Can you arrange that?"

I hesitated, not because I wasn't willing to help bring the two of them together, but because I was in awe. He'd just received devastating news, but he still had the heart to worry about a child he'd never met: a true man of substance.

"Of course. I'll set something up."

## 19

"Just remember, you're a PI, not a social worker," Charles said.

It had been four months since the close of Liza's case. Charles and I were sitting at Mickelson's, enjoying iced tea and fish and chips.

"I know. I just want to spark the healing process."

"That's very noble. I guess that's why you're a PI. You've got time to play the social worker if you want. How many cases you working right now?"

"Currently, I'm taking a bit of a break."

"That's not like you. Case took a lot out of you, huh?"

"Yeah, it was rough. Never expected it to turn out the way it did. Made me think about Martin and the—"

"Stop. You don't need to feel sorry about that. You did the right thing. It's better that he doesn't know all the details. Derek committed suicide. That's all he needs to know."

"Well, whether it's better or not, I'm not in a hurry to change things."

"How about a vacation? You could book a flight to

anywhere. A few weeks on a white sandy beach. Could be exactly what the doctor ordered."

It did sound like a good choice.

"Maybe after I straighten things out here. It would be nice to take some time and get away for a while."

"So, what's the plan for this afternoon?"

"I'm meeting Danica at her aunt's house. From there, we're going to Carson's. He's asked me to stay for the first part of the meeting, but if things go well, I'll take off and the four of them will be left to bond."

"You'll ride off into the sunset."

"That's right."

"Syl?"

"Yeah?"

"You're an angel."

Alyssa's Masters' home was buzzing with activity when I arrived. There were a few children riding bikes out front. I pulled up as a pre-teen flew out of the house, letting the screen door smack against the door frame. Danica was out front, cross-legged, sitting on the concrete, engrossed in her cellphone. She was wearing skinny jeans, a black t-shirt with "Yes" on the front, and a gray windbreaker. She looked up when I honked the horn and gave a slight wave before slipping the phone into her pocket and heading my way.

"Hey," she said, her voice shaking a bit.

"Hi, Danica. You ready?"

"Guess so."

"All right. Climb on in."

Summer had been filled with hot, humid days oscillating between torrential downpours, but the weather had recently turned. It was one of the first autumn-like days we'd experienced, and the weather was overcast and cool, with a hint of rain in the air. The change had put me in a relaxed, peaceful mood. A cool breeze crept into the car as Danica zipped up her windbreaker before climbing into the Taurus.

We drove in silence for the first fifteen minutes, but as we approached the on-ramp for M-14, Danica asked, "Do you think she'll ever forgive me?"

"Kara? Maybe—in time. Just give her time, and remember that she's hurting too."

"I do want to know her. We're family."

"Yes, you are. But just remember that you lived without knowing about one another for more than a decade, and your first meeting was not that positive."

"I just didn't know what to do. I was scared and sad."

I nodded my head, not sure how to respond. Danica had been through so much already, and she was just a teenager. Over the months I had forgiven Danica for lying about not recognizing the picture of Liza, and stopping by to interrogate my priest, but the crimes against Kara were much more egregious. There was a chance that Kara would never want to see her again. I wasn't sure what would help soothe her pain.

"Forgive yourself," I said. "Do that first. After that, work on mending relationships."

CARSON WAS outside when we arrived. He was clean-shaven and dressed in neat, pleated khakis and a blue polo shirt. Before we got out of the car, Carson crossed the driveway and stood beside my car door.

"Sylvia—it's good to see you," he said in a low, subdued tone.

Carson Stark had become something of a friend. It probably wasn't the best idea to mix business with pleasure, but all payments had been made and we were both lonely adults, hurting and missing our dead spouses. I nodded and smiled.

Danica opened her car door and stepped out onto the gravel.

"Carson Stark, meet Danica Masters," I said, motioning for Danica to come over to our side of the car.

"Hello, Danica," Carson said, holding out his hand. Danica took it and gave him a firm handshake, but she wouldn't look up at his face.

"Well, we have a lot to catch up on. Is it okay if we head inside? I have a few people I'd like you to meet."

"Sure," Danica muttered.

I followed behind the two. Carson looked back, giving a look that said it was okay to leave.

"I am going to run a few errands. Danica, is it okay if I come back in an hour to pick you up?"

The confused look on Danica's face caused me to wonder if I'd made a mistake getting involved in helping Carson and Danica connect.

"Danica, do you—?"

"It's okay."

∾

I RETURNED forty minutes later to find Danica and her half-siblings playing with Legos. Carson was watching with a smile on his face. The visit must have gone well, because Danica ended up wanting to stay longer than an hour. After she said goodbye to her brother and sister and Carson, we headed out. Before I could close the door, Carson called my name.

"Yeah?"

"If you have time tomorrow, maybe we can get lunch? My treat."

I hesitated. "Carson...I..."

"It's just lunch, Syl. I'm not on bended knee or anything like that."

We both laughed. I needed more laughs; more friends in the world, so, I said yes.

SIGN-UP for my Exclusive Reader Club! We are currently reading *The Girl in Blue*, a prequel to the Sylvia Wilcox series in serial form. You will receive a chapter of the story each month. It's totally free and you may unsubscribe at any time.

Exclusive Reader Club Sign-Up

**Let's Get Lost In Stories Together!**

Braylee

## OTHER BOOKS BY BRAYLEE PARKINSON

Made in the USA
Columbia, SC
13 November 2020